Never Thwart a Thespian

by Edie Claire

Book Eight of the
Leigh Koslow Mystery Series

Dedication

For Jami, Jan, Justin, Kim, Mark, Rick, Sarah, Trina, and
all my other beloved acting buds with AOG.
It was the best of times.
Period.

Chapter 1

"Isn't it the most glorious place you've ever seen?!" Bess crowed, spreading her arms wide above her head and nearly toppling backwards off the crumbling concrete steps in the process. "Just look at it!"

Leigh pulled back the hand she'd flung out in case her aunt actually did topple backward, then looked. Bess's ability to view the decrepit monstrosity of a building before them through rose-colored glasses came as no surprise. The fact that the lenses of her current pair of 80s-vintage plastic sunglasses were, in fact, tinted red was pure coincidence.

"I'm looking," Leigh replied drily.

Bess turned to her niece with a glare. "No negative Nellies!" she admonished. "I have your mother for that. You have to open up your mind to the *possibilities!*"

Leigh took another look. The sight was by no means new to her; growing up in West View, a suburb north of Pittsburgh, she had passed by the red brick building on the borough's main drag thousands of times. But she couldn't remember ever being impressed. Even during her childhood, its bizarre facade had raised questioning eyebrows. The structure had originally been built as a church, which would explain the large, square tower to the right of the double front doors. According to Leigh's mother Frances, the top of the tower had once been edged with brick and mortar crenelations surrounding a giant wooden steeple and metal cross. After the building was sold to a fraternal order, however, a few of their more boisterous members had tried to remove the steeple with a wrecking ball while "under the influence," knocking off not only the spire but a good bit of the surrounding masonry besides. The result was a tower that looked like it had a giant mouth open to the sky — a mouth with half its teeth knocked out.

Leigh struggled for an optimistic comment. "Maybe it looks better inside?"

Bess's lips twisted ruefully. "Not really," she admitted. "But it will when we're done with it!"

Leigh tensed. "We?"

"Why, of course," Bess replied, leading her niece up the remaining steps toward the front doors. "You didn't think I would be so crass as to cut you out of such an important family project, did you?"

Leigh's steps halted. "You do realize that putting the words 'family' and 'project' in the same sentence makes me want to run screaming, right?"

Bess merely chortled. "It's going to be marvelous!" She inserted a key into the door lock, struggled with the mechanism a moment, then pushed open the creaking wooden door. "After you, kiddo," she insisted, stepping back and gesturing Leigh inside.

Leigh complied. Her aunt's affectionate use of the term "kiddo" had bothered her when she was a teenager, but now that she was on the gray side of forty, she took it as a compliment. She stepped through the doorway into what must once have been a church vestibule. A few ancient-looking metal coat racks were crammed along the far wall, while other doorways led left and right. The scuffed black and white tile floor was littered with shards of plaster and curls of paint that had peeled from the butter-yellow ceiling and walls.

Leigh stepped over the debris and moved hesitantly toward the right doorway. "Shouldn't we be wearing hardhats or something?"

"Oh, piffle!" Bess retorted, pushing her sunglasses to the top of her head and moving on into the next room. "It may look a bit shabby at the moment, but it's not like it's been *condemned* or anything! If it had been, I could never have convinced Gordon to buy it — not that I didn't have to sell that miser half my soul in any event." She let out a huff. "Two different inspectors agreed that despite its appearance, the building *is* structurally sound. It just needs a little TLC; that's all."

Leigh hid a smile. From what she knew of Gordon Applegate, who happened to be one of her husband Warren's financial management clients, the man was no miser. He was one of Pittsburgh's most generous philanthropists.

He was also — ordinarily — not an idiot.

"I've been meaning to ask," Leigh said tentatively, stepping into the old sanctuary after her aunt while keeping a watchful eye toward the ceiling for falling beams. "How *did* you get Mr. Applegate to invest in this little venture?"

Bess gave a dismissive flick of her left hand while her right hand searched for a light switch. "The man's got more money than God and he's had the hots for me ever since I played Gertrude in Hamlet. Oh, here we are. Ta-da!"

The lighting in the cavernous room changed from eerily dim to slightly less dim. Leigh took a couple steps forward and looked around. The space was as wide as it was deep, with large windows on either side and a raised platform at the opposite end. Behind the platform was an empty odd-shaped area bounded by half-walls that Leigh suspected had once housed a choir loft and organ pipes. Doors on either side of the former chancel led back into the rest of the building. The high, arched ceiling was bedecked with ancient rotating fans, a few of which were missing blades. The entire room was coated with a thick layer of dust and the worn brown carpet beneath their feet was beyond filthy. All in all, Leigh was pleasantly surprised. Knowing her Aunt Bess, the room could just as easily have contained a disassembled carnival ride or an elephant graveyard.

"Interesting," Leigh conceded. "How old is it?"

"Going on a hundred years," Bess replied proudly, her eyes twinkling. "The cornerstone was laid in 1915. By an independent Baptist congregation, I believe."

Leigh walked further out into the room. Her gaze rested on the area behind the chancel, and a queer prickling started at the base of her neck. She stopped moving.

"Unfortunately, the people who built it didn't stay here very long," Bess continued. "It was owned by several different congregations, but all of them seemed to have trouble meeting the mortgage. I barely remember, when I was little, these windows having stained glass in them. There was a particularly pretty one out over the front doors — it showed the women at the empty tomb on Easter morning. But all the stained glass was removed and sold ages ago."

At the word "tomb," a wave of cold slid down Leigh's spine. Her shoulders shivered. What was wrong with her?

"The last congregation that owned it put on the classroom addition in the back — that was in 1961," Bess explained. "I bet that decision made for some lively church meetings, because they'd hardly used it two years before the loan went into default—" she broke off her lecture and took a step closer to Leigh. "What's up, kiddo? You feeling all right?"

"I'm fine," Leigh insisted, trying to make it the truth. "I just got a weird vibe or something." She gave herself a shake and looked around again. It was just an empty room. "After the last church defaulted, is that when the Narwhals bought it?"

Bess chuckled. "Oh, you remember them, do you?"

"Their sign was hard to miss," Leigh answered, remembering the giant wooden plaque that had occupied the front-window space throughout most of her own childhood. The Fraternal Order of the Narwhal, a group of businessmen her normally charitable father had once derided as "morons of a feather, flocking together," had commissioned a local painter to immortalize their mascot, a medium-sized species of whale with a single horn sprouting from its forehead. The result was a freakish cartoon that Leigh and her cousin Cara had argued bitterly over during their elementary days. Cara had been certain that the painting showed a volcano spewing lava — Leigh thought it looked like chocolate pudding with a spoon sticking out.

"Ah, yes," Bess agreed. "The Narwhals. Bunch of puffed-up dandies, pretending to be entrepreneurs. 'Successful local merchants,' indeed. They wound up defaulting just like everyone else! But to answer your question, no, they weren't the first fraternal order to buy this place. That would be the Adders, back in the sixties. They were even crazier — used to conduct meetings wearing rubber snakes around their necks." She gave an exaggerated shudder that jiggled her generous curves. "I dated one of them once. Lord help me, I'd have been better off with the snake."

Leigh grinned. Her thrice-married aunt's exploits with the opposite sex were legendary. Where reality ended and legend began was anyone's guess, but Leigh knew better than to underestimate. "So they were the ones who got drunk and knocked off the steeple?"

"Bingo!" Bess said cheerfully, stepping up onto the platform. She turned around and faced an imaginary audience, lifting her hands to either side. "Thank you. Thank you all so much!" She moved her hands over her heart; her eyes filled with actual tears. "It's true. I always believed in this place. And now, tonight, in your presence, the dreams of the North Boros Thespian Society have finally been realized. After twenty years of rented gymnasiums, barns, school auditoriums, and church basements, at long last we have our very own dedicated theater extraordinaire! Bless you. Bless you all!" She blew a kiss to the audience, then with a sweeping flourish took a bow so low and so dramatic she wound up collapsed on one knee, emotionally spent.

Leigh applauded, throwing in a whistle for good measure. Her aunt didn't move. "Um... Aunt Bess?" she asked after a moment.

"Yes?" Bess answered, her face still to the floor.

"You can't get up again, can you?"

"Not a chance, kiddo."

Leigh stepped onto the chancel and gave her aunt a hand. As Bess regained her footing, Leigh glanced around the empty choir loft and organ pipe area with a frown. What *was* it about the place that creeped her out so much? "You really think you can turn this building into a theater?" she asked skeptically.

"Of course!" Bess declared, affronted. "It's the perfect space. All we need to do is clean it up a little. We may not even have to rent chairs! There are loads of them in the basement, left over from when the place was a banquet hall. The society already owns some basic lighting equipment and flats and curtains and such. Getting everything ready for opening night in eight days won't be easy, but it's definitely doable!"

Leigh whirled to face her aunt. "Eight days? Opening night? Are you kidding me?" The room might not be filled with rotting elephant carcasses, but every possible surface was choked with dust, peeling paint littered the filthy carpet like snow, and she was pretty sure the spots on the choir railing behind her were bat guano. "You can't get a show together in eight days *and* get this place suitable for the public!"

"I don't see why not," Bess countered. "The cast has been rehearsing for weeks already. All they need is a venue!"

Leigh started to get the picture. "So you've been planning all this for a while now."

Bess smirked. "My dear, I've had my eye on this building for a *decade*. I bit my fingernails to the bone waiting for the borough to get possession of it and get it to a sheriff's sale after that hustler

Marconi took off and left it to rot. Blast that man... so many wasted years!"

Leigh searched her memory for the reference. "Oh, you mean the guy who wanted to turn it into a strip club?"

Bess's expression soured. "That's him."

Leigh tried not to laugh. She remembered all too well the degree of apoplexy her mother had suffered upon learning that a "gentleman's club" was moving smack dab into the middle of their beloved and heretofore perfectly Godly hometown. Frances Koslow had mobilized every women's and/or religious organization in the borough (including both the Girl Scouts and the Indian Princesses) to protest against it, leaving no yard without a sign, no business without a publicly visible statement of support for the cause (lest their customer traffic mysteriously decline), and no zoning board member with a good night's sleep until the necessary permit was denied. The fact that Frances's twin sister Lydie, Cara's mother, had joined the crusade was not surprising, since the two were always supportive of each other. But Leigh had been puzzled at the zeal shown by her Aunt Bess, who rather than being one to jump onto her younger sister's moral high horse, usually enjoyed knocking Frances off of it.

"So *that's* why you joined the 'West View Citizens Against Indecency and Moral Turpitude!'" Leigh cried.

Bess's lips pursed. "Let's just say sacrifices were made."

Leigh grinned. "I hope the North Boros Thespian Society appreciates you."

Bess smiled slyly. "Oh, they will. We'll get this theater yet, don't you worry!"

"Yet? You don't have it already?"

Bess's expression sobered. "Gordon Applegate has it; the society doesn't. We're flat broke, as usual. Gordon has agreed to let us rent it indefinitely, for a pittance, *if* we can turn it into a cultural attraction the North Boros can be proud of. If not, he's made no bones about the fact that he's got a second offer waiting in the wings."

"A second offer?" Leigh exclaimed, flabbergasted. The gnarly deposits on the choir railing were definitely bat guano. Now that her eyes had adjusted to the dimness, she could see at least one of the furry mammals snoozing on an overhead light fixture. "Who on earth else would want the place?"

Bess's eyes narrowed. "At the sheriff's sale, nobody. That's why Gordon got it so cheap. But now some shark of a real estate attorney wants it. She's already offering more than he paid, and Gordon is champing at the bit." She sighed. "He doesn't mind giving money away, but refraining from making an easy buck — now *that* goes against his DNA."

"Why does the attorney want it?" Leigh asked, deciding to investigate the organ pipe bay.

"She doesn't want the building," Bess said disapprovingly. "She wants the lot. She won't say why, but Gordon thinks she has some inside information about another buyer. A fast food franchise or a drug store, maybe. This place has great visibility and plenty of space for parking, which is hard to find on this stretch of road, you know."

"So why didn't she bid at the sheriff's sale?" Leigh asked, surprised to find the area behind the chancel empty. The whole place was still creeping her out, but she was determined to overcome the feeling. She walked toward one of the rear doors to see where it led.

"Well," Bess answered, her voice taking on an uncharacteristic sweetness. "She meant to, I suppose. She did show up, but the poor thing met with a little mishap in the ladies' room, and she *just* missed the bidding."

Leigh stopped walking. "Aunt Bess!"

Bess's eyes widened innocently. "Yes?"

Leigh shook her head. "Never mind." She turned and moved towards the door again.

"Ooh!" Bess cooed, pulling up beside her. "Let's go see the bathrooms. And the basement, of course. That's where you and the kids come in!"

Leigh found nothing in that statement to like. "Excuse me?"

"Just come along and see!"

Leigh followed Bess through the doors and into a curved hallway. A set of stairs leading up appeared on her right; a door ahead bore a faded sign that read "Office." They walked around the curve to the left, past another staircase leading down, and through an open doorway to the annex, which was clearly newer, although not apparently in any better condition. "Oh, ignore all this," Bess instructed as they walked around a collection of twelve-foot two-by-fours, miscellaneous plastic pipes, and giant rolls of black plastic. "The bathrooms are here. See? Not so bad as you might think!"

Leigh looked through the door Bess held open to observe a dust-caked restroom with three pink metal stalls, one grimy sink, and a mirror that was smeared with what looked like red lipstick. A paper towel dispenser hung half off the wall, its cabinet open and gaping, and a waste can in the corner sat piled to overflowing with brown paper towels. How long the trash had been there was anyone's guess. For all Leigh knew, the last women in the building had been pole dancers auditioning for the mysterious Marconi. "Charming," she responded.

"It needs work," Bess admitted. "But the real problem is, neither of these bathrooms closest to the auditorium are handicapped accessible. The stalls don't meet the new standards. In order to open to the public, we'll have to fix up the big unisex bathroom in the basement. The basement *is* accessible, barely, by the ramp coming off the alcove opposite where we came in. It's just that—" she hesitated a little. "Well, sending people through the basement at all presents just a *teeny* little challenge."

Leigh waited for it.

Bess's left eye gave the slightest twitch. Leigh knew the sign well. It meant that her aunt was either nervous or lying through her teeth. Often it meant both. "Follow me!" Bess chirped with false confidence. "And all will become clear!"

They walked back down the corridor, out of the annex, and to the head of the staircase that led down to the space underneath the former sanctuary. "The basement has loads of possibilities for receptions and such," Bess twittered as they descended the stairs. "It even has a kitchen! But at some point someone decided to store some things down here, and... well... you know how people can be!"

Leigh followed Bess down the last steps and looked out into the room. It was all she could do not to turn around immediately and go back up. "What the—"

"Yes," Bess interrupted. "It is rather impressive, isn't it?"

Leigh gaped. The space was as big as the sanctuary above it, but its ceiling was low — at least those sections of ceiling that were visible. The entire space, from wall to wall and floor to ceiling, was completely crammed full of *stuff*. It didn't look like a storage room, with orderly piles and rows and aisles. It looked like a charity donation clearinghouse that had gotten hit by a tornado, pulled up into the funnel, shaken like a martini, and sat back down again.

"Where did it all—"

"Well, the building has served a lot of different purposes, like I said," Bess interrupted again. "Churches, the two fraternal orders, and a couple times it was a banquet hall. See the chairs?"

Leigh did see folding chairs. Some folded, some unfolded. Some broken in half. One was hanging off a crooked hat rack, another was partly buried underneath a clear plastic bag filled with Styrofoam packing peanuts. All of them were thoroughly entangled in a web of other items under, around, and on top of them. The vast sea of accumulated objects before Leigh's eyes looked like a child's "find this" puzzle book on steroids.

"I... do see chairs," she conceded.

"We just have to get them out, you see," Bess continued. "And... er... all this other stuff, too."

Leigh turned toward her aunt. "We? All this? Out?"

Bess offered her best fake smile. "Of course. Our patrons will need to get to the accessible bathroom, you see." She pointed across the room.

Leigh looked. "I don't see any bathroom."

"Yes, well," Bess replied, her smile starting to droop a little. "You would if you walked back upstairs and came down on the other side. But it's... um... kind of hard to get there from here at the moment."

"You don't say," Leigh deadpanned, moving past a wet/dry vacuum with no hose to get a closer look at a long, smooth pole that hung off a stand on one end and dragged the floor on the other. "Isn't this a ballet barre?"

Bess stepped forward with her. "I do believe it is! This place was a dance studio for a while, too. Didn't I mention that? Back in the nineties."

Leigh's better judgment still urged her to run screaming back up the steps. But the bizarre nature of the cornucopia of accumulated crap before her couldn't help but spark her curiosity. She picked up a shaggy piece of brown fur from off one end of the ballet barre. It was shaped like a hood and sported a stub of paper mache from which the tip had obviously broken off.

"Narwhal horn," Bess explained.

"Since when do whales have fur?"

"Since the men of the order got hat envy over the Moose and the Elk."

"Gotcha." Leigh dug deeper into the pile. She opened a small cardboard box, then shut it quickly. New ballet slippers might look pretty, but apparently used ones could reek of foot odor indefinitely. "Any chance there's anything of actual value in here?"

"Oh, absolutely!" Bess cried. "Seems like every occupant left it in a hurry. No one's used the basement or the old kitchen in ages... even when the place was a banquet hall, all the food was catered and they used the newer kitchen in the annex for reheating and dishwashing and such. The basement's only been used for storage."

Leigh pulled a folded section of newspaper from the bottom of a ceramic planter decorated with pink flamingos. She checked the date. "May 17th, 1974!"

"You see?" Bess said proudly. "This place is practically a museum! The Pack will love it!"

"The Pack?" Leigh questioned. She knew perfectly well that Bess was referring to Cara's two children and Leigh's own twins, whose nickname was well earned. Not only had the foursome roamed their North Hills neighborhood as one ever since Leigh and Warren moved in next door to Cara and Gil, but when the kids combined their brainpower, any unsuspecting adult prey were in serious, serious trouble.

"Yes, I've been meaning to speak to you and Cara about that," Bess began, her voice suddenly demure. "I know the kids are off on spring break next week, and I heard that none of you are going anywhere, what with Allison's surgery and Gil's conference in Nuremberg. So I thought, what could be more perfect than their dear young aunt finding them a fun and exciting job to do?"

Leigh's head filled with visions of her precocious eleven-year-old year daughter climbing around on shaky scaffolding trying to live-capture a sleeping bat. "Aunt Bess, I don't—"

"Under constant supervision," Bess cajoled. "And with pay?"

Leigh gritted her teeth and considered. She *was* wondering how she could keep the kids safely occupied with school being out all next week. Pittsburgh in March was still wet and cold, most of their friends were headed out of town, and the eye muscle surgery Allison was scheduled for — while not restricting her physical activity per se — was expected to leave her eye red and puffy for a few days. The girl wouldn't be feeling very social, nor would she be able to spend her usual hours reading or staring at a computer screen. As for Ethan, he still owed twenty bucks for the window he and his cousin Mathias had busted out playing disc golf. "Keep talking," Leigh replied.

Bess's eyes twinkled. "I need their brains as much as their brawn. There are bound to be some real gems in here for the theater group — it's a veritable treasure trove of props! But the room has to be completely cleared out by opening night, and I can't possibly sort through it all myself and whip the rest of the building into shape besides. I've already hired a crew of men through the Community Outreach Center to help with the heavy lifting and cleaning and such, but I can't trust them to tell the wheat from the chaff — yesterday I caught one of them throwing out a perfectly good walking cane topped with a carved fish head!"

Leigh reserved comment. "So you want the Pack to help you sort through all this and decide what to keep and what to pitch?"

"Exactly!" Bess beamed. "I'll give them my criteria and they can take it from there. They've got a good eye for treasure, all of them. They just need to catalog the 'keeper' stuff and get it squirreled away in the annex, then stack the trash for the crew to haul out. They can earn a little money and it would be such a tremendous help to the society. What do you say?"

Leigh took another long look around the cluttered, musty-smelling basement. She didn't need to wonder what the kids would think of their great aunt's proposal. Hunting treasure was already one of their specialties — getting paid to do it would be nirvana. But what if, buried amidst the broken chairs and the smelly shoes, there was anything... dangerous?

"You have no idea what's in here, do you?" Leigh asked, wading deeper into the clutter and shifting aside a metal shelving unit stocked with bags of silk flowers. She had spied the corner of what looked like a steamer trunk, and she couldn't resist checking it out. Antique steamer trunks could indeed be valuable.

"Well, what I've seen so far has been pretty predictable," Bess assured. "The churches left hymnbooks and Christmas decorations and candles and such. The banquet facilities left chairs and dishes and some sound equipment. There are all sorts of things from the dance studio — apparently that owner skipped out in the middle of the night and left everything. But as for the fraternal orders..." her voice trailed off as she held up a giant orange plastic toilet seat. "I daresay we might be in for a few surprises."

"As long as there's nothing... toxic," Leigh offered, pushing a mound of wadded up black fabric off the top of the trunk. It *was* a steamer. And an antique. It seemed to be in reasonable condition, too, except that the latch was missing. She smiled as she reached down to open it. Perhaps a little treasure hunting could be fun, even if the building itself did give her the creeps.

"Does that mean you'll let me hire the Pack?" Bess asked hopefully.

"I'm sure they'd be delighted," Leigh answered, lifting the heavy lid.

"Oh, goody!" Aunt Bess crowed. "I'll come over and see them after school, then. I'll have to speak with Cara too, of course —"

Leigh didn't hear anymore. Her ears had shut off the instant her eyes saw human bone. Tattered cloth. Gaping, empty eye sockets.

She let the trunk lid fall shut with a bang. She stepped backward, tripped over a plastic topiary, and tumbled sideways over a patio grill.

"What on earth?" Bess questioned, scrambling forward to offer Leigh a hand.

Leigh pulled herself upright, then pointed a shaking finger toward the trunk. She made a strangled sound in her throat, but no words came out.

Bess turned toward the steamer. Leigh reached out to catch her aunt's arm, but was too late. Bess was already opening the lid. *No! Stop!*

Bess smiled and reached down. She pulled out a length of twine, then hoisted her arm high to lift out the remainder of the plastic skeleton. Her merry voice cackled with laughter. "Well, that's a stitch, isn't it? Almost looks real! What with the clothes and decaying flesh and all. I guess I forgot to mention... the last couple years, when the borough had possession, they let the Young Businessmen's Chamber use the building for their haunted houses at Halloween." She looked deeper into the trunk. "Oh, and look here... rubber brains! And fake vomit!"

Leigh sank back down on the grill and tried to rein in her racing heartbeat. "Aunt Bess," she said weakly as her aunt inadvertently dangled the skeleton's rib cage inches from her face. "Please put that thing away."

Bess dropped the skeleton and turned to look at her. "Oh, you couldn't possibly—" She stopped suddenly. "Oh, my. I'm so sorry, kiddo. I totally forgot about your... um.... *proclivity*."

Leigh frowned. How anyone in the family could forget for one minute her epic talents at unintentional corpse location, she had no idea. How many murder investigations did one innocent ad copywriter have to get dragged into before everyone admitted it was *not* her doing, but some kind of horrible genetic curse?

"That's okay," Leigh muttered, standing up and rubbing her arms. "But I'm done here. If the Pack wants to spend their spring break sorting through this mess, that's fine, but I have to tell you — I have a bad feeling about this place. And knowing my history, that could be significant."

Aunt Bess waved a dismissive hand in the air. "Nonsense. It has character, that's all! All theaters do. And I'm telling you, this building was *meant* to be a theater — even if it has taken a hundred years to make it happen!"

"If you say so."

Bess's eyes gleamed. "Can't you feel it? The history? The aura? The mystique! Why, every respectable theater has to have its ghosts, and from what I—" She broke off suddenly and threw a furtive glance at Leigh. "Never mind."

Leigh stiffened. "Oh, no you don't!" she warned. "There's something about this place you're not telling me, isn't there?"

Bess's large, almond eyes blinked. "Why, no. Of course not. At least not anything that would concern you, seeing as how you don't believe in ghosts." She smiled angelically. "So, no worries!"

Leigh groaned. Her aunt had her right where she wanted her, as usual. There was no rational reason to be apprehensive, and she prided herself on being rational. She cast another glance around the dim, musty, ill-fated building that Bess was so clearly infatuated with.

It seemed to look back at her.

With a smirk.

She sighed, long and slow. Bess was right. Leigh Koslow
Harmon most certainly did *not* believe in ghosts.

But bad karma was a whole different matter.

Chapter 2

"Koslow!" Maura Polanski exclaimed, looking up from the stack of papers on her lap with a smile. "Didn't expect to see you tonight. How did Allison's surgery go?"

Leigh plopped down in the recliner that had been pulled up close to the detective's bedside. Leigh's longtime friend, who was not quite eight months pregnant, had been ordered to stay on strict bed rest because of premature amniotic membrane rupture. Being sentenced to physical inactivity was pure torture for a woman who chased down murderers for a living; but, being pregnant for the first time at forty-two, Maura was not inclined to take chances. Nor was her city police lieutenant husband, who had made it clear to the county homicide squad that any co-worker who tempted the detective into putting so much as one toe on the ground would be busted down to reading parking meters for the rest of his or her career.

"Allison handled it all like a trouper," Leigh answered. "Everything went fine; she's just tired. She dropped off to sleep early, so I thought I'd pop over. Tried to sneak you in a nail file, but Gerry frisked me at the door."

Maura chuckled. "Yeah, he's been a little overprotective. But at least he let Dodson schlep all this in here. I'd be going insane without it."

Leigh raised an eyebrow at the mountain of manila folders and papers piled up on a card table at her friend's other side. "Are you kidding me? What is all this? You can't possibly have gotten this far behind on your reports!"

"They're not mine," Maura responded, closing the folder in her lap and tossing it onto the nearest pile. "At least, not many of them. They're cold cases. The kind nobody has time to look at otherwise, at least not on the current budget. Right now, I've got nothing *but* time."

"Baby staying put?"

Maura patted her abdomen, which slowed only the slightest of bumps. "Oh, yeah. Junior knows how to follow orders," she said proudly.

"Yeah, well," Leigh smirked. "Enjoy *that* while it lasts. At least you finally look pregnant. I was afraid Cara and I were going to have to come over and strap a pillow on you."

"Oh, come on," Maura protested, her eyes twinkling mischievously. "I'm huge!"

Leigh's eyes narrowed. They had all been worried about Maura's having a baby at her age and with her job, but up until her recent hospitalization, the burly six-foot, two-inch detective had sailed through the process with little more than occasional indigestion. The fact that she hadn't needed maternity clothes until well into month seven was of particular annoyance to Leigh, who had looked and felt like a beached whale for the duration of her own pregnancy. "Do not make me hurt you," she growled. "I looked more pregnant than you six months *after* the twins were born!"

Maura laughed. "Yeah, you did, didn't you?"

Leigh gave an exaggerated frown. "Remind me why I bother to come and visit you?"

"Because you know how desperately I need a laugh," Maura replied. "So, what's up with the family? Besides your mother getting her silver fillings pulled and melted into a necklace?"

"Who told you about that?" Leigh asked with surprise.

"Your mother, of course. While she was dusting the bedroom. She even showed me the necklace. It was... an interesting twist on recycling. She's coming back tomorrow to wax the kitchen floor. She said mine was way cleaner than yours, by the way, and that you use an overpriced cleanser that isn't appropriate for your floor surface."

Leigh rubbed her face in her hands. Of course Frances would offer to come and clean for Maura while she was indisposed. Frances would clean anything, at any time. Having the chance to dish on her daughter's insufficiencies while doing so was just an incidental perk. "Well, that's nice of her and fortunate for you," Leigh conceded. "I bet she brought you guys a casserole, too."

"Actually, she brought three." Maura smacked her lips. "Delicious!"

"If she talked to you the whole time she was cleaning, you probably know more about what's going on with the family than I do," Leigh suggested.

"Well, let's see," Maura said with enthusiasm, leaning back against her pillow. "The kids have a week off school, during which you *should* be staying home taking the time to teach them things like how to fold their clothes properly and how to entertain themselves without electronic devices."

Leigh slumped in her chair. "Oh, yeah. Heard that one."

"And we're all proud of Warren because he's doing such a great job helping out all the local non-profits with their financial management, which is a major sacrifice on his part, because he *could* have become President of the United States, you know. Sadly, he had no choice but to stay closer to home and be the most devoted husband and father in the world, seeing as how his wife insisted on having a career of her own rather than dutifully supporting his."

"Standard fare: selfish daughter marries man who can do no wrong. Next?"

"Your father works too many hours at the vet clinic and he's not as young as he used to be."

Leigh nodded. "Husband avoiding being at home; mysteriously not looking forward to retirement. Check."

"And your Aunt Bess has apparently taken on 'another foolhardy project which will only come to grief in the end' and is using 'inappropriate means' to make it happen." Maura's lips twisted with thought. "I was plenty curious about the 'inappropriate means,' but Frances got distracted by a cobweb on the ceiling and had to leave before we got back to the topic."

Leigh chuckled. "Well, I can't say Mom's too far off, there. Aunt Bess showed me her little 'project' yesterday, and it's a doozy. As for whether her methods are inappropriate — that kind of depends on whether Gordon Applegate is complaining."

Maura's eyebrows rose. "Old-money Applegate? Last of the steel baron dynasty? Now you've really got me curious."

"He's a client of Warren's," Leigh explained. "But I didn't realize my Aunt Bess knew him. Apparently he's a bit of a theater buff. Somehow or other — the 'other' being what my mother disapproves of — Bess talked him into buying a hundred-year-old building in West View so that her thespian society could rehab it into a theater. But the place is a total mess... and creepy as hell, besides."

Maura pulled her head up. "What building are we talking about?"

"That red brick monstrosity that used to be a church. Right on Perry Highway, between the funeral home and the dry cleaners."

"Andrew Marconi's place!" Maura cried.

Leigh stared. "You know about him?"

Maura raised an eyebrow. "A guy buys a building in the middle of West View, proposes to open a strip club, starts a major community uprising, and then disappears? No one for two boroughs in any direction is likely to forget that! And perhaps you haven't heard, but I also work as a county detective?"

Leigh sighed. "Sorry, I keep forgetting that other people actually had lives back then. I remember the hoopla it caused in the family, but the twins were toddlers in those days. Whenever I try to recall something from the world outside my house, all my brain serves up are blurred images of dirty diapers and macaroni and cheese."

"So I've heard," Maura replied drily, turning to study her tableful of files. "Marconi never did turn up again, you know. I was just looking at that case yesterday. It wasn't mine, but it always bothered me." She pointed toward a stack just out of her reach. "Can you look in that pile, there? Should be labeled Marconi. Got a couple sticky notes hanging out the side."

Leigh rose, located the file, and handed it over. "Have you been inside the building?"

Maura shook her head as she flipped through the folder.

"It has bad karma," Leigh informed.

The detective frowned. "Don't start with me, Koslow." She found a page with a pink sticky and pulled it out. "I never was happy with this case. The lead investigator wasn't the greatest — he'd been good early on, but then he had some personal problems that got in his way. I always suspected he left a lot of stones unturned with this one, and now I know he did. He never even interviewed your mother!"

"My mother?" Leigh replied, startled. "Why on earth would he? I mean, I know she led the protests against the strip club, but—"

Maura put down the paper and gave Leigh an appraising look. "You really don't remember all this, do you? All right, sit back down and I'll refresh your memory. At least of what's on the public record."

Leigh dropped into her chair.

"To hear the locals tell it now, Andrew Marconi was some glitzy shark from the West Coast who invaded West View with every intention of turning it into the next Las Vegas. But none of that was true. Marconi was a local boy — grew up in Shadyside. His family were big-money lawyers going back several generations, and Marconi was the last of the line. He was also the definition of a black sheep. Failed out of law school, got arrested a couple times for petty stuff, couldn't hold a job. Only success he ever had was when his dad died and he used what little inheritance he'd been granted to buy himself a business. Turns out he had a knack for the adult entertainment industry. He started off with one adult video and novelties store downtown and within a few years had opened a strip club on the South Side and two more novelty shops down in Washington county on the interstate. He bought the building in West View hoping to be the first to offer quality titillation closer to home for the relatively wealthy gentleman of the northern suburbs. But he made a critical error."

Leigh smirked. "He underestimated one Frances Koslow."

"Indeed," Maura agreed. "By all accounts, the public outrage totally blindsided him. He knew there would be some disapproval, but he was naive about his ability to sway the local zoning board. He'd paid more for the building than it was worth, and he was in hock up to his eyeballs after expanding his other businesses so rapidly. The zoning board's decision was critical to him."

"So when he got the bad news he took off, rather than face his debts?" Leigh suggested.

"Well now," Maura said smoothly, "that's just it. That's what everyone assumed. But the fact is, not a single person went on record saying they'd seen Marconi for a full thirty-six hours *before* the decision came down. He didn't attend the final hearing; only his lawyer was present. The president of the zoning board said publicly that he had tried to reach Marconi with the verdict, but was unable to contact him. So yes, Marconi could have heard the verdict through the grapevine, or just seen which way the wind was blowing and took off to parts unknown. But there's not a shred of evidence *proving* that he ever actually found out the news he was waiting so desperately to hear."

Maura eyes met Leigh's with a level gaze. "And in all the years since, the guy's never been seen or heard from. The borough tried to find him — they had to in order to process all the legal rigmarole to get possession of the property he abandoned. He left all his other businesses in the lurch as well — had no further contact with family, employees, or his handful of friends."

Leigh felt a prickle of angst. "I never knew he *disappeared* disappeared. I just thought he skipped town."

"So did everyone else, at first," Maura continued. "But his family raised the alarm when his car turned up abandoned somewhere in McKees Rocks, looking like it had been stolen and dumped several times over. When the investigators found no sign that Marconi had recently drawn out any cash and that he wasn't using any of his credit cards, it began to look more like foul play."

Maura tapped the file with a finger. "The case got assigned to homicide, but it never went anywhere. The detective in charge found zippo and eventually it went on ice." Her expression turned wistful. "I always wanted to take a crack at it. I could see that Doomas was tunneling the thing."

Leigh shifted uncomfortably in the recliner. She preferred the story she *thought* she knew. "What's tunneling?"

Maura's reverie continued a moment before she answered. "Tunnel vision. You've got a guy named Marconi who's into strip clubs and adult retail, and who owes a lot of money, and he mysteriously goes missing. What does that say to you?"

Leigh shrugged. "Loan sharks? Mob hit?"

"Exactly," Maura proclaimed, smiling crookedly. "That's what the detective went looking for. And those things are possible, sure. But what if his name was Steinmetz and he sold organic potpourri and scented candles?"

Leigh's forehead creased. "Not following."

"Just because a guy has an Italian name and sells sleaze doesn't mean he's connected," Maura explained. "Nothing in Marconi's file points to that. And he owed a lot of money, yes, but he owed it to legitimate lenders and he wasn't in any immediate crisis. So his name might as well have been Steinmetz and he might as well have sold candles. And if that was the case — *then* what do you think might have happened to him?"

Leigh considered. "Lover's spat? Mental breakdown? Random mugging gone wrong?"

"Assault by a crazed community organizer wearing orange lipstick and carrying a giant handbag?" Maura smirked. "You get my point. The detective spent almost no time looking at the other possibilities. He was too focused on what the stereotype dictated. Tunnel vision."

Leigh got antsy. She rose from the recliner and began to pace. She'd never met Andrew Marconi and couldn't pretend to care about him personally, but whenever the M word came into play her feet itched — and justifiably so — to run the other direction. "So you think he was... you know?"

"Oh yeah," Maura said matter-of-factly. "I'd bet money he's dead. What's curious is why his body never turned up."

"Okay!" Leigh said loudly, throwing up her hands. "TMI, detective. I don't need to hear anymore. Can we talk about something else, please? Like, say... food?"

Maura had sunk her head back into her pillows again. She was staring at the ceiling, looking contemplative. "I asked Doomas back then if he was going to search the building, and I remember what he said. He looked right at me and said 'For what?' like it was a stupid question! I guess he thought the mob was so good at disposing of bodies that even bothering to look for one would be a waste of his precious time."

Leigh put a hand on the doorknob. "I'd better get going."

A frown creased Maura's face. "He did wind up doing a search, but how thorough was he? If only I could get up and out of here, I'd go down there myself right now and—" Her gaze rested on Leigh, whose presence she seemed to have momentarily forgotten. Ever so slowly, the detective's frown melted into a smile. "Then again, I don't need to get up, do I?"

Leigh didn't care for the gleam in her friend's eye. "Did I mention that I have to go?"

"How much time have you spent in that building?"

"Allison may wake up and need me."

"Koslow!" Maura exclaimed, sitting up. Her cheeks were suddenly rosy. "*Why* did I never think of this before? All these years I've been cursing your sheer dumb luck, when I could have been making use of you! Why, you're better than a damn cadaver dog!"

Leigh's face grew hot. "You *are* kidding, aren't you?"

Maura chuckled. "Of course, of course."

Leigh studied her another moment. "No, you're not!"

"Well, not completely," Maura admitted, still smiling. "You have to admit, it would be terribly convenient."

Leigh rolled her eyes with a groan. The irritable, swearing, stomping Maura she had known and loved since her college days she knew how to deal with — but ever since the detective had heard her baby's heartbeat, she had turned into an incurably happy camper whose peaceful, laissez-faire demeanor was curiously disturbing.

"I'd feel a whole lot more comfortable if you'd just yell at me and tell me to stay the hell away from there," Leigh declared.

Maura shrugged. "No can do, Koslow. Stress is bad for the baby. But if it bothers you, just forget I said anything. Go on back with your Aunt Bess and scrape paint off the walls, redecorate, hang curtains — whatever you would otherwise do." She smiled innocently.

Leigh turned to leave.

"If Marconi's there," Maura muttered with cheer, "I'm sure you'll run into him."

Chapter 3

"Are you positive you're up to this?" Leigh asked her daughter worriedly as the Pack scrambled out of the van.

"I'm fine, Mom," Allison assured, twirling her neon pink eye patch around on her finger. "My eye just feels a little scratchy, that's all. Do I have to wear this thing? The doctor said it was 'optional.'"

Leigh studied her daughter tentatively. Allison had been born prematurely and was small for her age, but the image of frailty she presented was only skin deep. The child had a mind like a steel trap and the curiosity of about six cats — a most uncomfortable combination, at least for her parents. "He also said you should avoid dust," Leigh reminded. "Which will be completely impossible in this building without it. Now, put it on, please."

Allison sighed, adjusted the patch over her left eye, then put her glasses back on.

"I think it looks cool, Al," her brother Ethan encouraged. "Makes you look dangerous, in a girly sort of way."

Leigh smiled at her son, who had been born just as prematurely, but was big for his age. At eleven, he was nearly as tall as Cara's son Mathias, who was thirteen and relatively tall himself. For much of the boys' lives they had been the same size, but Mathias had recently hit a growth spurt.

"Is it really dusty?" Cara's daughter Lenna, also eleven, asked. "Maybe I shouldn't have worn these leggings." Her large blue eyes blinked with distress, and Leigh stifled a sigh. Neither she nor Cara had a clue how any girl born with Morton genes could be such a shrinking violet. Pathological anxiety in general was understandable — in that Lenna was like her Great Aunt Frances. But fear of insects, dirt, sweat, reptiles, and fashion faux pas put the child in sharp contrast to the rest of the Morton women, who — while sporting a variety of other neuroses — were uniformly audacious.

"They'll wash," Leigh assured, closing the last of the doors and locking the van with her remote. "Let's go on in and check it out. If anybody doesn't want to stay and work, I can take you back home. It's up to you."

The Pack looked at each other. Leigh knew full well that none of them would back out now, but she couldn't resist making the offer. Just looking at the outside of the accursed building was enough to give her the heebie-jeebies. But she could hardly justify keeping everyone else out of it based on nothing but bad vibes and a bad joke. At least, she *hoped* Maura had only been joking. How could the detective be serious, when any number of people, including the police and a bevy of building inspectors, had been in and out of the place multiple times in the years since Marconi had gone missing? There was no rational reason to worry about... *that*.

As Leigh led the Pack toward the building, a side door to the annex was opened, apparently by a giant bag of Styrofoam packing peanuts with legs. The figure stumbled to the rental dumpster and the bag was tossed up and in, revealing the shabbily dressed torso of a bulky man in late middle-age with a wild head of graying hair and broken black eyeglasses repaired with duct tape. He caught sight of the group and stared a moment, his jaw slack. "You here to see Ms. Bess?" he asked, his words slow and drawn out.

"That's right," Leigh answered. "She's here, isn't she?"

The man nodded. "She's in the sanctuary." His gaze turned to the Pack, and as he stared at them his eyes began to bug as if the children were armed and dangerous. "Are you the kids gonna work in the basement?" he asked tentatively.

"They are," Leigh responded, assessing him. The man did not appear to be mentally challenged, but his odd manner could certainly be described as "socially awkward." She decided that he must be one of the men Bess had hired through a local charity to help with the manual labor. "I'm Bess's niece, Leigh. Nice to meet you."

"I'm Ned." He said simply, then he turned around and began walking back inside. Leigh looked over her shoulder to see Mathias elbowing Ethan in the ribs and whispering something in his cousin's ear.

Ethan grinned. "Yeah, he does!" he said out loud.

After the man was out of earshot inside, Leigh turned around. "He does what?"

Ethan looked slightly embarrassed. "Oh, it's just that he looks like this character in a show we used to watch all the time."

"What show?" Lenna asked.

"You know," Mathias answered. "The Scooby Doo episode where—"

Lenna shrieked and covered her mouth with her hands. "The creepy janitor!"

"Stop that," Leigh ordered, speaking to herself as much as the kids. "There's nothing creepy about him. He's just a man trying to do an honest day's work. I suggest you leave him alone and let him do it."

Stay away — far, far away, Leigh added mentally. She could hardly admit it to the kids, but the man *was* creepy. Which meant that everything about him fit into his current surroundings perfectly.

They had just reached the door when the cool spring sun slid behind a cloud, darkening the sky. Leigh gritted her teeth and pulled on the door handle, fully expecting a hundred bats to come flying out in her face, just like in the Scooby Doo opening credits.

The door creaked open uneventfully.

It's just a building! She reminded herself. So what if every blasted thing about the place was creepy?

"Come on in," she said with false cheer, holding the door open for the Pack and then pointing the way to the sanctuary. "Go see if you can find your Aunt Bess." She would have made a joke about the — very real — bats waiting in the rafters, but she didn't care to hear Lenna shriek again.

The kids took off toward the sanctuary without looking back, and Leigh lingered in the hall a moment, wishing she hadn't had quite so much diet cola on the drive down. Bess had said that the plumbing in the bathrooms was functional, but there was little else to recommend them. Would they even have toilet paper? Leigh grimaced as she opened the door to the women's room and stepped inside.

Her nose was struck immediately by the distinctive scent of lemon mixed with ammonia. She looked down to see a black and white tile floor not only clear of debris, but shining in the harsh fluorescent light. Looking up revealed bright pink stalls, gleaming white sinks and a spotless mirror. The metal trash can in the corner had disappeared, replaced by a white wicker bin with a neatly tied-off plastic liner. The towel dispenser hung straight on the wall, exposing an appropriate two inches' worth of brown paper.

Leigh stood still and stared. It was Saturday morning. She had just been here on Thursday. There could be only one explanation for such a phenomenal transformation.

A toilet flushed. Leigh watched as a woman's behind backed out of the stall, clad in fake-denim, elastic-waisted work pants with a cleaning smock tied around the back. The woman straightened and turned towards Leigh. Her carefully coifed hair was covered with a clear plastic rain bonnet, and she held a toilet bowl brush in one hand and a bottle of cleanser in the other.

"Hi, Mom," Leigh greeted. "Wow. You've been busy."

Frances's lips pursed. "Your aunt has gone too far this time. You do realize that this scheme of hers isn't feasible?"

Leigh considered the question rhetorical. "The bathroom looks great."

Frances harrumphed. She set down her tools in a bucket by the sink and removed her gloves. Then she pulled off the bonnet, tucked it in a pocket of her smock, and fluffed her limp curls. "Decent restrooms are the least of Bess's problems."

Leigh short-circuited the rant she feared was coming by slipping into a stall and attending to her business. When she emerged, her mother was no longer in the bathroom. Smiling at the success of her tactic, Leigh washed her hands with the provided industrial-strength antibacterial hand soap and stepped back out into the hall.

"What Bess does not realize," Frances continued from her position just outside the door, "is that a building this size cannot just be cleaned once. It will require constant diligence both in cleaning and in repairs, absolutely indefinitely. Her rag-tag group of part-time thespians cannot possibly manage such a task, nor can they afford to pay to have it done properly. Why, if your aunt had any idea how much it would cost to hire a so-called 'professional' to perform all the cleaning services so desperately needed around this—"

"Did you see the bat guano in the sanctuary?" Leigh interjected hopefully.

Frances's eyes narrowed, and Leigh fought the urge to shrink. She could live to be a hundred and the sight of her mother's keen eyes glaring out of slits would still make her feel like a preschooler with a stolen cookie. *"Bat guano?"* Frances repeated in a gravelly deadpan. "You have seriously seen the droppings of bats, *inside* this building?"

Leigh smiled weakly. "On the choir railing."

Frances departed, bucket in hand.

Leigh breathed a sigh of relief and headed slowly down the hall. It was one thing for Bess and Frances to bicker with each other for well over a half century; it was another to have to hear about it. If she was lucky, the bat guano would distract Frances for at least twenty minutes, which should be more than enough time for Leigh to get the kids settled and herself the hell out of here before the next harangue.

She entered the sanctuary to see the kids and Bess just on their way out of the room, heading through the far door to the basement staircase. Frances was already drenching the choir railing with some substance in a spray bottle, and two men were pulling up the filthy carpet and cutting it into strips. As one man jerked up a particularly nasty section, dust exploded into the air so thickly that it looked like Bess had rented a fog machine. Leigh coughed.

"Sorry about that," the man apologized. He seemed to be in his late twenties or early thirties, with blond hair, blue eyes, and a boyish grin. "One thing about being a smoker, your lungs are used to the abuse!" he laughed merrily. "But for anyone else, this dust is killer. When the YBC — that's the Young Businessmen's Chamber, you know — when we were doing the haunted houses and used the fans, the dust got so bad we had to start wetting down the carpet first. Hey, Gerardo!" he called eagerly, looking at his coworker. "We should try that now!"

He made a bizarre gesture that Leigh assumed was meant to indicate spraying the carpet with a hose, but looked more like he was waving an imaginary handgun. Gerardo, a tall and rather handsome Hispanic man in his mid to late thirties, raised an eyebrow and stared dubiously.

"Oh, never mind," the younger man said, laughing at himself again. He turned to Leigh. "He doesn't speak English. That's Gerardo, and I'm Chaz. Are you another relative of Bess's?"

"I'm her niece, Leigh. Nice to meet you, Chaz." She turned to the other man with a nod. "You too, Gerardo."

Gerardo nodded back at her politely. He remained mute, his face neutral of expression, but his dark eyes surveyed her with a knowing look she found unnerving. Leigh coughed again, then glanced up at the chancel area to see how her mother was faring. She needn't have worried, since Frances was already in "haz mat" mode, attacking the guano with gloves, a paper smock, and one of her husband's surgical face masks. She was scrubbing away like a mad woman, paying no attention whatsoever to anyone else in the room.

"Did you ever see any of the haunted houses?" Chaz chattered, dropping his end of the carpet and releasing another cloud of dust. Gerardo made a snorting sound, pulled the carpet strip his way, and began to roll it up alone.

Leigh shook her head. "Sorry. I missed them."

"They were really awesome!" Chaz continued proudly. "I'm in the YBC, you know. Or at least I was. I worked three Halloweens here. So if you need to know where anything is, just ask me. They used to call me 'storage guy!'" He laughed at himself once more, holding his side for effect. "It was hysterical!"

Leigh shot a glance at Gerardo, and she could swear the man returned a look of wry humor before swiftly averting his gaze.

Leigh tensed. Though neither of the two men seemed threatening, something was not right with the picture Gerardo presented, and Chaz was rapidly proving himself to be a brainless chatterbox. Before she had so much as a second to disengage herself, Chaz launched into a long story about how he had once lined up a bunch of fake sarcophaguses along the sanctuary wall and then someone else had made them fall like a line of dominos, spilling the plaster mummies out on the carpet and nearly breaking the top of his own foot, which was so badly bruised he had to borrow another guy's shoes because his instep was so swollen he couldn't get his work boots back on...

Leigh nodded and said "oh, really?" at regular intervals, looking for an opportune pause in which to make a polite exit, but the man was clearly a master of the game, ending each phrase with an upward inflection so that no sentence ever really ended. She was about to give up and treat him like family — with a rude, full-out, mid-sentence interruption — when something he was saying actually penetrated her gray matter.

"You know, like happened with the real murder. But some

people thought that was in bad taste, so what we ended up doing instead was—"

"Real murder?" she barked without apology. "What real murder?"

At last Chaz paused and took a breath. His eyes twinkled with delight. "Oh, surely you've heard about *that!* The way the body was found and all — I thought everybody in West View knew!"

"Clearly not," Leigh deadpanned, her limited patience dwindling rapidly.

"Of course, that was *ages* ago. Maybe you were too young to remember." His blue eyes teased her. He knew damned well she was a least a decade older than he was. If she didn't know better, she'd swear the guy was flirting with her.

Gerardo let out an odd sound. Leigh looked up to find him smothering a supposed cough, but the look in his eyes told her he was laughing.

She returned his smirk with a glare. *Like hell you can't speak English!*

"Look, Chaz," she said sharply, deciding to table the issue of Gerardo's deception — for now. "I grew up in West View, but I haven't lived here since college and I obviously don't remember any murder. Are you talking about Andrew Marconi?"

Chaz's blond eyebrows lifted. "The mob guy? Oh no, I'm talking about the first one."

Leigh's knees felt suddenly weak. "The *first* one?"

He nodded vigorously. "Way, *way* back. When this place was still a church." He moved to the wall and lounged against a windowsill. "My grandma said the church members tried to keep the whole thing hush-hush, you know. There were all sorts of rumors flying around about human sacrifice and devil worship and all that. My mom says that part was probably all nonsense — and maybe it was. But Grandma says the basic facts of it were true, at least. And the church never recovered from the scandal. They sold the building and it was never used as a church again. Because you know, like Grandma says, once something really evil happens in a place—"

"Your mother was absolutely right, young man," Frances interrupted, glaring down from the edge of the chancel with her hands planted on her hips and her face mask pulled down to yield an extra chin. "There was not, nor has there ever been, any *devil worship* in West View! That was a ridiculous rumor started by a bunch of gossip mongers with nothing better to do with their time than stir up trouble, and we should not be repeating such nonsense, even now."

Leigh was beginning to see how she might never have heard of this before.

"But the body *was* laid out on the altar," Chaz argued in a sulky tone. "That much was definitely true. Grandma says everybody said so."

"Where an intruder chooses to commit a random act of violence is neither here nor there," Frances insisted. "At the time, this was a God-fearing church with good, decent people in it. *End of story.*"

Leigh begged to differ. "Excuse me, but could someone please tell me what the hell murder we're talking about?"

Frances's glare could freeze lit charcoal. "You will watch your language in a house of worship, young lady!"

Leigh bit her lip. The building in which they were standing hadn't been a house of worship for longer than she had been alive, and she was pretty sure that even when it was, the word "hell" was broadcast from the pulpit on a regular basis. But she had no interest in arguing either point with Frances.

She turned back to Chaz. "What exactly did your grandmother tell you about a body?"

The twinkle returned to his eyes. "It was the church custodian. He was working here all alone one night, and he never came home. When the minister or whoever came in the next morning, they found him right up there" — he gestured to the empty chancel area — "laid out on top of the altar. *Dead.*"

Leigh looked at the empty space near where her mother stood. The same space she'd been standing in two days ago when the hair on the back of her neck had lifted.

The same hairs crept up again.

"Stabbed through the heart," Chaz finished darkly.

"Oh, poppycock!" Frances protested hotly. "The poor man died from a blow to the head!"

Chaz's expression turned sulky again. "Well, yeah, maybe." He turned to Leigh and winked. "But stabbing makes a better story, don't you think?"

"Don't you think," Frances said scathingly, "that you young men — whom my sister is paying by the hour — ought to *get back to work?!*"

Chaz jumped to attention and started tugging on another loose corner of carpet. Gerardo followed suit. Frances uttered a loud harrumph and turned back to the choir railing.

Leigh stood still a moment, digesting the unpleasant information. Bess knew all about the building's history, clearly. She just hadn't seen fit to tell Leigh about it. And why not?

She turned away from the workers and headed for the door her aunt and the Pack had gone through earlier. It opened to an alcove with both a narrow staircase and a wheelchair ramp leading down to the basement. The concrete ramp was clearly an afterthought, having been built outside originally and then enclosed later with inexpensive aluminum walls and storm windows. As Leigh headed down the twists and turns of the seemingly endless incline, she noticed that the sky had turned gray, and scattered raindrops thumped noisily above her head as she descended.

Blasted creepy building, she muttered to herself, having no trouble imagining Bess's theater group flooding the basement to put on *Phantom of the Opera.* Add a couple candles and a rowboat, and the atmosphere would be perfect.

She emerged into the basement to see Bess perched imperiously on a three-legged stool, rendering judgment on the fate of various objects that the Pack filed forward to present. "This birdcage is a gem, Allison!" she cooed. "It wouldn't hold a bird, of course, but it would look lovely on a Victorian set. Put it in the 'priority props' pile. Oh heavens, Matt dear, throw those stinky things away." She raised her voice to announcement level. "All ballet shoes go in the trash pile! Unless they don't smell in the *slightest.*"

"There's nothing here that doesn't smell in the slightest!" Lenna called back with a giggle, wrinkling her perfect little nose.

"Some smells are more acceptable than others," Bess said lightly, taking a closer look at the bizarre globe-shaped mass of paper mache that Ethan held out to her at arm's length. It was covered with red and white globs of crepe paper and had a black circle painted on one side. "Good Lord, child," she said disparagingly, "what on earth was this supposed to be, do you think?"

Ethan shrugged. "Giant eyeball?"

Bess's own nose wrinkled. "Trash pile."

"Check," the boy said cheerfully, moving off.

Leigh sidled in as soon as the children were out of earshot. "Aunt Bess," she whispered, "you did *not* tell me there was actually a murder in this building!"

"Didn't I?" Bess said innocently. "I presumed you already knew. It's hardly a secret, after all. It's been common knowledge since the sixties. What of it?"

"What of it?" Leigh repeated incredulously.

Bess's level gaze didn't falter. "Yes, what of it?"

Leigh's face reddened.

"How about this, Aunt Bess?" Lenna asked, bounding up with an enormous purple crushed-velvet robe trimmed with brown fur. It was big enough for a very large man. Or a small whale.

"Narwhal ceremonial gear," Bess pronounced. "Put it in 'costumes.' You never know — maybe Herod could wear it in *Superstar!*"

Lenna skipped off, and Bess turned back to Leigh with a castigating look. "Really, kiddo, I'm surprised at you. People die in hospitals and nursing homes all the time, and those buildings don't bother you, do they?"

"But that's—"

"And you can't possibly be worried about finding the poor man's body, since it was buried over half a century ago."

"Well, in my case, that doesn't necessarily—"

"One can't very well avoid any building where anyone ever kicked it," Bess continued. "Heavens, I can't even avoid places where you've personally found—"

"Can we not bring all that up, please?" Leigh begged, her cheeks still flaming. "I just want to make sure the Pack is safe here, that's all."

Bess frowned. "And why on earth wouldn't they be? They're with me, aren't they?"

Mathias appeared before them holding a chain saw that was encrusted with a red substance disturbingly reminiscent of blood. "This must be from the haunted houses!" he enthused. "Can I turn it on and see if it works?"

Leigh opened her mouth to speak, but Bess beat her to it. "You know perfectly well you may not. In any event, it has no chain and is almost certainly out of gas. Still, put it in the donation pile for the veterans. It might be of use to somebody."

"Okay, but can I scare Grandma Frances with it first?"

"By all means."

Mathias trotted happily toward the stairs.

"Matt!" Leigh chastised. "Your aunt was only joking!" The boy stopped with a pout, and Leigh turned to face Bess again. "It's more than just what happened in the sixties," she whispered fervently. "The police aren't so sure that Andrew Marconi took off of his own free will. They think he might have been murdered as well!"

Bess shrugged. "So what if he was? It's not like it happened here in the building."

Leigh threw her aunt a hard look.

Bess's expression turned thoughtful. "So they're not sure where it happened, are they? How very interesting. Still, that was almost a decade ago. There wouldn't be much evidence left of him now, would there? I mean, after that length of time, with the building's being mostly shut up and without air conditioning... I would guess all you'd find now would be bones, perhaps with hair on the—" Bess jumped. "Heavens, child! I didn't see you there. What do you have for me now?"

Leigh looked over at Bess's opposite elbow, and her pulse pounded. Allison stood inches away, smiling innocently. She had, as always, crept up as quietly as a cat in a sandbox. How much had she overheard?

Leigh's teeth gritted. Who was she kidding? Allison had undoubtedly heard every age-inappropriate word.

"It's just one of the tablecloths," the girl answered. "I was going to put it in the donation pile with the others, but this one doesn't have any stains on it, and it's got this lace trim that's kind of pretty. You want it in the props pile?"

Bess smiled. "Absolutely, dear. Good call."

"Allison," Leigh said sternly. "How long have you been standing there?"

The girl looked back at her levelly. "Long enough to see Mathias sneak upstairs with the chain saw."

A blood-curdling shriek reverberated through the ceiling tiles, followed by boyish laughter and the heavy pounding of running feet.

"Oh, dear," Bess lamented, her eyes sparkling wickedly. "However *did* that boy slip past me?"

Chapter 4

Leigh sat outside in the rain. It was only sprinkling at the moment, and the highest of the front steps stayed reasonably dry under the eaves, so she was content. Never mind that the concrete under her butt was freezing. All that mattered was that she was *not* inside the specter-ridden building.

She gazed idly at the traffic that moved along Perry Highway. The appeal of the location to a fast food restaurant or a drugstore was obvious. Why couldn't someone else have won the bidding and torn the place down? Even as she chided herself for disloyalty to her aunt, the thought held appeal. The sorry brick building had had its shot, and had only ever seemed to attract misery. Why not let some shiny new burger joint inflict high cholesterol on the populace instead?

"Hey you, there!" a scratchy voice called. Over the steady din of the traffic, Leigh hardly heard it, but on the other side of the highway she could see an elderly woman standing on the porch of an old house waving her arms. An older man sat in a chair next to her, a four legged walker parked by his feet. "You, there!" the woman called insistently. "Come across?"

Leigh threw a quick glance over her shoulder. She was the only person in sight; the woman must be summoning her. Most likely, the neighbors had noticed the commotion around the building and wondered what was going on.

Leigh rose stiffly from the cold concrete, waited some time for a safe break in the traffic, then jogged across the two lanes and up the neighbor's sidewalk. The large brick house looked very much like the one Maura still owned in nearby Avalon. It had probably been built around the same time as the church and had once been a grand family home on the young borough's main thoroughfare. But now, like so many of its ilk, it had been converted into apartments and swallowed up by commercial zoning.

"Oh, thank you!" the woman gushed, waving Leigh up onto her half of the front porch. "I'm Merle Dubanowski, and this is my husband Earl." She cocked her head toward the man in the chair, who looked up at Leigh with a nod and a smile. "Sorry to bother you, but Earl and I've been dying to know what all's going on over there. Do you know? Have a seat, hun. Can I get you some coffee? What's your name again?"

"Leigh Koslow, and no thank you," Leigh answered, dropping into the proffered wicker loveseat, which was significantly more comfortable than her concrete step.

"Are you from around here? Do you know who bought the building? What they're gonna to do with it?" Merle questioned as she lowered herself into another chair opposite. Leigh judged the woman to be in her late seventies, skinny and weathered looking but a shrewd intelligence behind her dark brown eyes. Her clothes were worn and surroundings modest, but all were kept scrupulously tidy, in contrast to the porch on the opposite side of the house, which was liberally cluttered with plastic toys, broken furniture, and dead houseplants.

Leigh attempted to sort through the relevant questions. "I grew up in West View, but I live in McCandless now. The building was bought by a philanthropist, and it's being rented to the North Boros Thespian Society. They want to turn it into a theater."

Merle's eyes widened to saucers. "A *theater?*"

"A theater?" Earl repeated, scratching his bald, age-spotted head. He was a short man, round in the middle but with arms and legs like sticks, and he sunk into his plastic Adirondack chair as if he'd been poured there. Leigh wondered how he managed to get out of it.

"That's right," she responded. She hadn't thought to wonder whether the immediate neighbors would take kindly to Bess's wild idea. She knew that despite her own mother's complaints, all the locals in her family were supportive of community theater in general and the idea of a new "cultural attraction" in West View in particular. Surely most of the local citizens would be happy just to see the building taken care of again.

"I was kind of hoping they'd just tear the damn thing down," Merle said bitterly.

Leigh sat up. "You were? Why is that?"

Merle's pale lips puckered. Her head shook. "We've never seen nothing good come out of that place, and we've lived here over thirty years."

"Thirty years?" Earl echoed uncertainly.

"Yes, thirty!" Merle replied, then turned back to Leigh. "Always been an eyesore. Bunch of drunken men dressing up like animals and playing like idiots — who wants that outside their front door? Then they rented it out for receptions and that, and we still had drunks puking on the sidewalks. And those god-awful haunted houses! Good Lord. Earl and me would go over and stay at my sister's whenever that happened."

"I thought it was twenty years," Earl mumbled.

"You know we moved here in 1979!" Merle insisted. She turned to Leigh once more, her expression troubled. "What kind of theater are we talking about? You don't mean somebody else is trying to open up one of them girlie peep shows—"

"Oh, no," Leigh interrupted quickly. "Not a strip club. Nothing like it. A community theater that puts on plays." Her mind searched for some agreeable titles. "Like *The Mousetrap* or *Arsenic and Old Lace.*"

Merle's frown lifted a bit. "Well now. That sounds all right, I guess."

Leigh smiled. Bess's group had actually done both those plays, so she wasn't being dishonest. There was no need to tell Merle what considerably more risqué shows Bess would produce if she actually got the chance, because there had always been enough reasonably sane individuals in the troupe to overrule her. Leigh could only hope there always would be, as she was pretty sure that any family member's participation in a nude version of *A Midsummer Night's Dream* would drive Frances Koslow to apoplexy.

"But I still wish they'd just tear the damn thing down," Merle repeated sulkily. "At least then we could stop worrying about what was going on over there. All night long, lights moving, strange noises... you know anybody could move into that place — drifters, whoever. We never know who's over there. But damned if there isn't always something going on."

"We moved in '87, didn't we?" Earl protested.

"No!" Merle argued. "That was when Jimmy moved to Texas. We came here in '79. The year after your mother died, remember?"

"That was your mother."

"No! My mother died in '76. You're thinking of Jimmy's mother-in-law having that heart attack right before he and Lori Ann went to Texas..."

Leigh's mind drifted. It was some time before the couple remembered her existence, and Earl never did concede on the year in which they had moved. But as soon as Leigh had her hostess's attention, she asked the obvious question. "You said something was always going on in the building. Something like what? You mean when it was abandoned?"

Merle's shrewd eyes held hers. "I mean always. Can't tell you how many times Earl or myself looked out our bedroom window and saw lights over there. Could be the middle of the night. Most of the time things were quiet, though, and as long as whoever it was didn't bother us, we didn't bother them, you know."

"You didn't call the police?"

Merle gave a shrug. "We never knew the owners — could have been them over there for all we knew. There was only one time we were sure it was vagrants — partiers, you know — what with the loud music and the voices and all. Earl was just about ready to call the police on them when they come running out the front doors like the devil himself was chasing them. Burst out in a big cloud of cigarette smoke, screaming and carrying on. Said the building was haunted and they could have been killed."

"Damn hippies," Earl said with grunt.

Merle nodded. "Earl and I heard every word of it — they were all right out in the street. Talking about how a man got murdered there once, and now the same murderer was chasing them. Or the ghost of the guy who got murdered — they didn't seem real clear. Of course, they were most likely drunk or stoned or something. But they scattered, the lot of them, and they didn't come back. And nobody else ever partied there after them, neither."

Leigh was beginning to wish she had accepted the offer of hot coffee. When had the spring air turned so chilly?

"How long ago was all this?" she asked, not sure she wanted an answer.

Merle gave another shrug. "Oh, long time ago. Before the Young Businessmen's Chamber started all that nonsense at Halloween. Back when it was rented out for receptions and that. Like I said, though, it doesn't seem to matter much who owns it. Funny stuff happens irregardless."

"There's somebody over there," Earl agreed with a nod.

Leigh didn't really want to know the answers to her next questions, but her traitorous mouth asked them anyway. "Somebody like who? What kind of funny stuff?"

Merle pulled her worn cardigan more tightly across her chest. "Well now, that depends on who you ask. What with that church custodian being murdered way back when, a lot of people around here say the building's just plain haunted. But Earl and me, we don't believe in none of that nonsense."

"No, we do not," Earl added with emphasis.

"We were still living over in Bellevue when it happened," Merle continued, "but we heard about it. Everybody did." She gave an exaggerated shudder. "All that talk of devil worship and human sacrifice! Nothing but rubbish, if you ask me, but no church wanted the place after that, and it's gone downhill ever since. We tell people what we see... with the lights bobbing around at night, and even vandals afraid to stay there — and they all say it's haunted. But me and Earl, we just think it's somebody messing with people. Who knows why. People are hard to figure sometimes."

"Lori Ann's a little overweight," Earl interjected.

Leigh waited a moment. Merle made no response, and Leigh couldn't think of an appropriate one, either. "The murder of the custodian," she asked instead. "The case was solved eventually, right? They found out why it happened like it did?"

Merle shook her head. "Never did figure that out. Not that I heard, anyway. Of course, the custodian was no prince himself, you know. Mean guy, nasty temper. They say the police were already watching him, ever since a buddy of his had gone missing a couple weeks before, right after the two of them got into a fistfight over a woman. So of course when the custodian got killed, everyone thought the buddy had come back and done *him* in. But the police never could find that other guy, dead or alive, and they couldn't prove a darn thing one way or the other, so that was the end of it."

"What church did that woman go to?" Earl asked loudly.

"What woman?" Merle asked louder.

"Lori Ann's mother!"

"Seventh-day Adventist."

Earl squirmed slightly more upright in his chair, leaned over toward Leigh, and pointed his finger at her meaningfully. "She was a Seventh-day Adventist."

Leigh nodded silently back.

"Haunted or not," Merle continued, "we'd both be a whole lot happier if the damn place was just torn down. It'd make such a nice park, you know. Plant some trees and set up a few benches and swing sets for the kids — now that's a sight I'd like to see out my windows. Wouldn't you, Earl?"

Earl was still looking at Leigh. "They have their services on Saturdays, you know."

"I've heard that," Leigh replied, just as a spot of strawberry blond drifted into her peripheral vision. She looked across the street and recognized her cousin Cara walking around the rear of the building and down the side street with a camera in her hands. Cara caught sight of her at the same time and waved.

Leigh rose with a smile. Her cousin always did have excellent timing. "It's been nice chatting with you," she told her hosts, "but I'm afraid I need to get back. I'll send my Aunt Bess over sometime to talk to you about the theater. I'm sure she can answer any questions you may have."

The couple smiled and expressed their thanks, and Leigh darted back across the highway.

"That looked interesting," Cara commented as she snapped a quick picture of the front windows. "Were the neighbors pumping you for information, or vice versa?"

"Both," Leigh answered. Assuming that Cara was planning to go inside, Leigh stepped in between her cousin and the door. "Look," she began, embarrassed by her inexplicable wussiness. "I don't mean to sound paranoid or anything, but with the Pack working here, I'm just a little... I mean... did you know there was a murder here once?"

Cara's attractive blue-green eyes blinked. "You mean that church custodian?"

Leigh blew out a breath. "Aunt Bess told you, then?"

Cara's forehead furrowed. Leigh's cousin was only two years younger than she was, but unlike Leigh, Cara's still-gorgeous face only showed wrinkles when she laughed. Or when she was confused. "Aunt Bess didn't need to tell me. Everyone knows that story."

"Well, I didn't!" Leigh protested. "But I knew something was wrong with the place the moment I walked in, just the same. I could *feel* it, Cara. I could sense where it happened, even!"

Cara's expression grew even more incredulous. "Don't be ridiculous, Leigh! Of course you knew about the murder. Everyone did. That story fascinated us when we were kids!"

Now it was Leigh's turn to blink. "It did?"

Cara smiled. "Of course. We weren't supposed to know anything, and we couldn't say anything in front of our mothers, but it was common knowledge. Classic spooky story material for all the West View kids. Don't you remember — one time you told a younger neighbor girl about it, in dripping detail, and she got so upset she cried. Her mother walked over and complained to my mother, and then my mother went over and told your mother —"

Leigh groaned and held up a hand. "Spare me the rest, please."

"You remember now?"

"No," Leigh replied, "but I'm sure that living through it once was enough." How could she possibly forget such a thing? She had always prided herself on being able to remember more detail from her childhood than most people could, including Cara. Her memory of the first few sleep-deprived years after the twins were born would always be vague, true. But she had thought her earlier memories were still solid.

Traitorous gray matter, she thought with chagrin. Being over forty was hell. What other information was getting wiped out of her brain by the minute?

"That story always did capture your imagination," Cara continued, rubbing it in. "I'm not surprised you felt a little unsettled walking into the sanctuary." She smiled, then had the gall to laugh. "Did you really think you were psychic or something?"

"Of course not," Leigh lied. She stepped out of her cousin's way. "What are you doing here, anyway? I thought I was supposed to bring the Pack home."

"You are," Cara answered, stepping not toward the entrance, but on across the front steps. "I'm only here to get a few quick pictures. Aunt Bess wants me to do a sketch of the outside to use on some promotional materials for the Society." She frowned at the missing crenelations on top of the mouth-like tower. "Hmm. This will take some fudging."

Leigh followed as her cousin walked slowly around the front

corner and up the parking lot side of the building, snapping pictures as she went. "Honestly," Cara said, frowning at the aluminum and acrylic housing that stuck out of the building's side to enclose the monstrous wheelchair ramp, "with all that added on and without the steeple and the stained glass the original church was designed to have, it'll be tough to make this building look anything less than hideous."

"Quite," Leigh agreed.

Both women were startled by a sudden movement from above. They looked up to see Ned, the man Leigh had met at the dumpster earlier, standing on the flat roof of the annex and leaning a ladder up against the back wall of the old sanctuary. With a roll of screen wire and a hammer tucked under one arm, he began to ascend the ladder.

"Oh, be careful!" Cara cried. "It's been raining."

Ned looked down at them both dubiously, his shaggy gray hair tousling in the breeze. "Ms. Frances says we gotta keep the bats out."

Right above where Ned had placed the top of the ladder was an attic vent boasting holes the size of fists. "I'm sure neither Frances nor Bess want you to do anything dangerous," Cara called back. "Maybe you should wait until the roof is dry?"

"Won't make any difference," came a husky voice from behind them. "He could fall through just as easily in the sunshine."

Leigh and Cara turned to see a woman barely five feet tall — and that while wearing four-inch heels — standing behind them in a crisp business suit. She carried a professional camera similar to Cara's and was wearing a hands-free earpiece so large in comparison to her tiny ear that it dominated the entire left side of her face.

"Excuse me?" Cara remarked. Her tone was superficially polite, but Leigh knew her cousin well enough to know that she had taken an instant dislike to the stranger.

"Sonia Crane, attorney at law," the woman rasped. Her voice sounded like something one might expect from a retired miner with emphysema, not a woman the size of a fourth grader. "Crane and Associates," she finished, extending a rigid, perfectly straight hand first to Cara, then to Leigh.

Leigh attempted to shake, but might as well have attempted to engage a slab of granite. The woman was probably around their own age, but her overzealously tanned skin was leathery and her perfectly tailored clothes reeked of cigarette smoke.

Leigh started to introduce herself, but Sonia cut her off. "It's only a matter of time before someone is seriously injured on these premises," the attorney pronounced. "And I can assure you that the lawsuits will be *crippling.*"

Leigh's eyes traveled upward again. Ned had reached the top of the ladder and was placidly tacking the screened wire over the attic vent, ignoring all three women.

"Were you planning to injure someone?" Cara asked sweetly.

Leigh fought back a grin. Cara didn't dislike very many people, particularly on first sight. Leigh knew it was petty, but she had always secretly enjoyed watching her nearly perfect cousin act less than perfectly; and for whatever reason, this tiny woman had Cara's rarely used claws just itching to be unsheathed.

Sonia's expression remained bland. "Crane and Associates doesn't deal with personal injury law," she stated, as if this answered the question. "We do real estate and property law. And I can assure you, with my over twenty years of experience in the field, that this building as it stands is an accident waiting to happen, ergo, an investor's worst nightmare."

Aha, Leigh thought. No doubt this was the attorney Bess had mentioned earlier — the one who wanted the property herself and who was, even now, trying to buy it back from Gordon Applegate.

"If you're here because you've been hired to do some promotional work for the Thespian Society," Sonia continued authoritatively, "I would suggest you rethink. This building will never open to the public. It won't pass inspection." She snapped a quick picture of Ned on the roof. "You there!" she called. "I wouldn't trust that ceiling if I were you! It could be rotted clean through!"

Ned granted her only the briefest of glances, frowned, and returned to his work.

Sonia harrumphed, then snapped another picture.

Cara started to say something, but Leigh cut her off. "We were told that the building was declared sound by two building inspectors," she said, intentionally sounding uncertain. "Is that not true?"

Sonia drew herself up to her full, pixie-like height and leaned closer to Leigh. "Private inspectors can be paid off," she said heavily. "But the borough has final authority in granting the necessary permit... or not. This place is clearly a firetrap, if nothing else. Regardless, if people don't feel safe coming here, the venture will fail. And people *won't* feel safe. Not with this building's history of... well, you know. *Black magic.*"

Leigh resisted an urge to smile. Though she would be the last one to deny the building's macabre atmosphere, Sonia's blatant attempts at undermining Bess's plans — by any means possible — were really too amusing. "Black magic?" she repeated, trying to sound frightened, even as she tapped her cousin's foot to warn her to play along.

Sonia's dark, perfectly plucked eyebrows waggled ominously. "It's common knowledge," she said in a low, conspiratorial whisper. "*Human sacrifice*. Practiced *Right. In. There.*" She cocked her head over their shoulders toward the building. "It doesn't get any darker than that. Not even that Marconi fellow could overcome this building's reputation. Ran him off to Timbuktu it did, and lost him a boatload of money besides. But Gordon Applegate is sharper than that. As soon as he gets a load of the file I'm constructing, he'll sell off this dump quicker than—"

Sonia suddenly straightened up and lightened her tone. "Well, that's what I hear, you know. From other people. Gotta go!" In a flash of navy blue — and with another burst of cigarette odor — she whirled away and hopped into a car parked nearby.

"Why were you humoring her like that?" Cara asked with annoyance.

"That sniveling little piranha!" Bess thundered, hurrying out from the door to the annex as Sonia drove out of the lot. "What does she think she's doing here? On *my* property?!"

Leigh declined to point out that the property did not, technically, belong to Bess. It was more interesting to speculate on why the mere sight of her aunt in the doorway had sent the brassy attorney scuttling away. "Aunt Bess," Leigh queried. "What exactly did you *do* to that woman at the sheriff's sale?"

Bess's lips drew into the subtlest of smirks, even as her eyebrows lifted with false innocence. "Me? Why I'm sure I don't know *what* you're talking about. Now, what exactly did she say to you? And what the devil was she doing with that camera?"

"All done, Ms. Bess," Ned called from the roof. He had finished his task and was standing near the roof's edge. "You want anything else? There's some leaves and junk up here that need cleaned out."

"That would be lovely, Ned, thank you," Bess replied pleasantly. She turned to the women and lowered her voice. "Not the brightest bulb in the factory, that one, but he's a good worker. The lady at Community Outreach said—"

"Aunt Bess," Cara broke in, uncharacteristically exasperated. "How do you know Sonia Crane?"

"Oh, we've met," Bess said dismissively. "What I'd like to know is what on earth she wanted with the two of you?"

"My guess would be to scare us out of doing publicity work for the project," Leigh offered. "She was probably also hoping we would spread the word that the building is unsafe. Or haunted. Or occupied by squatting devil worshippers. I don't think she cared which, really."

"She's obviously trying to convince Gordon Applegate that the theater can't possibly succeed," Cara added bitterly. "And if there's money in it for her, she'll stop at nothing to do it. I'd be wary of any photographs she happens to put in that 'file' of hers, for sure. She'll manipulate them to show whatever she wants him to see. Cracks in the foundation, water leaks, mold — I wouldn't put anything past her."

Both Leigh and Bess turned to stare at Cara. "You know her already?" Leigh asked.

Cara's eyes narrowed menacingly. "Oh, I know her all right. We went to college together."

"But," Leigh protested, "she didn't recognize you!"

Cara gave an unladylike snort. "If you knew her like I did, you wouldn't find that surprising. She's one of the most self-absorbed individuals I've ever had the displeasure to come across. You could walk up to her again two hours from now and she wouldn't recognize you, either."

"She certainly knew Aunt Bess," Leigh remarked.

Bess gave her salon-styled "big hair" a fluff with both hands. "Must be the doo," she said, her eyes twinkling with mischief. "Never mind. I'll have the men keep an eye out for her. But if she thinks she can fool a man like Gordon with a bunch of trumped-up nonsense, she's got another think coming."

With that, Bess turned with a flourish and hurried back into the building.

Cara looked after Bess quizzically. "She never did answer your question, did she? About why Sonia would get so spooked by the sight of her?"

"Nope," Leigh agreed. "And something tells me she's not going to. Which, knowing Aunt Bess, means you and I are almost certainly better off not knowing."

Cara murmured something unintelligible under her breath, then raised her camera and snapped another picture. Scattered raindrops began to pelt down again.

"You know,'" Leigh asked, her voice thoughtful. "It isn't all just 'trumped up nonsense.' A lot of bad stuff really did happen here, and the building's hardly in mint condition. What if this is one hare-brained scheme of Aunt Bess's that really *doesn't* turn out for the best?"

Cara's gaze whipped from the LED screen on her camera to the portion of the building she'd just photographed. "Where the —"

"What is it?" Leigh asked.

Cara tilted the camera screen her direction, shielding it from the rain with an outstretched arm. "Look. See him there?"

Leigh squinted at the image. Just visible at the edge of the flat roof, not far from where they stood, was a pale, disembodied head with wild gray hair. "Don't show me crap like that!" she protested, recoiling from the camera. "Like I need something else to creep me out today?"

"It's just a trick of the angle," Cara explained, studying the photograph more closely. "But still, it's odd. He must have been lying perfectly flat on the roof with his head stretched out. Yet when I looked up just a few seconds later, he was gone."

"Most people clean out gutters with their hands, not their chins," Leigh said darkly. "I think he's just plain weird, Cara. Which makes him fit right in around here." She gave an exaggerated shudder. "Now if you'll excuse me, I'm going back downstairs to hover over the Pack like a worried hen for the rest of the day."

"Sounds good," Cara said distractedly, still staring at her camera. "I'll see you later."

Leigh turned and walked toward the door with a grumble. Not

that she was paranoid. Or superstitious. Or anything. It was just that, all things considered, there were places she would rather be right now than inside this particular building.

Like, say, inside a barrel at the top of Niagara Falls.

With six cats and a Rottweiler.

Chapter 5

Fortunately or unfortunately, depending on how one looked at it, the Pack did not share Leigh's uneasiness with their employment venue. Rather, they were enjoying themselves immensely. They were also making concrete progress on the assigned task.

Leigh looked around the basement to see a good portion of the menagerie pulled from the jumble in the center of the room and sorted into neat piles by the stairs to the annex. The contents of the trash pile were being continuously gathered and hauled up the stairs to the dumpster by Gerardo, while Chaz whittled away at the props pile, commenting at length on various items in it and — occasionally — taking a handful of them off into the annex for placement in one of Bess's designated storage closets.

There was also, Leigh noted with chagrin, a pile for "keepers," which consisted of items the Pack wished to permanently adopt, and which Bess assured them they could, pending the almost-certain approval of Gordon Applegate. These included a dirty blender (which definitely would *not* be coming to Leigh's house), a dog bed (which her father's clinic probably could use), a fake horse harness covered with sleigh bells (say what?), a giant framed painting of a man with holes where his eyes should be (also hopefully bound for Cara's house), and an oversized plastic machete painted with fake blood (ditto).

"Why did the Young Businessmen's Chamber leave so much of their haunted house stuff here?" Leigh asked, frowning with disgust at a collection of fake rats with bloody fangs that Mathias was in the process of moving to the "keepers" pile.

"We always left everything here," Chaz piped in cheerfully. "We didn't know from year to year if the building would be available again, and we didn't have anyplace else to store it anyway. When the borough finally got ready to sell, they gave the President notice to come and get it, but he was a do-nothing jerk and it all just got left. And that was before *last* Halloween — the organization's disbanded now so there's nobody to do anything with it anyway."

"Very intriguing," Bess chirped, examining a leather case presented to her by Ethan that appeared to hold dental instruments. Instruments that were — like a disturbingly high proportion of items in the room — coated with some sort of fake blood. "We might be able to use this. I've always had a hankering to produce *Little Shop of Horrors*." She zipped up the instrument case and handed it back to Ethan. "Props pile, please!"

"Mom?" came Allison's small voice. "I think you should see this."

Leigh looked down to find her daughter standing quietly at her elbow, her nose twitching as she adjusted her heavy eyeglasses. The twitching was a subconscious gesture Allison shared with her grandfather Randall. But it was also a tell. They both twitched more when they were excited or alarmed, and it was often the only sign they gave of such emotion.

"What is it?" Leigh asked, her own alarm obvious.

Allison held up a man's leather briefcase, once stylish and probably expensive, but now scorched and blackened along half its width as if it had been tossed sideways into a barbecue pit. Leigh took the case from her daughter's hands, opened the various pouches, and looked inside.

"It's empty," Allison said simply.

"I see," Leigh replied, noting that all the zippers still worked. The charring was only superficial. Still, it would hardly be of much use to anyone in a professional capacity — unless they wanted to hear wisecracks about tripping into an open flame. "What about it?" she asked finally. "Do you want to keep it?"

Allison shook her head. "You didn't feel it. Here, right above the latch. See?"

Leigh moved her fingers to the area Allison pointed out. The scorching had made the lettering difficult to see, but the debossed monogram was still intact. Leigh traced the letters with her index finger. "A. J. M?"

Allison's eyebrows rose meaningfully. "Now you get it, Mom?"

Leigh's breath caught. *Andrew J. Marconi?*

But how could Allison know about —

She broke off the thought. The question of how Allison knew anything was, as always, rhetorical.

"I think it's strange that the police wouldn't have removed it from the building when they searched," Allison said calmly, twitching her nose again. "Don't you?"

"Yes," Leigh said uncertainly. "That is strange." Not that the monogram alone would be proof positive that the case belonged to Marconi — but it was certainly too good a possibility to ignore. "Maybe the case wasn't here when the police searched. Maybe it got tossed into the pile later. Where did you find it?"

Allison pointed to the same area of haunted house paraphernalia in which Ethan and Mathias were still digging. "It was tucked under the electric chair," she replied.

"The electric—" Leigh looked over to see a monstrosity that did indeed resemble an electric chair. She hadn't noticed it earlier, but that wasn't surprising, given that the boys were still in the process of unearthing it.

"This is so cool!" Mathias crowed. "Hey, Aunt Leigh, do you think my mom would—"

"Not a chance," Leigh said quickly.

"Ooh!" Chaz cried out, practically leaping across the room to reach them. "It *is* still here! That was my favorite room *ever*. The 'execution room!'" He plopped down in the seat and placed his arms in the fake straps, smiling from ear to ear. "See, what happened was, we had the whole thing set up just like an execution room in a prison. And when the people first walked in, it was really dim, and they could just see the chair. For a moment, nothing happened. They were just standing there in the dark. But then the chair started to spark and sizzle! And then — this is the really cool part — we had a plant going through with the group, see. He was one of us, but he was dressed up like a businessman who just got off work, with a briefcase and everything. And the people thought he was one of them. But in this room, he all of a sudden jumps the ropes and says, 'This is so bogus! That's not a real electric chair! Look, here's the switch!' And he goes over to the wall and reaches up and grabs this big switch, see, and then *poof!*"

Chaz yelled so loudly, the boys beside him both jumped. He cracked up laughing. "It went totally dark then, you see, and nobody could see anything. But when the light came on again, it was a red light, and a strobe, and there was heat and smoke and steam everywhere, and right where the dude had been standing, there was a charred corpse! Still holding his briefcase!"

Chaz dissolved into laughter again. "Scared the crap out of people, that did. They didn't realize until then that he was a plant, you see. But we had a swinging panel in the wall, and Josh, he just slipped out and went back to meet up with the next group at the front of the house again."

Leigh looked down at the briefcase. "So this was the prop you used?"

Chaz nodded. "Yeah, that was the burned one we stuck to the skeleton's hand. Josh had another one he kept with him."

"How did you make the smoke?" Mathias asked.

"It was just a fog machine," Chaz replied, "but we had red lights and space heaters, and a guy on a ladder behind the wall would toss ashes down over the corpse, so it looked and even *smelled* like smoke!"

"That is too cool," Mathias said with admiration.

"Do you remember where you got this briefcase?" Allison asked Chaz seriously.

"Oh, no, I never thought about it," he answered. "Probably somebody brought an old one." His eyes sparkled with sudden enthusiasm. "I remember burning it, though! We built a little bonfire out in the parking lot, and we tossed in the case and the extra suit and shoes. Not the corpse, though. It was plastic, so we just had to smear ash on it. But the other stuff we let burn for a while, and then we sprayed the hose on it. The guys wanted to burn other stuff too, so we made a second bonfire, but then some guy threw his lighter in it, and a neighbor wound up calling the police, and then the fire department—"

Chaz's trip down memory lane was interrupted by a string of Spanish words flung at him by an unhappy Gerardo. Leigh couldn't understand a word of it, and neither, she suspected, could Chaz. But Gerardo's caustic tone left no mystery as to his meaning.

Chaz stood up from the chair, his expression sulky. "Fine! I'm getting back to it!" Then he grumbled just loud enough for the kids and women to hear him. "Sheesh, what a slave driver!"

Chaz moved away, picked up an armload of props, and slowly began walking toward the stairs. Gerardo stood still at the bottom of the stairway, glaring at him. Chaz stuck out his tongue, then bolted up the steps. Gerardo shook his head with disgust and got back to work on the trash pile.

Bess leaned over to whisper in Leigh's ear. "I offered them all a significant bonus if the work gets done on time. But either they all get it, or no one does." She chuckled. "I don't have to say a word."

Leigh's gaze returned to the case in her hands. It was possible that a member of the Young Businessmen's Chamber could have donated the case to the cause. But she doubted it. The initials would be an unlikely coincidence; furthermore, the briefcase was real leather, well made, and in good shape before the pyromaniacs got hold of it. Why would its owner give it up? It made more sense that the case *had* actually belonged to Andrew Marconi, but that the police search had missed it somehow.

Leigh tried hard to think of a plausible, non-alarming reason why the man might have left his briefcase not at his home or his office or at one of his other established businesses, but in a vacant building. She failed.

"Mom?" Allison asked quietly, breaking into Leigh's distinctly unpleasant thoughts. "Do you think we should show it to Aunt Mo? Just in case?"

Leigh suppressed a sigh. "Yes," she answered bleakly. "I do."

"Chew Man!" Maura cried gleefully as "Chewie," Leigh's corgi, barreled into the detective's bedroom in a frenzy of bouncing, sniffing and surveying. Within seconds he had zoned in on an area of intense interest underneath the bed, and his front half disappeared from view.

"Found that flax seed cracker, did you?" Maura chuckled warmly. "I was wondering where that went."

After a few seconds, Chewie wiggled his elongated body back out, licked his lips, and jumped up to put his front paws on the side of Maura's mattress. "Come on up, boy!" she invited.

"I don't think he needs—" Leigh protested, but she was too late. Allison had already lifted up the dog's back end and propelled him onto the mattress, where he hustled toward Maura's head and cuddled obligingly beneath her arm.

"Dog therapy," Maura announced with a smile. "Perfect. Lowers the blood pressure, I hear."

"I thought you might like to see him," Allison said with a smile.

"You were right," Maura praised. "And I'm glad you came too,

Allie. Let's see that eye... Sheesh, that's nothing! I look worse than that after an all-night stake out. You feeling all right?"

Once Allison assured that she was feeling fine, Maura's gaze moved to Leigh. "Did I miss the memo? Are we having a meeting? Discussing methods of arson, maybe?"

Leigh looked down at the scorched briefcase in her hands. Maura always did take note of details.

"We found it at Aunt Bess's theater building," Allison explained, hopping up onto the foot of the bed. "The people who ran the haunted houses burned it on purpose, but nobody knows how it got there." She held out her hands for the briefcase, then passed it up the bed to Maura. "Look at the monogram, Aunt Mo!"

Maura turned the case over carefully, examining the zippers and peering into all the pockets as Leigh had done. When her fingers moved over the debossed monogram, the trace of a smile curved her lips. "Allie," she said smoothly, "hand me that file marked 'Marconi,' would you?"

Allison quickly located the manila folder on the card table and handed it to the detective, who was wedged between the dog on one side and the case on the other.

Maura opened the folder and glanced inside. Her smile widened. "Andrew *James* Marconi," she announced. "Good work, Allie. I think you may have something here."

The girl's face beamed.

"Tell me again what you know about it," Maura asked. "Are you sure it was found inside the building?"

Leigh and Allison explained what little they knew about the history of the briefcase, and Maura's brow furrowed. "Not much chance of decent prints," she said thoughtfully, "after all this time and so many people handling it. The fact that it's been smeared with ash doesn't help either. But I may send it to the lab anyway. It definitely raises suspicion that Marconi could have met with foul play at that location."

Allison puffed up with pride, but Leigh felt her heart sinking into her shoes. Call her crazy, but she would be happier if the number of unsolved homicides occurring inside her Aunt Bess's theater remained at its current total of one.

"You know, it's odd," Maura continued, musing. "If this is Marconi's case, he wouldn't have carried it around empty. At some point, somebody else must have dumped its contents, and it's highly likely that something in those contents would have identified him by name."

"It could have been somebody working at the haunted house who'd never heard of Marconi or the mystery about him," Allison suggested. "They could have just seen it as one more piece of junk in the pile."

"True," Maura agreed. "Although I'd wager a guess that most of the population of West View is familiar with the name, what with all the press about the strip club and the entire community pretty much waging war on the man."

"People know the name, yes," Leigh remarked, suddenly thoughtful. "But that doesn't necessarily mean they would assume this briefcase was important to the police. Now that I think about it, everyone I've talked to about Marconi has had the impression that he skipped town. Whether he's dead or alive now, no one seems to know or care, but they don't talk about him like he was a victim of..." Leigh hesitated. She really did hate even saying the word. "Murder."

Maura nodded. "You're right about that, Koslow. In the department, we saw the investigation turn from missing person to possible homicide, but in the community, the story was already legend as it stood. The little people had won the battle, and the big bad Marconi had run away like a thief in the night. The suggestion of foul play against him didn't surface for some time, and even then, what evidence did trickle in never got much traction in the press." She patted the briefcase at her side. "Not until the Morton women came on the scene, anyway," she said wryly, her eyes twinkling at Allison.

Leigh's imagination flashed with an image of her daughter wearing a blue uniform and leaping about with a gun. She felt a strong surge of motherly panic. "Allison wants to be a veterinarian," she blurted.

Both Maura and Allison turned and stared at her.

"Yes, well," Leigh murmured, before either could comment. She stepped forward and retrieved Chewie from where he had nearly fallen asleep, his tawny muzzle draped across Maura's baby bump. The dog eyed her reproachfully as she set him down on the ground and reattached him to the leash in her pocket. "We need to get back home, Allison, and your Aunt Mo needs her rest."

Maura made a rude snort. "Rest? What do you think I *do* all day?"

Leigh threw her friend a meaningful look. She had more she wanted to discuss, including the claims of the neighbors regarding mysterious after-hours activity inside the building. But she had no intention of adding any more tidbits to the building's already-macabre history within 500 yards of Allison's hearing. *Can I call you later?* Her gaze begged. The kids were enjoying themselves, they were earning money, and with luck they would be done in two or three more days. She could accept that situation if she must, but surely the less they knew about the building's dark side, the less likely they'd be to go looking for trouble.

Maura responded to Leigh's unspoken plea with a tight-lipped frown. "I guess maybe I could use another snooze," she said dutifully. "But thanks for coming, Allie, and for the dog therapy. Oh, and thanks for the physical evidence in the cold case — not just everybody delivers that sort of thing to my bedside, you know."

Allison smiled back at the detective, and her dark eyes flashed. A look of understanding passed between the two of them.

Leigh sighed. The sooner the Pack got the basement cleaned up, the sooner they — and she — could get the hell out of that building and start spending the rest of the kids' spring break someplace a little more wholesome. Someplace brighter, maybe. More uplifting.

Like, say, a mortuary.

Chapter 6

Leigh watched as her son stepped backwards, wound up his pitching arm, and hefted a thoroughly disgusting mold-ridden, broken-spoked umbrella up into the air and towards the top of the now-towering trash pile. The missile hit a ceiling tile, displacing it sideways and chipping its edge off. Then the umbrella bounced down onto the top of the stack and slid along its length to the bottom, creating a mini avalanche of refuse that spread out across the floor underneath a shower of dust and fiberglass from the ceiling.

Ethan grinned sheepishly. "Oops."

"We really can't add one more thing to this trash pile," Lenna said with authority, coming to her cousin's defense. "It's too big. Everything just slides back down again. And we're running out of room."

"We should just start hauling the trash outside ourselves," Mathias suggested, flexing his still-negligible adolescent biceps. "It's not that hard."

"The dumpsters are already overflowing," Leigh informed, looking hopefully at her watch. She was starving, and Warren had promised to bring them all some of his famous enchiladas for dinner. The Pack had worked all day Saturday, half of Sunday, and now most of Monday as well, and they were all weary of delivered pizza. She couldn't wait to dig her teeth into some warm tortillas — and to get this whole wretched project over with.

Unfortunately, they had already filled up not one but two rented trash containers, and Bess was unable to get another delivered until Tuesday. So while the kids continued to sort and pile, the hired men had been pulled away to help with the sprucing up of the former sanctuary. According to Bess, this alteration to the plan was just as well, because the director of the Society's upcoming production was absolutely adamant that the cast be allowed to rehearse in their actual performance space... starting tonight.

"We'll have to start a second trash pile further from the steps,"

Leigh ordered. "Just make sure you can walk between them and that it doesn't block anything."

Ethan immediately flung a chipped vinyl record like a Frisbee, sending it skidding into an area they had only just managed to clear that morning. "How about there?" he suggested.

Leigh frowned. "The spot is fine, but surprising as this may sound, trash does not strictly *need* to be airborne. Carry it, please. Before somebody gets whacked in the face with half a coffin lid."

Ethan gave a sigh and started back to work, but Lenna froze in her tracks. "Nobody really found a coffin in here, did they?"

"Yes, Len," Mathias answered sarcastically. "We found coffins. And bodies, too. Dozens of them. Where were you?"

As Lenna's inevitable shriek hit the basement's stale air, followed by a whine of complaint at her brother's mistreatment, Leigh headed for the steps. "I think it's time for a break. Dinner should be arriving any minute; I'm going outside to keep a lookout. Why don't you guys go wait in the annex kitchen? Get yourselves some drinks and we'll bring the food in there."

Leigh did not have to dismiss the Pack twice. They flowed around her like galloping mustangs and were out of sight within seconds. She walked the rest of the way up the stairs and through the annex toward the door to the parking lot. Her heart leapt to see her husband through the window, approaching the door with a foil-covered tray in one hand and a gorgeous bouquet of spring flowers in the other.

Her lips curved into a smile. Oh, but she did love this man!

She hurried forward to unlock the door. They had been keeping all the doors locked after the handymen had left for the day and were no longer trooping in and out, but the security measure did nothing to soothe Leigh's ever-present angst, since she was certain that she and the kids would be safer on the opposite side of the doors.

She let her husband in and greeted him with an enthusiastic kiss on the lips. "I was happy enough with the enchiladas," she teased, reaching for the bouquet. "Here, let me take these off your hands."

Warren released the flowers and shifted the tray of food into a more comfortable two-handed grip. "Um... I really wish I didn't have to admit this, seeing how fabulous a greeting they just earned me, but the flowers aren't for you."

Leigh's cheer deflated. "Seriously?" she whined, burying her nose in the bouquet and inhaling the first pleasant scent she had experienced all day. "What if I take them anyway?"

He leaned over to plant an apologetic kiss on her cheek. "I'll buy you another one later if you like. I'll buy you five of them. But this one I need. It's an emergency. Trust me."

She looked up at him curiously. "Emergency flowers? For who?"

His reply was interrupted by the sound of a slamming door in the parking lot. Leigh looked out the glass panel to see a chauffeur closing the door of a limousine behind a small, white-haired man in a tailored suit.

"Oh, no," Warren lamented, snatching the bouquet back from Leigh and placing the tray of food into her hands instead. "He's early."

"Who's early?" she asked, confused. "Is that—"

"Gordon Applegate," he answered tersely. "Come to make even more trouble for me, I'm sure. Would you mind carrying the food inside? You and the Pack go ahead and eat. Looks like I'm going to be tied up for a while here..."

As Warren opened the door to admit his client, Leigh slipped away down the hall. She felt no particular compulsion to impress Mr. Applegate, but given that the man was dressed so impeccably, she would at least like to remove any shards of ceiling tile from her hair before their first introduction.

She delivered the warm tray to the waiting Pack, threatened all manner of unrealistic punishments if all the enchiladas were eaten before she returned, and rushed into the bathroom to make herself as presentable as possible, which was not very. But her appearance would have to do. She was undeniably curious about the richer-than-God and — to quote her Aunt Bess — "randy as a sailor" Gordon Applegate. She also wanted to know why in hell her most-certainly heterosexual husband was buying flowers for another man.

She emerged into the annex corridor and followed the sound of the men's voices to the curved hallway behind the sanctuary. She stopped just short of being seen.

"She's got to know something I don't," Gordon Applegate's thin tenor said insistently. "Damn woman's hounding me like a pit bull over this ridiculous old fire trap. She thinks the property's worth something and she's looking to turn a quick buck. I'd bet anything she's deluded about its worth, but the fact remains: whether or not she could turn a profit on this place, there's no question that I could, just by unloading it on her right now."

Leigh did a double take. At first she assumed the "damn woman" Gordon was cursing in hushed tones must be Bess, given her aunt's natural association with the verb "hounding." But now she realized he must be talking about the real estate attorney Sonia Crane, who had evidently confronted him after Leigh's encounter with her on Saturday. Was Gordon seriously considering selling the building out from underneath the Society, mere days before their first opening night?

"You could certainly profit from a sale at that price," Warren said smoothly. "But haven't you been insisting all along that financial gain is not your goal here?"

Gordon Applegate's only response was a gruff exhale. The men were quiet for a moment, and Leigh decided to show herself. She backtracked a few steps, quietly, then walked on into the hallway. But when she got to the place where the men had been standing, she found they had already moved into the sanctuary.

"Gordon!" she heard her Aunt Bess exclaim. "Oh, how wonderful that you're here! Come in, come in. You have to see!"

Leigh hustled forward and entered the sanctuary a few paces behind the men. She watched as Gordon Applegate stepped out into the auditorium and was immediately pounced upon by her exuberant aunt. "Well?" Bess cooed, taking his arm and leading him out into the room's center. "Not bad for less than a week's work, hmm?"

As Gordon studied the transformed room around him, Leigh studied Gordon. He was a slight figure, on a level with Bess and considerably slimmer, but his bearing was that of a confident man who knew what he was about and brooked no dissent. He appeared to be somewhere around seventy, with snow-white hair on each side of his head and nothing whatsoever on top. His light blue eyes were piercing, set far back under prominent brows and narrowly on either side of a long, thin nose. To say that the man was handsome would be pushing it; to say that he reeked with the aura of wealth would not.

Gordon surveyed the room for quite some time, and Leigh could imagine the differences he must be seeing. The worn carpet had vanished to reveal original hardwood of a rich oak that, while permanently marred in any number of ways, shone with cleanliness and a fresh coat of varnish. The walls looked equally bright and clean, still wet in places with the latest coat of a warm, peachy rose color. The clear glass windows sparkled. Aside from the painter's scaffolding and supplies, the room was still perfectly empty. Yet the same space that had seemed hollow and foreboding mere days ago now pulsed with new life and invitation.

"Well?" Bess repeated, her merry eyes twinkling as she held Gordon's skinny arm close to her side. "Tell me I'm a miracle worker."

Gordon drew in a long breath, then let it out with a smile. "My dear, you are indeed. This place is unrecognizable." He took her hand in both of his own and favored her with a lusty look. "Bravo," he whispered.

"I agree," Warren said, his own surprise obvious in his voice. "You've done a fabulous job here, Bess."

To Leigh's surprise, Bess's eyes ceased their fawning over Gordon and turned to Warren with a look of practiced disdain. *"Mr. Harmon,"* she said coolly.

Warren's face fell. "Now, Bess—" he began.

"Gordon, dear," Bess crooned, cutting Warren off and pulling her benefactor toward Leigh. "You must meet my niece. Gordon, this is Leigh Koslow; she and her children have been helping out with the project downstairs. Leigh, this is Mr. Gordon Applegate, the most generous man in the world. Discuss!"

For a moment, Leigh found herself at a loss. Her aunt's performance was applause-worthy, as neither of the men seemed to realize what total B.S. she was shoveling at them. "It's nice to meet you, Mr. Applegate," Leigh forced out finally. Then, remembering the conversation in the hallway, "I understand you've made a very generous donation to the Thespian Society. I'm sure the entire community will appreciate it."

Bess's face gleamed with approval. Gordon's eyes held Leigh's without modesty, false or otherwise. "Well, I suppose we'll see about that," he said noncommittally. He looked from her to Warren, then back over to Bess. "But I'm a businessman first, you know."

"Oh, psshaw!" said Bess, trapping his arm at her side again.

"You're as tender-hearted as they come. You just make oodles of money despite yourself!"

Gordon frowned at her, even as his lips twitched toward a smile. "Don't start up with all that again, Bessie. I told you before the sheriff's sale, either it flies or it doesn't. I won't have my name attached to some slipshod, second rate—"

A phone rang in his pocket with one of the loudest, shrillest, most obnoxious ringtones Leigh had ever heard. It might as well have been a recorded voice shrieking *wherever you are and whatever you're doing, I am more important! Answer me NOW!*

And Gordon did. "Excuse me," he said, pulling the phone from his breast pocket and glancing at the screen. "I have to take this." He put the phone to his ear and moved off toward the stage area.

"Bess," Warren said beseechingly as Gordon stepped out of earshot. "Don't be like this. I told you I was sorry. Look—" he extended the bouquet. "These are for you. And... I brought enchiladas. Even made a couple with sour cream and green onions, just for you."

He turned his liquid-brown, puppy dog eyes on his aunt-in-law with full force, and Leigh knew that inside, Bess was melting to a puddle. But her outward expression stayed hard. She reached out with a mechanical motion and took the flowers from his hands, her cool stare leaving his face only just long enough to glance down at the bouquet. "Grocery store?" she inquired sharply.

He shook his head with a smile. "Florist."

The corners of Bess's lips twitched.

Warren's smile widened. "Am I forgiven, then?"

Bess's lips continued to twitch, but she threw her nose in the air and turned around with a flounce. "Forgiveness *pending,*" she said haughtily. "I'm going to go put these in water," she called to Leigh over her shoulder as she headed for the door. "If Gordon finishes with his call before I get back, send him toward the restrooms, would you? Francie has truly outdone herself on those urinals..."

Bess departed toward the annex muttering, and Leigh turned to face her husband. "What on earth was that all about?" she asked, baffled. Bess, like all the other Morton females, absolutely adored Warren. In their eyes, he was *the man who could do no wrong.* Which, although perfectly lovely now, had been annoying as hell in the years when Leigh had only considered him a friend. How she could have been the last one in the family to succumb to his charms was still hard to figure. "I can't imagine what you could have done to her," Leigh mused, her own lips twitching. "I would guess maybe you ran over one of her cats, except if that were the case, you'd be dismembered by now. What gives? What *did* you do?"

Warren let out a long, exasperated sigh. "I gave a paying client sound financial advice, that's what."

Leigh followed his tortured gaze out over her shoulder to where Gordon stood hissing into his cell phone.

"Oh," she said heavily.

"Yes. *Oh*," Warren agreed. "Gordon asked me about this venture and what it would cost him — not just up front, but over time. Bess keeps telling him that the Society can bring in enough revenue to at least cover the insurance and upkeep, but he doesn't think that's realistic. He thinks it will be — to put it poetically — the gift he keeps on giving."

"And you think so, too," Leigh surmised.

Warren cocked an eyebrow. "From a financial perspective, this place is the definition of a money pit. He might as well throw suitcases of cash off the side of the Fort Pitt Bridge."

"That's not true," Leigh argued. "Other people will be getting something out of this — the community will be getting a theater. If he really won't miss the money, it could turn out well. Couldn't you tell him—"

"Leigh," Warren said miserably. "I'm not going to lie to a client. But for the record, I didn't try to talk him out of it, either. I just laid out the reality of the situation in dollars and cents. The irony is that Bess thinks he's reluctant because of *my* advice, when the truth is he would never have gotten involved in the first place if he weren't besotted with *her!*"

The sincere grief in his voice tugged at Leigh's heartstrings. "Don't let her get to you," she said warmly. "It's 95% pure play-acting; you do realize? She's not really mad at you. She's only trying to make you feel guilty so you won't say anything else that could hurt her case with Gordon."

"You think?" he asked, looking relieved.

"I know," she assured.

"Well, I certainly hope so," he replied, lowering his voice as Gordon wrapped up his call. "Because I get the feeling her case is about to take a turn for the worse."

As if on cue, they heard a sharp rapping on the front doors to the sanctuary. Gordon responded by looking at Leigh expectantly. Fighting her annoyance at being considered the defacto "help," she crossed to the back of the church and into the alcove and opened the door. She had the feeling that the arrival of whoever was knocking was fully anticipated.

She was right.

"Hello," the tiny woman said brusquely, pushing past Leigh and into the vestibule. "Sonia Crane, Esquire." She extended the rocklike hand again.

This time, Leigh refrained from trying to shake it. "Leigh Koslow," she offered. "We met two days ago, in the parking lot."

Sonia's hawklike eyes showed not a glimmer of recognition. "I'm here to see Mr. Applegate," her deep voice rasped. "I'll just show myself inside."

Leigh saw no benefit in arguing. She merely followed as Sonia strode into the sanctuary and made a beeline for Gordon, extending her rigid hand before her like the cattle guard of a train engine.

Gordon greeted the lawyer with equal briskness, then turned to Warren as if to make an introduction. But as soon as Sonia glanced in Warren's direction, her face lit up. "Why, if it isn't the County Councilman himself!" she purred, taking his hand in both of hers. "Lovely to see you again, Mr. Harmon." Her crocodile smile cracked the makeup around her eyes like clay in a desert, and Leigh watched with growing ire as the woman's thumb caressed the back of his hand.

"I'm afraid I can no longer lay claim to that title," Warren responded smoothly, extracting his hand with a practiced gesture that fell just short of a rebuff. "I retired as chair of the council years ago, as I'm sure you're aware, Ms. Crane. But I thank you for the compliment." His smile was equally practiced; friendly, but noncommittal. Leigh relaxed her clenched jaw muscles. A little. She was well aware that her recovering-politician husband was consummately skilled in handling all sorts of pandering and manipulative people, and she trusted him implicitly. But that didn't stop her from wanting to heft this particular woman into the nearest dumpster.

She stepped to her husband's side. "That's Leigh Koslow

Harmon," she said pointedly, amending her previous introduction.

Sonia Crane ignored her completely.

"Warren is my financial consultant," Gordon said impatiently. "I want him to hear whatever it is you have to say, Ms. Crane, so let's just get to it, shall we?"

"What the — " came a voice from the doorway to the hall. The threesome turned to see Bess manage — just barely — to stifle the next word on her lips. Her eyes trained on Sonia and flashed fire. "What is *she* doing here?"

Sonia's confident expression quickly faltered. "Excuse me, Mr. Applegate," she said in a hushed tone, moving closer to him as she spoke. "I was under the impression we would be meeting alone."

Gordon looked from one woman to the other in confusion. "What the devil difference does it make?"

Bess strode forward. "I believe I told you in no uncertain terms, Ms. Crane, that you are *not* welcome on these premises!"

Sonia leapt to a position fully behind Gordon.

"I invited her to meet me here," he insisted, holding firm against Bess's steady advance. "And last I heard, I *am* the unlucky owner of this firetrap!"

Bess halted. Her lips pursed thoughtfully. "I suppose you do have a point, Gordon, dear."

His ice-blue eyes twinkled at her. "Why, thank you, Bessie."

The two exchanged a private look, causing Leigh to wonder suddenly just how much of her aunt's flirtation was play-acting. The man *had* called her "Bessie" twice now and lived to tell about it. *Interesting.*

"Now, as I said," Gordon repeated, stepping around to face Sonia again. "I want to get this over with. You said you had another offer. Let's hear it."

Sonia's eyes darted nervously toward Bess again. She cleared her throat, but said nothing.

Gordon sighed. "Bess, dear, would you and your niece mind excusing the three of us for a moment?"

Bess gasped. "You won't — "

Gordon held up a hand. "Just let me hear her out, then you can show me whatever it is you want to show me. All right?"

After a moment's indecision, Bess relented. She turned toward the door and gestured for Leigh to follow her. "I suspect our dinner is getting cold, anyway," she said with a sniff.

"Bess?" Warren called just as the two women reached the door. "I marked your enchiladas with those red cherry peppers you like. The Pack wouldn't dare touch them."

Leigh watched as her aunt's eyes glowed softly, then began to moisten. Bess turned around just long enough to give a curt nod, then swept herself quickly through the door. "Damn, he's good," she muttered, swiping at one eye.

Leigh laughed out loud. "Yeah, tell me about it."

"Well?" Leigh asked later when Bess appeared, alone, in the doorway of the old Sunday school classroom the Pack were using as a staging area for prop inventory. "Was Gordon impressed with the tour?"

Bess dropped down into an empty folding chair with a sigh. "I believe so, yes. He never thought we could accomplish this much this fast, that's for sure."

"And his meeting with Sonia?"

Bess gave Leigh a sideways glance. Her lips twisted ruefully. "That horrid little woman. I swear to you, she'll stop at nothing to get this place back from Gordon. She's upped her offer, do you believe that? *Significantly*. And she insists that time is of the essence. She wants this place *now*, or not at all."

"What did Gordon say? Is he considering it?"

Bess sighed. "I don't know. He wouldn't tell me. He and your husband are deep in discussion over the topic, even as we speak." She raised a carefully manicured fingernail to her lips and began to nibble.

Leigh gently reached up and pulled the hand away. "Don't fret, Aunt Bess. Gordon doesn't strike me as the type who's easily pressured by the likes of Sonia Crane. If he promised you he wouldn't make a final decision until after opening night, I'm sure he'll stick to that. Particularly now that he's seen the result of all your hard work."

Bess's expression hardened. "He had darn well better! And if that grasping, pint-sized she-devil doesn't lay off between now and then— "

"That reminds me," Leigh interrupted, lowering her voice. The

Pack seemed otherwise occupied, but she'd been burned by that charade before. "Sonia Crane doesn't strike me as a woman who's afraid of much, yet she's obviously terrified of *you*. Now, tell me what you did to her. I really don't want to have to bail you out of jail over this."

Bess drew herself up indignantly. "What exactly do you take me for? I never laid a finger on the wench! She's a lawyer, for heaven's sake. If I had accosted her in any way, don't you think she'd sue the pants off of me?"

Leigh considered. She was about to try another tack when a cell phone dinged. Bess reached into her pocket and looked at the screen.

"Oh, dear," she murmured, rising. "Camille's outside."

"Who?"

"Camille Capone, the director of the show." Bess glanced around quickly at the piles of props. "All right, staff!" she announced, raising her voice. "I have your first requisition. The actors will be here for rehearsal shortly, and as you know, I promised we'd have everything set up in time. I need the following. Are you ready?"

The Pack looked up at her eagerly. Allison grabbed a pad and pencil (items which she always, mysteriously, seemed to have close at hand) and Mathias drew up to his full height. "Ready!" he answered.

"We need to make the stage look like a church sanctuary that's seen better days," Bess announced. "So first off, we'll need to bring in that old wooden lectern, the candelabras, and that hall table I said could pass as an altar. Then I'd like some buckets and mops to scatter about. Maybe a dusty drop cloth. We need to put some silk flowers and anything else that could be used as a wedding decoration in a cardboard box. And if they get to Act Two, we'll have to find something that looks like an acolyte's candle lighter..."

Leigh rose. "Are you kidding me?" she said incredulously. "You spent all this time turning a decrepit sanctuary into a nice looking auditorium just so you could turn it back into a decrepit sanctuary again?"

Bess blinked back at her. "Well, that's the genius of it, don't you see? I knew we'd be in a time crunch, so for our first production I picked a play that's already set in an old church. No need to put up flats, or even a curtain. How perfect is that?"

Leigh bit back a retort as the Pack divvied up the tasks and began to scatter. She had been trying hard not to let herself dwell on the building's grisly history. The sanctuary looked so different since it had been cleaned and repainted, she had almost succeeded. And now the Pack had been charged with turning the stage back into an eerie looking chancel all over again?

She needed another enchilada.

Unfortunately, there weren't any left.

"Come with me, kiddo," Bess urged, tugging her niece toward the door to the hallway. "I need you to be there when I let Camille in."

Leigh's eyebrows lifted. "Why?"

"Because I've been wanting to strangle the woman for at least a decade," Bess answered matter-of-factly. "And today really has been quite trying already. Would you mind?"

Chapter 7

"I was rather hoping the audience could sit in wooden pews," the figure on the stage said wistfully. "They would do so much to set the mood!"

"Yes, well," Bess responded tightly. "The original pews were all stripped out ages ago, along with the organ pipes and the stained glass."

Camille Capone's large gray eyes blinked vacuously. She appeared to be older than Bess, but was still a very striking woman, with long silvery blond hair and a tall, lithe figure that seemed to float rather than move. "Well, let's look around for them, then. I'd like to put them back."

The muscles molding Bess's face into an artificially pleasant expression began to twitch. "Although I can't say I've searched for any of those things specifically, Camille," she replied with strain, "one does not generally find several tons' worth of wooden furniture and metal piping hidden behind a dust pan."

Camille appeared to consider the information. "No, I suppose not. But perhaps we could rent—"

"No," Bess said firmly. "You've seen the budget. We're lucky to have found enough folding chairs. Now, will these props do for the chancel?"

Camille frowned at the narrow hall table that was currently serving as an altar. "Some colorful altar cloths would be nice."

"Linda is already checking to see if Greenstone will lend us some of their old ones."

"Purple, I think," Camille mused. "With piping in canary yellow. And as for the embroidery—"

"We'll take whatever they offer," Bess declared. "Anything else you need for tonight?"

Camille rotated her head slowly around the room, taking in the furnishings the Pack had moved onto the chancel, the assorted personal props in a pile beside the stage, and the small grouping of folding chairs provided for the cast. Her gaze then moved upward, sweeping across the ceiling. With measured slowness, she began to raise her arms until both hands were high above her head. Then she tossed back her chin and shouted at the top of her lungs. *"Let there be light!"*

Leigh, Warren, and the Pack all started in surprise.

Bess merely rolled her eyes. "I told you already — Kevin can't load the lights in until tomorrow. For tonight, we'll just have to make do."

Camille hadn't moved. Her face was still pointed toward the ceiling. "Yet it be true that darkness approacheth, Elizabeth, in all its cruel and gentle beauty. Shall we light candles, then?"

This time, Bess gave a start. Then she looked up and uttered an expletive. "The lights!" she moaned. "I completely forgot! Three of the four right over the stage are burned out. Once the sun sets, the actors won't be able to see a thing!" She glanced toward the door to the annex, then snapped her fingers with annoyance. "And the men have left already, of course. I found two bulbs in the old choir room; I was going to have Ned put them in this afternoon—"

"I can change the bulbs for you, Bess," Warren offered, rising. "Assuming you can reach them from the attic?"

Bess's face brightened. "Why, yes," she said warmly. "The inspector mentioned that; he showed me the access panel. Would you mind, terribly?"

Warren flashed a killer smile. "My pleasure."

"Let there be light!" Camille repeated, still holding her pose.

The Pack, which up to now had been admirably silent, dissolved into muffled giggles.

"You don't *have* to do this, you know," Leigh whispered into Warren's ear. Her husband had a brilliant mind for both finances and politics, but when it came to being "handy" around the house, he was as worthless as she was. Any task requiring more than a screwdriver had always resulted in a call to her Aunt Lydie. Changing a light bulb required no great technical acumen, true, but he had dressed for a business meeting.

"Small price to pay," Warren whispered back.

"I can help you, Dad!" Ethan said eagerly, rising.

Leigh had a sudden image of her exuberant son putting a foot through the drywall and crashing thirty feet to the sanctuary below. "I don't think so," she said quickly. "I can help."

"You boys can go get the ladder," Bess instructed. "The one that's in the old church office. Take it up those stairs in the curved hallway to the second level. We'll meet you there."

The boys headed off, and Bess leaned over toward Allison and Lenna. "I'll need you two to turn the lights off and on and let us know if the new ones are working. And..." she said heavily, tilting her head toward the stage where Camille now drifted in rapid circles around the chancel, muttering to herself. "Keep an eye on *her*, could you please?"

The girls nodded. "Don't worry Aunt Bess," Allison said solemnly. "I'll watch her."

Leigh and Warren followed Bess out into the curved hallway and up the staircase. "Okay," Leigh said when they reached the second floor. "I have to ask. How exactly did Camille Capone get to be a director for the North Boros Thespian Society?"

Bess stifled a low groan. "Because Charlie Capone caters our dinner theaters every November, that's why. He's got a fabulous reputation and he charges us next to nothing, which is the only reason we make any real money. The revenue from the dinner theater makes up more than half our yearly budget."

"Gotcha," Leigh replied.

"We only let her do one show a year," Bess continued. "Generally, whichever one she can do the least damage to. This show's pretty easy, and she was overdue, so my objections got overruled."

"Is this the panel, Bess?" Warren asked, pointing up to a warped ceiling tile covered with water stains.

"That's it," she answered. The boys appeared with the ladder, and she instructed them to put it under the tile. "The inspector just lifted it and pushed it to the side. Then there's a wooden trap door that opens straight up. Be careful, though. He did say we have a bit of a bat problem."

Warren, who had taken two steps up the ladder already, stopped abruptly. "Bats?"

"A few," Bess qualified. "But I'm sure it will be fine now that Ned sealed up the holes in the vent." She smiled encouragingly.

Warren's face paled a bit, but he nevertheless climbed the rest of the way up the ladder and hefted himself through the trap door.

"I'll grab the bulbs," Bess offered, opening a door in the hallway and disappearing inside.

"What do you see, Dad?" Ethan called up curiously.

In the hole above they saw the flash of a white beam of light from Warren's cell phone app. "A whole lot of dust," he replied without enthusiasm.

Leigh grinned. Warren had always been far more fastidious than she was, and when he had lived alone in his own apartment, the place was always spotless. Marriage and kids had increased his tolerance for dirt and grime significantly, but the man still had standards. "Maybe the bats will have eaten all the spiders," she teased.

He made no response.

"Here are the bulbs," Bess announced, returning. "Now, Warren," she called, "the inspector said that you just lift straight up on the fixture. You should be able to reach the bulb without removing any of the housing. But if anything looks broken — don't touch it! We'll need an electrician, then."

"Got it," Warren answered, his voice sounding farther away.

"I'll take the bulbs up to him," Ethan offered, reaching out toward Bess.

"Nice try." Leigh grabbed the bulbs herself. "I don't trust this ceiling, Ethan. One step in the wrong place —"

"The inspector said the beams were sound," Bess interrupted. "And there are planks laid out to walk on."

Leigh threw her a stern look.

"But your mother's probably right," Bess amended wryly. "Maturity and a healthy respect for danger are what's required for such a task. Innate athletic ability doesn't matter much. Or lighter weight."

Leigh growled under her breath and stomped up the ladder. She laid the two bulb boxes to the side of the hole and hoisted herself up as Warren had. Then she looked around and froze.

She wasn't sure what she had expected, but her surroundings looked like something out of a horror movie. The kind where expendable guy #1 gets accosted by banshees, electrocuted, and sucked to death by spiders all at the same time.

The ceiling was relatively high in the middle, tall enough for her to stand, but requiring Warren to stoop a bit. Metal beams shot up to the slanted roof at a variety of angles, while more numerous wooden supports crisscrossed the floor amidst a sea of insulation so filthy and clumped that its surface looked like moon rocks. Extending from the trapdoor where Leigh stood to the gable at the front of the church was a flat area about twelve feet wide, in the middle of which a series of walking planks were laid out like railroad tracks. At the edges of the flat section the floor began to slope, descending steeply to the eaves where it joined the pitch of the roof. The sun had not yet set, and its last dim rays filtered through the window in the opposite gable, casting gloomy shadows throughout and making myriad cobwebs shimmer. The floor was dotted everywhere with discarded plastic sheeting, twisted strands of metal, torn-open bulb boxes, random lengths of unconnected electrical wiring, and cast-off pieces of wood and insulation. And everywhere, *everywhere*, dust lay so thickly that Leigh feared to move.

"Charming, isn't it?" Warren greeted. He was bent over about six feet away from her, surveying the floor with his phone light. Every step he took left a visible footprint on the dusty planks.

Leigh grumbled under her breath again. "Let's just get this over with, shall we? Where are the fixtures we're dealing with?"

He shone his light over a round metal canister buried in the sloped part of the floor to her left. Two wide planks were conveniently nailed over the beams that led to it. "The two closest to the wall are both burned out," he explained. "I say we go for those. They're closer."

"Sounds good to me," Leigh agreed.

"I'll crawl down and pull up the fixture," he proposed. "You stay here and hold the light. When I'm ready you can come down just far enough to hand me the bulb." Warren walked to the edge of the flat part of the attic, then crouched down. He got to his knees and crawled a few paces out onto the planks toward the light fixture, then leaned out the rest of the way to grasp the metal canister.

"Watch out for bats," Leigh said grimly. The more her eyes adjusted to the darkness, the more "dust" she suspected was actually guano. She thought briefly of scanning the rafters above her head, but decided some things were better left unknown. One look at the attic window, which not only let in light through gaping holes around its casing but also had whole panes of glass missing, made clear that Ned's screen cover on the opposite vent was useless.

"Can we not talk about that, please?" Warren said worriedly, extracting the light fixture and laying it on its side on a plank.

"Sorry, but I saw one hanging off one of these very lights last week," Leigh answered. *And no wonder,* she thought to herself as she shone the beam onto the fixture. The canister base had large gaps around the bulb mechanism — easy as pie for the little furballs to fly through the broken windows and head straight down. She could only hope that none of them had done so recently.

"All right, I'm ready," Warren declared, both speaking and moving a little more quickly. "Hand me one of those."

Leigh unwrapped a bulb and crawled toward him with it. He traded her the old one, then screwed in the new with surprising efficiency. Within seconds, the fixture was back in place. Clearly, the man had no wish to prolong their adventure.

"Why don't I start on the other one?" Leigh suggested as he began the trek backwards. Why should the man do all the dirty work? After all, she was lighter than he was. Furthermore, her balance was better.

"You don't have to do that," Warren insisted. "I'm already filthy."

"So am I," Leigh retorted, setting down the phone light. "This way we'll get done faster." She moved to the opposite side of the flat area, then began crawling carefully down the slope on the other set of planks. After a moment, Warren reached the phone and held the light for her.

She could hear him exhale heavily. "I *hate* bats," he muttered.

Leigh grinned to herself as she reached the fixture and balanced herself to heave it up. "Wuss!"

"You didn't marry me because I was macho," he defended. "Have we not established this?"

"Allison would tell you that they're cute," Leigh said as she pulled. "And beneficial to the ecosystem. Of course, she's not the one cleaning up the—"

Her words broke off as a flurry of flapping darkness and flying drops of liquid exploded into her face. In one motion she cried out, dropped the fixture, and flung herself backward out of the way.

"Leigh!" Warren's call of distress reached her ears just as she realized, with a sickening rush, that she was no longer on the planks. She had landed on her back across the bare beams, with the bulk of her flailing body now lying halfway between them... where there was nothing to hold her up but insulation and drywall.

"Get on the beams!" Warren shouted, moving towards her.

Leigh came to her senses quickly and tried to scramble back toward the planks. The wooden struts of the roof were only a few feet above her head, and she reached up to steady herself by grabbing the nearest one, noticing in the instant before her hand made contact that its surface seemed oddly lumpy. She touched it, and the lumps came alive.

The next four seconds consisted of sheer, screaming chaos, which Leigh not-so-proudly met with pure, unadulterated panic. The very air around her seemed to explode — filled to choking thickness with flapping, furry wings. She had no idea where she was or what she doing. She knew only that, at the end of those four seconds, she found herself all the way at the bottom of the slope in the eaves, face down in a pile of extra insulation and refuse. Warren seemed to have a hold on her ankle and there suddenly appeared to be at least a chance that, if she ceased panicking, she could still survive.

"Stay still a minute," Warren said, attempting to sound calm even as his own voice wavered. "Don't try to move yet. Just catch your breath."

Leigh's eyes were closed, but her mind still reeled from the flapping. Flapping, flapping, and more flapping. The bats weren't just on the light fixture she had pulled up. They were everywhere. And she was pretty sure the first one had peed on her. "I'm all right," she assured, her eyes still closed.

"You're not going to fall," Warren assured. "I've got you. I can pull you over diagonally till you get back to the planks. Okay?"

"Sounds great," she squeaked. "Just let me open my eyes first."

She rotated her head just enough to get her face out of the insulation and opened one eye. The bats were still flapping. A half-dozen of them, at least, hovered around the vent Ned had covered with screen wire. There had been many more of them before, dozens at least, most of which must have found their way out through the broken window already. But the few who remained seemed determined to exit through the blocked vent, and they were plenty agitated. She watched as one of them gave up suddenly and swooped down through the open trapdoor instead. "There's another one!" she heard Mathias shout from a distance.

Fabulous. How many others had flown downstairs?

"Are you ready?" Warren asked.

"Just a second," Leigh answered. "Let me get my hands underneath me." Her nose itched. And no wonder, since she'd just done a faceplant in fiberglass. She could only hope it wasn't asbestos. She pulled up a hand and shoved the loose chunk of insulation in front of her away to the side.

Six inches from her nose lay a human skull.

She scrabbled backward on hands and knees like a madwoman.

"Slow down!" Warren advised, "You'll put a foot through the floor!"

Leigh was back on the planks. Her breath heaved. Above her head, bats still flew. She watched as one found the broken window and swooped off into the dusk. A second followed.

Maybe she was wrong. She *could* be wrong, couldn't she?

"Let's get out of here," Warren insisted, urging her ahead of him.

"Do you have the light?" she squeaked, not moving.

He placed his phone in her hand. "Now can we get moving? I may appear calm to you, but appearances can be deceiving. You just took a good ten years off my life, and I'd already lost six to the bats. *Let's go.*"

Leigh crawled up the planks and moved out of the way just enough to let him get back to the flat part of the attic, too. But then she stopped. She raised one unsteady arm and shone the light on the area of the eaves where she had rolled. The pile of spare chunks of insulation, loose plastic, and other trash that had gathered in that particular spot looked like no more than a random accident of gravity. But it could also have been placed there to cover something. Something about six feet long.

She moved the beam of light to where her own head had rested.

The enchiladas threatened a reappearance.

Leigh clicked off the light and shuddered.

Warren paused halfway to the trapdoor and looked back at her. "Why aren't you coming? You aren't seriously still worried about the stage lights!" He crawled toward her; he couldn't raise himself any higher without putting his head in the bats' traffic lane. "Look, I'll shine my phone app on the actors all night if I have to, but these bulbs are going to have to wait until this attic is officially rabies free." His voice turned suddenly sober. "You didn't get bit, did you?"

Leigh shook her head. As far as she knew, none of the bats had actually touched her, despite the startling proximity of their beating wings to her face. She wanted to explain that to her obviously worried husband, but her voice wasn't working.

The gruesome image in the eaves was burning itself into her brain.

What she had seen was real. The plastic skeleton in the basement trunk might have fooled her for a moment, but Halloween props didn't usually wear striped polyester sport shirts. And their bones were still connected. And they didn't tend to be hidden in places where they might never be found.

"Leigh," Warren said heavily, putting an arm around her shoulders. "What is it? What were you shining the light on just now?"

The answer was on the tip of her tongue, but for the life of her, she couldn't speak it.

Andrew J. Marconi.

Chapter 8

Leigh stood at the bottom of the ladder. Warren closed the trapdoor behind them, descended the ladder himself, and turned to look at her. "You aren't in shock, are you?" he asked with concern.

Here, in the relative normalcy of the adequately lighted, reasonably tidy corridor, her voice at last returned to her. "No," she managed. "I'll be fine. I just need to catch my breath."

His brown eyes studied her. He did not seem convinced. "Well, I hope you're not in shock," he replied. "Because I'd like to reserve that right for myself, thank you very much."

She returned a weak smile. "I'm afraid you'll have to wait a bit. It's going to get worse before it—" She broke off abruptly as a large bat careened wildly down the corridor, narrowly shot past them, then disappeared into the room where Bess had found the bulbs. They both realized, in that moment, that the noises that previously hadn't registered in their shell-shocked brains were *not* coming from a nearby television, nor from a crowd out on the street. The boyish shouting, girlish shrieking, pounding footsteps, banging doors, and inexplicable strains of a soprano aria were echoing up the stairway from the building below their feet.

"Bats," Warren said simply.

Leigh nodded.

They hurried down the steps to find Ethan and Mathias sprinting toward them from the annex with a burlap bag and a broom. Warren stretched out a hand to stop them, and a few paces behind came Allison, breathing heavily, her small face bright red with agitation. "Leave those bats *alone!*" she ordered. "You're going to hurt them!"

Her brother turned. "We're not going to hurt them, Allie!" he insisted. "We're just going to help them get back outside!"

Allison stomped her foot. "You will too hurt them, and they don't *need* your help!" she raged.

"Your sister's right," Warren interjected, relieving the disappointed boys of the bag and broom. "Leave the bats alone.

They'll find their own way outside. Nobody needs to get bit."

Allison's small shoulders slumped with relief. "They won't bite unless they're cornered, Dad," she informed, her color subsiding a bit. "And less than 1% carry rabies. They're really just misunderstood. Did you know that—"

Bess burst into the hallway. "Done!" she proclaimed, breathing nearly as heavily as Allison. "I've got every door propped open and every window raised that I could raise. There's a nice breeze coming in and I've seen at least three fly out already." She turned an appraising look on Leigh and Warren. "Are you two all right?"

"We'll survive, I think," Warren answered. "Where's Lenna?"

"Incoming!" Mathias shouted as another brown shape winged its way through the hall. They ducked in unison and the bat flapped over their heads and off toward the staircase.

A high soprano note shrilled through the air. The noise seemed to be coming from the other side of a door near Leigh, and she quickly stepped over and opened it. There, in the back of a small, otherwise empty closet, Lenna huddled under the protective arm of Camille. "Aunt Leigh!" Lenna shrieked, looking up at her with frightened eyes. "Are they gone yet?"

"Not quite," Leigh answered honestly. Her gaze turned to Camille, who stopped singing just long enough to smile at her pleasantly.

"Verdi," the woman said with a wink, as if the one word explained all.

Leigh heard Ethan shout behind her, and her peripheral vision caught another pair of beating wings moving along the hallway behind her.

"Ooh!" Lenna whined, "Shut the door, Aunt Leigh! Shut the door! But she did not wait for Leigh to shut the door — Lenna reached forward herself, grabbed the knob, jerked the door forcefully from her aunt's grasp, and slammed it back upon the two of them.

Camille started singing again.

"We all need to get out of here," Warren said sensibly. "There'll be no practice tonight."

"I suppose you're right," Bess said with disappointment. "I'll text the cast. Though some of them are probably already on their way."

Leigh felt suddenly sick. The fact that it took her a moment to realize why, she could only credit to the increasingly mushy neurons in her forty-something brain.

Or maybe she really was in shock.

"Warren," she said calmly, "Can you take the Pack home? I'll follow you later."

He looked at her suspiciously. She felt a stab of guilt at delaying his education, but *someone* had to get the Pack out of here, and Bess, unfortunately, would need to be present when the police arrived. "Please?" she begged, her eyes heavy with meaning. *I can't talk in front of the Pack, but I'll fill you in later. I promise.*

Warren's eyes narrowed back at her, but with a gruff exhale, he relented. *You'd better.* "Are you a hundred percent sure you didn't get scratched or bitten?" he asked again. "Maybe we should take you to urgent care and get you checked out."

"I'm positive," Leigh assured. "None of them touched me."

"Bats don't fly into things accidentally, Dad," Allison informed calmly. "They have amazing precision in the air — if they didn't they'd never be able to catch moving insects."

Warren cleared his throat. "I'm sure." With one last, skeptical look at Leigh, he withdrew his car keys from his pocket. "Let's get out of here, guys." He opened the door to the closet. "Come on, Lenna," he soothed. "I'll take you home."

Lenna burst from the interior of the closet and attached herself to her uncle's waist like a suction cup. "Can we run?" she whimpered.

Warren cast a look at Camille, who seemed content to stay where she was. *"Il trovatore?"* he asked.

Camille's pretty face beamed. *"Stride la vampa,"* she answered.

Warren nodded in approval. "Carry on."

Camille smiled at him, closed the door on herself, and complied.

Bess let out a frustrated groan.

As soon as Leigh was certain that Warren, the Pack, and Camille were all safely out of the building — the last being accomplished only after Bess insisted she had seen a bat flying *into* the closet — Leigh herded her aunt into the relative safety of the high-ceilinged sanctuary and sat her down in a folding chair.

"Aunt Bess," she said tiredly, dropping down into a chair beside her. "There's something I need to—"

"We'll have to call the police, I suppose," Bess said with

annoyance.

Leigh blinked. "Excuse me?" Her aunt could not possibly know.

Bess swiveled to face her. "Well, we'll never get all the bats out if we don't leave the doors and windows open, but we can't just go off and leave the place like this, either. If I explain everything to the police, do you think they'd be willing to drive by and keep an eye on the building overnight?"

If Leigh hadn't wanted so badly to either scream or cry, she would have found herself laughing. "You know," she said obliquely, resting her head on the back of the chair and staring up at the ceiling. "I think they just might."

Twenty-one seemingly endless hours later, Leigh flung her upper body flat on the foot of a bed and stared up at another ceiling. She exhaled loudly.

"I really wasn't serious, you know," Maura insisted.

"You cursed me," Leigh accused.

"Don't be so superstitious," Maura said blithely. "It could have happened to anybody."

Leigh sat up and stared at her. "Who *are* you, and what have you done with the real Detective Polanski? You know — the short-tempered, foul-mouthed one whose mantra for the last two decades has been 'blame Leigh first and asks questions later?'"

Maura merely shrugged. "She may turn up again someday. Right now, I'm just not feeling it."

Leigh lifted one eyebrow suspiciously. "Well, when she comes back, can you make sure she blows off some cumulative steam before she runs into me again?"

Maura chuckled. "No promises."

Leigh flung herself back on the mattress. "Have you heard anything yet?"

"Yep. About a half hour ago."

Leigh turned to face her friend, but didn't lift her head. "Well?"

"Andrew J. Marconi."

Idle curse words rattled around inside Leigh's brain. "I knew it."

"Well, I should hope so," Maura said matter-of-factly. "Unless maybe you were expecting someone else?"

Leigh shuddered. "One is enough, thanks. Actually it's *two* now for that wretched building! And Bess is determined to continue with her plans, of course."

"Of course."

Leigh rolled over and propped herself up on one elbow. "Don't the police need to keep the building roped off with yellow tape or something, like, forever?"

Maura smiled patiently. "The techs have done their job. The detectives, too, although there's not much they can do. Whatever happened to Andrew Marconi happened nearly a decade ago, and literally hundreds of people have tromped through the building since then. If there's any evidence left to gather, it will come from Marconi's remains, not from your Aunt Bess's auditorium."

Leigh's stomach lurched. It had been doing that a lot since last night. "They identified him awfully quickly," she commented.

"It's easier when they're fully dressed with their wallets still on them," Maura quipped. "But in his case, we had all the info we needed lined up in the file and ready to go. The autopsy results will take a while longer, but as far as his identity goes, the dental evidence was conclusive. Open and shut."

Leigh blew out another breath. "So he was murdered in his own building, and the killer didn't want his body found. I have to say, it was a pretty darn good hiding place."

"Maybe," Maura said thoughtfully. "Since the building was unoccupied at the time, and the body wasn't visible, even to someone changing the light bulbs. But a thorough police search *should* have found it. Clearly, that's not what happened. Detective Doomas didn't even find the damned briefcase, and it had to have been there all along. Between you and me, I'm not convinced he searched the building at all, despite his report. He for sure never bothered to pop open the attic door. There would have been a hefty smell up there, at least in the first—"

"Spare me, please!" Leigh interrupted. "I get the picture."

Maura considered a moment. "Sorry. I keep forgetting you're not used to the shop talk. Which reminds me, how's the Pack taking it? And Warren?"

"About like you'd imagine," Leigh answered. "Lenna screamed for fifteen minutes when she found out, even though she was never anywhere near the attic. Mathias was upset that, *as an adult*, he wasn't informed immediately. Ethan was upset because Lenna was so upset. And Allison just sat there and stared at me with her nose twitching. God only knows what she was thinking."

"What about Warren? I still can't believe you didn't show him what you'd found, when he was right there with you."

Leigh's lips pursed. "Yes, well, that didn't go over so well with him, either. I tried to tell him, right after we came down, but then all hell broke loose downstairs, and I just wanted to get the Pack home."

"Understandable," Maura replied. "But it's going to bug him anyway."

"Yeah, I know," Leigh said glumly. Maura's perceptiveness where Warren was concerned was no surprise. The three of them had been friends since college; next to Leigh, Maura was as close to Warren as anybody. "And he did such a nice job of keeping me from falling through the ceiling, too," Leigh admitted. "Very knight in shining armor-ish."

"So what happens now?" Maura asked. "With the show preparations, I mean."

Leigh grumbled.

"Wait!" Maura interjected. "Don't tell me. I got this. Not only is your Aunt Bess bound and determined that 'the show must go on,' but the Pack wants to keep helping, too. Even Lenna."

Leigh's eyebrows perked. "How'd you guess that?"

Maura smiled. "Lenna is braver than she lets on; she just likes the attention. There's a lion biding its time inside that mouse, you wait and see. The rest of them were born fearless. Not to mention stubborn as their moms."

Leigh frowned and was silent a moment. "Do you think we should let the Pack go back? Aside from the obvious macabre aspects of it, do you really think the building is a 100% safe place for them to be?"

"Koslow," Maura answered heavily. "No place is 100% safe for a bunch of curious, high-energy preteens and one thirteen year old who thinks he's an adult. No place is 100% safe for you or me, either. But the risk of future foul play in that building is no greater than in any other building or street or park bench where any other crime occurred once upon a time — which is a whole hell of a lot of places. If anything, the risk of whoever killed Andrew Marconi returning to the scene to cause more mayhem is *less* than it was before you found him. Theoretically, the guilty party could have tried to prevent his body from being found. Now, it's a moot point."

A sudden idea shot through Leigh's muddled brain. She pulled herself up with a jerk. "That sneaky she-devil of a lawyer!" she bellowed.

Maura looked back at her with a wry expression. "You mean Katharine Bower?"

Leigh's jaws clenched. She could be celebrating her fiftieth wedding anniversary and hearing the name of Warren's sexy, redheaded ex-girlfriend would still make her body temperature rise. "No!" she corrected. "And I'll thank you never to speak that name in my presence again. I'm talking about a real estate attorney. Sonia Crane."

Maura shook her head. "Never heard of her."

"She's been desperate to buy the building ever since she failed to nab it at the sheriff's sale," Leigh explained hastily. "Just this week she upped her offer! What if she's the one who put Marconi in that attic? Maybe she saw how thoroughly Bess was rehabbing the building and started to get nervous!"

Maura considered. She grabbed a notepad beside her and scribbled something down. "Worth checking into," she agreed. "You say she got outbid at the sheriff's sale?"

Leigh bit her lip. She really should start a family emergency fund for bail money. Her Aunt Bess was bound to need it sooner or later. "What I heard," she said carefully, "is that Sonia intended to bid, but didn't get there in time for some reason."

"You know of any link between this woman and Andrew Marconi?"

Leigh shook her head. "No, but she could have been involved in his purchasing the building."

"Or possibly the zoning battle," Maura added.

"Case closed!" Leigh said cheerfully. "Good. I never liked that woman." She thought again of Sonia Crane's overexuberant greeting of Warren, and it occurred to her that she had completely forgotten to question him later about how they knew each other. *Damned mushy brain!*

"It could be a woman," Maura mused, thinking out loud. "Carrying dead weight up a ladder and shoving it through a trap door wouldn't be easy for most, but Marconi was a little guy. Just

five feet five and a hundred and ten pounds. A strong woman could
do it."

"Sonia's no bigger than Lenna," Leigh admitted. "But she could
have had an accomplice."

"I'll check her out, Koslow," Maura promised. "In the meantime,
don't talk to her. Don't talk to anyone else about her, either. It will
be interesting to see how the news about Marconi affects her desire
to buy the property."

Leigh couldn't help but smile. Generally, when she found bodies,
the killer ended up being some obscure player she never suspected
until the last possible moment, usually after she had somehow
gotten herself thoroughly embroiled in the mess, unwittingly
endangering herself and possibly even getting arrested. But this
time was different. This time she had the obvious answer right out
of the gate and no reason whatsoever to be any more personally
involved. She could merely sit back, relax, and watch the
professionals get their woman.

What could possibly go wrong with that?

Chapter 9

"By the way," Leigh said later that night as Warren got ready for bed, "you never did tell me how you know Sonia Crane."

Her husband threw her a guarded look. "Didn't I?"

"Um... no," Leigh responded, stroking the black Persian cat that lay purring on her stomach as she reclined. Mao Tse was as old as the hills and barely weighed enough to be a paperweight, but in her few waking hours, the cat still had spark. "Obviously, you met when you were chairing the County Council. My guess is she wanted something from you."

Warren had the nerve to smirk.

"Stop that!" Leigh said irritably. "You know what I mean. Now tell me what happened with her. And *why* you didn't tell me before."

"I did tell you before," he said calmly. "I told you about it when it happened, four years ago. Remember the huge flap over that condominium development on the North Side? Sonia's firm stood to make a lot of money if the project got approved, but there was strong opposition from some local interests, as well as competition from a rival development company out of state. The woman drove me and everyone else on the council absolutely crazy with her lobbying. She would show up outside every meeting with these crazy-high heels on and start handing out plastic pens with dollar signs on them. We would go to the parking garage to find our cars mysteriously washed and polished with another pen stuck under the wiper blade. Fruit baskets appeared outside office doors — casseroles at people's houses. The day of the vote, a skywriter spelled out "Say yes to progress!" over Point State Park. Never mind what was ethical, the woman skirted on the absolute edge of what was legal — and probably crossed it a few times, though she never did so blatantly enough where we could prove it."

Leigh started to sit up, but when Mao Tse unsheathed her claws to hang on, Leigh quickly lay back down again. "Wait... I do remember. That was when I found the carton of baked ziti on our doorstep and some weird pen stuck behind the mailbox flag. Right? But I thought the lawyer doing all that was a man!"

Warren tried, but failed, to conceal another smirk. "Did you? I don't know why you would. I'm quite sure I never mentioned a gender one way or the other."

Leigh growled under her breath. "You are..." Then a thought struck. "Wait a minute. You approved that development!"

"As it turns out, yes."

"You let her get away with it!"

Warren frowned. "I didn't let her get away with anything. There were very sound reasons to approve the project. The joke was on her, actually, because her efforts were a complete waste. I knew from the beginning the proposal was almost certain to pass."

"But you didn't tell her that?"

"Why would I?"

"Gee, I don't know, maybe so she'd keep her clothes on?"

Warren sighed and sat down on the bed. Mao Tse lifted her head toward him and spit-hissed.

"Good kitty," Leigh responded, stroking her lovingly. There really was something magical about having a cat that worshipped you and hated the entire rest of the world. "You should have told me it was a woman at the time," she said sulkily.

"Leigh," Warren began patiently, "being pestered by lobbyists was always a part of my job when I was in politics. You know that. You also know I could handle it. Was it so wrong for me to shield you from some of the more unpleasant details about some of the more unpleasant people I had to deal with? There was no benefit to your knowing — it would only upset you."

Leigh growled under her breath again. "So what you're telling me is, to this day, Sonia Crane *thinks* her efforts to schmooze you were successful. That's why she was fawning all over you when she saw you at the building."

He shrugged. "Possibly. I don't care what she thinks."

"Even if she murdered Andrew Marconi?"

Warren made a face. *"What?"*

Leigh summarized her conversation with Maura that afternoon, confident that "don't tell anyone" didn't include Warren. "So," she finished, "if Sonia's enthusiasm for buying the building suddenly cools now that word about Marconi is out, we'll have our woman."

Warren looked skeptical. "Not buying it."

"Why not?" Leigh questioned, annoyed. "It makes perfect sense!"

"No, it doesn't," he argued. "If she had managed to buy the building, what would she do with the body then? Who says she could dispose of it any better the second time? And if she didn't, she'd be the obvious suspect — much more obvious than if she'd left the whole thing alone. You just said that before now, she wasn't a suspect at all."

Leigh considered. She gnashed her teeth. "I still think she did it. Which is a good reason to keep the Pack out of there."

"We've been over this," he countered. "The Pack made a very eloquent case earlier for why they should be allowed to finish their jobs in the basement. There is absolutely no reason that a murder committed nearly a decade ago should pose any risk to anyone working in the building today. Maura agreed. *You* agreed."

"Under duress, and against my better judgment," Leigh maintained. "There are some things kids shouldn't be exposed to."

"I agree, but the fact remains that they've already *been* exposed, and unavoidably so. Under the circumstances, I think it's healthier for them to go back and work through it than avoid the place forever. They said so themselves. You should give them more credit." His brown eyes turned suddenly resentful. "You should give *me* more credit."

Leigh didn't pretend not to know what he was talking about. "Warren," she began apologetically, "I *told* you, my first instinct was to tell you about the body; I would have told you as soon as I could talk, but we got distracted."

"You had plenty of time before I left," he insisted. "You could have taken me aside where the Pack couldn't hear."

Leigh felt terrible. Then she got inspired. "Was it so wrong for me to shield you from some of the more unpleasant details of my career as a corpse magnet?" she posed. "There was no benefit to your seeing the body — it would only upset you."

Now Warren's teeth clenched. His brown eyes, however, betrayed a sparkle. "Fine. I'll let it go. No more guilt trip. But you have to promise the same. No more questions about me and my ancient history with Sonia Crane — or any other female lobbyist, for that matter. Deal?"

Leigh considered. "Deal."

Warren smiled at her and leaned in for a kiss, but Leigh suddenly drew back. "Wait! Just one more question. Sonia didn't really ever take her clothes off, did she?"

His eyes twinkled with amusement. "No. She did not."

"Okay, then," Leigh said, sitting up a bit to finish the kiss without crushing the cat on her abdomen. "We have a deal."

Mao Tse spit-hissed again. But this time, neither of them paid attention.

The message Leigh received from her corgi was clear. *I can do this all day, you know. I've got nothing but time.* For the last half hour she had been pacing restlessly from one side of her house to the other, staring out the windows at nothing and doing a U-turn around the kitchen table. With every step Chewie had been attached to her heels, hoping against hope that this time, when she got to the kitchen, she would reach into the bin on the counter and give him a treat. He had hit the jackpot twice already.

"You've had enough to eat today, Chewie," Leigh announced, stopping a moment. "Why don't you go lie down and relax?"

The dog stopped when she stopped. Then he sat politely and stared up at her with the same intense, eternally hopeful expression with which he looked at anyone who ever said anything to him at any time.

Feed me.

"You need to get out of the house, boy," Leigh declared, stooping to scratch behind his giant perked ears. "We both do. All this peaceful silence is driving me bonkers."

If she thought she would enjoy a day of restful solitude in an empty house without kids or husband, she was wrong. Ordinarily, it would sound like heaven. But she had taken a week off work at her advertising agency, not knowing how things would go with Allison's surgery, and even if she chose to renege now, she had nothing at home to work on. Warren was busy with meetings in town and virtually the entire rest of her family was *there*. Cara had insisted on supervising the Pack herself today, removing any need for Leigh to return. And Bess had both Frances and Lydie busy there today as well. Tonight was the first real rehearsal, and Bess was in a tizzy over having lost an entire day from her renovation schedule due to what she dismissively referred to as "the unpleasantness."

Leigh's yard needed work, but it was raining again. The house needed— She broke off the thought with a snort. *To hell with that!* She was still technically on vacation. Computer work was out; she was too restless. But what else could she do with herself?

Feed me.

"Chewie, my man," Leigh stated, "Grab your leash. We're going for a drive. Maybe we'll go surprise your Aunt Mo."

The corgi didn't move a muscle.

Feed me?

Leigh looked into his earnest brown eyes and sighed. Chewie took in a lot of human words. He just assumed they all meant the same thing.

Her cell phone rang. She crossed over to pick it up from her desk and looked at the screen. It was Bess. *Whatever she wants,* Leigh coached herself, *just say no.*

"Hi, Aunt Bess."

"Hey, kiddo! Listen, you're not busy are you?"

"Swamped. I have—"

"Good, good," Bess interrupted. "Look, I made an absolute mountain of lasagna to feed everybody tonight, since the Pack wanted to stay late again and see the beginning of the rehearsal. But then I drove off this morning and just left it all there in my refrigerator. Could you be a dear and swing over to my house and fetch it for us?"

"You can—"

"And would you mind letting Chester out while you're there?" Bess plowed on. "He can use the dog door, but he's gotten so skittish about the rain lately, sometimes he'll wait for hours until someone encourages him to go out—"

"I'm not—"

"And you know that's not good for an aging bladder. Your father says it makes him more susceptible to infections. And with his liver already being—"

"Aunt Bess!" Leigh broke in firmly.

"Yes?"

"We both know perfectly well that you're only trying to get me back in that damned building."

"Well, *duh*."

Leigh exhaled with a groan.

"Come on, kiddo," Bess cajoled. "We've been through this before. Neither you nor I can possibly avoid every place you've ever found a body. It simply isn't practical."

Leigh closed her eyes and groaned again.

"It's better to get right back on the horse, as they say," Bess continued. "Not to mention the fact that I really did leave the lasagna at my house, and it's going to take a while to reheat. And your father did say that Chester —"

"All right, *fine!*" Leigh capitulated. "I'll do it. But I'm *not* staying."

"Yes, you will," Bess said confidently. "Ta-ta!"

Leigh hung up the phone and gnashed her teeth. She was such a pushover.

Chewie, who had sat at her feet like a tin soldier throughout the entire conversation, nudged her shin with his nose. *Feed me.*

Leigh gave up. She tossed the dog another treat, grabbed his leash, and headed for the car.

Nearly an hour later, she pulled into the building's parking lot, looked around, and sighed. It was happening, all right. She'd been paying enough attention to the media to know that news of Marconi's body being found, after all these years, in the very building he'd unsuccessfully tried to turn into a strip club, had hit all the local radio and television stations by dinnertime last night and made page one of both of Pittsburgh's daily newspapers this morning. The community battle over Marconi's adult entertainment enterprise and the intrigue over his sudden disappearance had never gotten off the local pages, but throw in a skeletonized corpse and suddenly the story was *everyone's* business.

Judging by the traffic jam caused by rubberneckers on the street, and the fact that Gerardo had to guard the open door beside the dumpsters against intrusion by the people loitering on the sidewalks and in the parking lot, Leigh was guessing that her Aunt Bess's folly was now the biggest local topic of conversation since the Big Dips coaster burned down in the old West View Park.

At least this time, her own name had not been included in the press reports. The police were aware of it, of course, but with them she was already legend.

She attached Chewie's lead to a belt loop, then balanced the giant tray of lasagna in both arms. She had tried carrying things with the dog's lead around her wrist before: *lesson learned*. She slammed the car door with her foot, hit the remote lock button, and strode toward the door.

Gerardo met her with a somewhat silly grin, his dark eyes oddly vacuous, and sprang to open the door for her. She studied him warily, certain she was watching a deliberate ruse. The spark of intelligent awareness she'd seen in his eyes the day she met him might be easy enough to cover up, but it could not be invented from whole cloth. She was certain the man was whip-smart, and quite possibly spoke English better than she did. "Hello, Gerardo," she said pleasantly, slipping inside. "Thanks."

He responded with a smile and a nod, then quickly turned away and closed the door. Leigh frowned. What *was* the man trying to hide? She should have told Bess her suspicions already. She had just been too darn preoccupied.

No sooner had the door closed behind her than she saw a group of older teenagers approaching it from the parking lot. "No go in!" Gerardo shouted fiercely, loud enough for Leigh to hear through the door's glass pane. "Call police!" He added something indecipherable — and no doubt colorful — in Spanish, and the youths moved off.

Leigh felt a jerk at her waist. The Pack's voices were echoing up from the basement, and Chewie was pulling that direction with all his might. "Not yet, Chewie," Leigh insisted. "We've got to get this in the oven first."

She tugged the dog backward a few steps, then turned and nearly collided with her mother. Frances surveyed her daughter, the dog, and the aluminum tray with a mixture of surprise and disapproval.

"You're coming back?" Frances asked rhetorically.

"Bess made me," Leigh retorted, realizing too late that she sounded like a five-year-old. Frances had, according to Leigh's father, taken her daughter's most recent corpse discovery with remarkably less hysteria than usual. She hadn't even suggested that Warren keep his wife locked in the house with an ankle bracelet for a month, which was her usual response. This time Frances had spent the first few hours afterward staring at her husband over a snifter of brandy mumbling, "Where did we go wrong? Where?" Then she had gotten up and scrubbed all the floors in her house and all the floors in her sister Lydie's house next door. Then she had gotten over it.

It was progress.

"So what are you and Lydie working on today?" Leigh asked, attempting a smile.

Frances glowered. Despite her frequent protestations of doom and gloom for Bess's proposed theater, she was psychologically unable to resist cleaning it, which was — of course — why Bess had invited her over in the first place. "Fresh bat guano," she said heavily.

"Ah," Leigh replied.

"And now," Frances continued critically, casting a glance toward the floor. "Dog hair."

"I brushed him this morning!" Leigh protested, even as she looked down to see a tumbleweed of tawny fluff detach itself from Chewie's rump and float gracefully to the tiles below.

Frances raised a single eyebrow. They both knew that brushing corgi hair was pointless, as it could replace itself in a matter of seconds. Frances stooped over and plucked up the tuft of fur. "If it were up to me," she said with authority, "none of us would be here. But my mule-headed sister has decided she knows better, and so naturally we will all put ourselves at risk for her sake. For the good of the family."

Leigh adjusted the tray in her hands. It was getting heavy.

Frances eyed it suspiciously. "You didn't make that?" she asked, the dimmest glimmer of hope daring to shine in her eyes.

"Um, no." Leigh admitted. "Aunt Bess did."

Frances frowned. "Of course." Then she studied her daughter's face, and her voice softened. "You are... feeling all right. Aren't you?"

Leigh smiled. "Yeah, mom. I'm fine. I guess you could say I'm... getting used to it."

Frances' lips twitched, seemingly undecided between pursing and smiling. "I think we'd all be happier if you got *over* it, instead."

Leigh chuckled weakly. "So would I, Mom."

"Chewie!" Ethan whooped, running down the hall and skidding

to a stop before them. He detached the dog from Leigh and swept him up. "Can I let him run around the basement with us?" he asked.

Frances growled under her breath. "I suppose if the dog must be inside the building, that's the least destructive place for him," she conceded. "Since we haven't cleaned down there yet. But don't you dare let him —"

"We won't, Grandma!" Ethan promised, skating off the way he had come on the shining, newly polished floor, dog in hand. Two more bunches of corgi fluff wafted through the air in his wake.

Frances harrumphed and took off after them, and Leigh continued toward the annex kitchen. She unloaded the lasagna into the oven, set it to warm, and made her way reluctantly back toward the old sanctuary. Her Aunt Bess was right. If this building did ever become the theater the Thespian Society was dreaming of, Leigh would not be able to avoid it forever. At least not the sanctuary. The attic, she could and would avoid forever. And she would make sure the Pack did, too.

"Leigh!" Bess cooed, hustling over to her from the stage, which was now fully decked out to look like a church chancel. "I knew you'd come! Did you get the lasagna in the oven?"

Leigh nodded, surveying the scene over her aunt's shoulder. Camille was flitting about the chancel, adjusting and readjusting the altar cloths. Ned and Chaz were on its opposite side, setting up folding chairs and wiping them clean with wet rags. In the rear of the sanctuary stood several tall light trees and a mobile spotlight. Other light trees were set up on either side of the stage, and myriad electrical cords covered with brown duct tape traveled across the floor.

"Isn't it looking splendid?" Bess said excitedly, practically bouncing as she talked. "And guess what? No more bats! That's one favor the police did us. They got a wildlife expert in here to properly seal up the attic. They had to, of course, so that the technicians could —"

At the look on Leigh's face, Bess broke off mid sentence. "Anyway, Kevin's got the lights all ready to go tonight, and the cast should be here soon." She threw a thoughtful glance over her shoulder, then pulled her niece away from the others and out into the curved hallway. "The board had an emergency meeting last night," she explained. "It was touch and go for a while, but good sense won out. We're proceeding full speed ahead! I told them we really had no choice. The show's been advertised for this weekend already; and in any event, Gordon's more antsy than ever now and he won't tolerate a delay. But if we can pull off a sellout crowd under these circumstances, he'll have to believe the theater can succeed!"

Leigh struggled for a response, but false enthusiasm was hard to muster. "I've been meaning to mention," she said instead. "There's something about Gerardo that bothers me. I think he —" she was interrupted by her Aunt Lydie coming around the corner wearing a fully stocked tool belt and holding a tape measure.

"Hello, Leigh, dear," she said fondly, her soft eyes transmitting sympathy she was unlikely to put into words, but which was abundantly clear regardless. Although Lydie appeared superficially to be a thinner version of her identical twin Frances, the women were nothing alike in temperament.

"Hey, Aunt Lydie," Leigh greeted, smiling with reassurance. "What are you up to?"

"I'm about to measure the attic window for replacement glass," Lydie answered, then turned to Bess. "Frances was right, there was definitely some water damage around the window in the women's room, probably from the ice this winter. Whoever patched it up cut some corners, but I can take care of that as soon as I make another supply run. About the glass — you said you'd send one of the men up with me to hold a light?"

"Absolutely," Bess answered. "I'll have Ned take you up. Follow me."

As Leigh walked back into the sanctuary behind the two other women, she opened her mouth to protest. But she could think of nothing to say. The broken windows did need to be fixed, and the sooner the better if they were to keep the bats out permanently. Lydie had plenty of experience at replacing glass (thanks to Ethan's and Mathias's love of flying objects) and she was clearly not bothered by the prospect of going into the attic. What was there for Leigh to protest?

"Ned?" Bess called as they walked back into the sanctuary. "Could you grab that big flashlight in the office and take Ms. Dublin up to the attic so she can measure that window for new glass?"

Ned dropped the chair he'd been holding with a clatter. His pasty face paled further. For a long moment, he merely gaped at Bess with wide eyes. Then he collected himself and shook his head. "Not going up there, Ms. Bess. There's bats!"

"There are no more bats inside the attic," Bess said confidently. "The wildlife specialist assured us of that. For the time being, at least, they have all been sealed out."

Ned shook his head again, causing his wild gray locks to quiver about his head. "I'm not going up there," he repeated firmly.

"I'll go!" Chaz shouted, tripping over the chair he had been wiping as he lunged forward. "I'd love to help!" He moved toward the door, practically prancing with enthusiasm. "I'll run and get the light, Ms. Dublin," he called to Lydie. "Meet you at the top of the stairs!"

He darted through the door, and Lydie gave a shrug to Bess and then moved off after him.

"That is odd," Bess said to Leigh, her voice low. "I wouldn't have predicted Ned to be the squeamish type. I don't believe for a minute that he's afraid of bats, or he wouldn't have gone up on that ladder and covered the vent the other day."

"Aunt Bess," Leigh argued. "I don't think there's anything weird about Ned not wanting to hang out in a place where a body lay rotting for nearly a decade. In fact, that's actually the *least* weird thing I've seen him do since I got here. You have to admit, all three of those men are a bit on the weird side."

Bess waved a hand dismissively. "Ned isn't *weird*," she insisted. "He's a tad bit socially awkward, yes. But he's a hard worker and he doesn't complain. Gerardo is an excellent worker, too, when he bothers to show up, although I've been a little miffed at his irregularity lately. As for Chaz, well, he sort of came with the building. Ned did too. The Outreach recommended them both because they'd worked here before. Chaz helped with the haunted houses, as you couldn't possibly have avoided hearing, and Ned did janitorial work here when it was a dance studio. You must admit, for all Chaz's faults, his knowledge of the props has been helpful, and if it weren't for Ned's insisting to me that there was a decent hardwood floor hiding underneath all that padding and grime, I might have wasted a ton of money recarpeting the sanctuary. So all in all, they were good hires. The Outreach checks all their clearances, so no worries there."

"Aunt Bess?" A small voice piped up behind them.

Leigh jumped, then cursed under her breath. She really wished her daughter would stop doing that. When had Allison slipped upstairs into the sanctuary, anyway? Leigh could swear the child had not been there seconds ago.

"Yes, kiddo?" Bess replied.

"Aunt Cara said to tell you that we're done with the trash. It's all been carried out to the dumpsters and it all fits."

"Excellent!" Bess praised. "Once all the props are moved into the classrooms, we can start getting that basement cleaned."

Allison nodded.

"All right," Bess continued. "If you're done going in and out, you can tell Gerardo to lock that door and come up here. I'm expecting some people at the front doors shortly, and I'll need him to keep a watch out that way instead."

For a long moment, Allison looked at Bess without speaking, her dark eyes seemingly perplexed. "Okay," she said finally, then turned and hastened back down the stairs.

Leigh's stomach churned with fresh anxiety. "Aunt Bess," she asked, "were you planning on her delivering that message in English or Spanish? Because they don't start foreign language until middle school."

"Oh, poo," Bess sputtered. "I wasn't thinking. I usually just gesture to the man, and eventually he gets it." She paused a moment. "Well, she didn't seem too worried, did she?"

Leigh knew she should be proud of her daughter's obvious perceptiveness. But the truth was, it worried the crap out of her. "I think Allison suspects that Gerardo understands English better than he lets on," she explained. "And I think so, too."

Bess looked at her with surprise. "But the director at the Outreach said —" she broke off her own statement, considering. "He was a late addition to the project, actually. They didn't have a track record with him yet, but they insisted he came highly recommended. How odd. If he needed the work so badly, why would he handicap himself by hiding the fact that he was bilingual?"

Leigh's unease grew. Before Marconi's body had made its grisly appearance, Gerardo's deception had seemed like a lark. So had

Sonia's persistence, Chaz's enthusiasm for the macabre, and Ned's looking and acting like a character from a spooky kid's cartoon.

Now it all seemed darker.

A shiver slid up Leigh's spine.

Stop that!

She gave herself a shake. Whatever violence had befallen Andrew Marconi had befallen him a very long time ago. She would not allow herself to start seeing murderers everywhere she looked. That way lay madness.

"I don't know, Aunt Bess," she answered, attempting to lighten her tone. "Maybe spending time in this building just brings out the wacko in people."

Her gaze fell on Ned, who had stopped wiping down the chairs and was standing, stock still, staring up at the ceiling above. His eyes were wide and fearful; his mouth hung slightly open.

Camille started singing again.

"I rest my case," Leigh sighed.

Chapter 10

Chewie sniffed eagerly around the small patch of overgrown grass at the base of the building's front steps. Many dogs had visited the accommodations before him, and he was delighted to sign the guestbook.

Leigh wished he would hurry. She had waited until the street was free of loiterers before coming out, and she had no desire to meet the next wave. Her gaze drifted up towards the attic window, and she noted with chagrin that the wood trim along the eaves of the gable was liberally coated with little brown lumps.

Bats. They might have gotten locked out for the day. But they obviously weren't giving up easily.

"Yoo hoo!" A familiar voice called. "Come on over!"

Leigh glanced across the street to see Merle leaning far out over her porch railing and waving a hand. Earl, beside her in his usual chair, waved his own hand high above his head, beckoning with equal enthusiasm.

Leigh couldn't bring herself to refuse. As soon as Chewie finished his business, she picked him up and darted across the highway.

"Ooh, hasn't *this* been a week!" Merle said with a grin, her eyes sparkling. "Earl and I've become the most popular people in West View!"

Leigh looked around to see that a variety of new places to sit had been added to the porch, including two lawn chairs, four dining room chairs, and one tired-looking bean bag. And although she was the only guest at the moment, a collection of used plastic cups and dirty ash trays gave evidence to previous crowds.

"I'll bet you are," she agreed. And if today was exciting, coming after the recent headlines, yesterday must have been even better — a veritable parade of local police, county detectives, crime scene technicians, a coroner's van, reporters with television cameras, random gawkers, and some dude in a pickup that said "wildlife management."

Oh, my.

"Have a seat! Have a seat!" Earl insisted, gesturing to the oak dining room chair next to him. Leigh wondered if they had left anything inside to sit on. Most likely, they'd been taking their meals out here.

"Bring your pup on up, too. It's fine," Merle insisted. "We love dogs!"

Leigh settled in the chair Earl had indicated and plopped Chewie down on the porch, where the corgi immediately set about the critical task of crumb removal.

"So now you have to tell us!" Merle said with enthusiasm, sitting down on Leigh's other side. "What's your Aunt Bess going to do about the theater? She came over the other day, you know, before all this happened. Introduced herself and invited us to opening night. Even promised us free tickets!"

"Nice woman," Earl commented with a nod. "*Quality.*"

Leigh tried not to chuckle. What he meant by that last part, she wasn't sure, but she had the feeling Bess would get a kick out of it.

Merle gave her no chance to answer, but plowed on. "We were a little concerned about a theater over there, you know, but Bess assured us it was all going to be quite sophisticated. No alcohol, no partying, just people from all over dressing up to come see a good stage production. Now, we could go along with that!"

"It would be a *cultural attraction,*" Earl said knowledgeably.

Leigh's smile broke through. So that was how Bess had played it, had she? Classing up the neighborhood. As for the "no alcohol" part, Leigh would believe that when she didn't see it. "Bess is determined to make it as nice a venue as possible," she said honestly.

Merle and Earl both looked at her hopefully. "You mean, *still?*" Merle asked.

"Oh, yes," Leigh answered. "Nothing stops Aunt Bess when she sets her mind to something. *Believe* me."

The couple grinned at each other. "Well, that's just wonderful!" Merle crowed. "We'd just got to thinking how nice it would be to have it all fixed up, but after what happened yesterday, we were sure it'd just go empty again!"

"Nope," Leigh assured. "Last I heard, opening night was still a go."

"Marvelous!" Merle replied. Then her expression turned suddenly dour. "I just hope all the publicity doesn't wreck it. It's unbelievable that that man Marconi could ruin this building's prospects even after he's dead! We always thought he was murdered, you know."

Earl nodded gravely. "Only thing that made sense."

Leigh nodded. She was quite sure that neither of them had even mentioned the name of Andrew Marconi in their last conversation, despite considerable talk of strange occurrences in the building, including murder. She suspected that despite their protestations to the contrary, they had, like most of the population of West View, assumed that Marconi had skipped town and then basically forgot about him.

Until now.

Earl's eyes suddenly widened with surprise. His chair, in a series of jerky motions, was steadily scooting away from Leigh.

"I'm so sorry," she apologized, jumping up to unwind Chewie's leash from around the chair legs. What the dog had found, she had no idea, as he was already tossing it back with a giant gulp when she located him behind the bean bag.

Merle laughed out loud. "Oh, just let him go," she insisted. "It'll save me a sweeping later."

"I thought we was having an earthquake," Earl said without humor. "Damn fracking wells. Those gas companies will kill us all."

Leigh dropped Chewie's lead and moved to a chair where she could catch him if he tried to leave the porch, although she considered it highly unlikely. Whatever he'd eaten had left a grease spot.

"Were you there when they found the body?" Merle asked.

Leigh's heart skipped a beat. "I was in the building, yes," she said vaguely. "But we cleared out pretty quickly when the police came." The less anyone knew about her or Bess's personal involvement in the matter, the better. Certainly anything she shared with Merle or Earl would become public knowledge within the hour.

"So, who do you think killed Andrew Marconi?" Leigh asked lightly, more to prevent further questions than to get an answer.

"Serial killer," Earl said confidently.

Merle made a rude snort. "Where's the others, then?"

Earl looked confused. "What others?"

"Well, you've got to kill a bunch of people to be a serial killer, don't you?"

Earl thought a moment. "There could have been more. We don't know."

Merle gave a huff and settled back into her chair. She turned her attention to Leigh. "If you ask me, and you just did, I'd say it was one of those religious crazies."

"Religious crazies?" Leigh asked, perplexed.

"Could have thrown 'em in the river," Earl proposed.

Merle ignored him. "You know, all those people who tried to stop his opening up that bawdy house of his, the ones preaching about indecency and whatnot."

Leigh felt a slight clenching in her chest. "You mean, West View Citizens Against Indecency and Moral Turpitude?"

"That's them. Not that I didn't agree with their aim, you understand," Merle said pointedly. "I had a sign on my lawn, too, you'd better believe. Last thing Earl and I wanted was nonsense like that happening right outside our door. But you put it somewhere else, see, and I don't give a damn. Men want to waste their money being men, that's their business, as long as they pay their taxes and follow the law. That's the way I see it."

Earl leaned toward Leigh and pointed a finger. "Lori Ann used to be a stripper."

Leigh quickly covered her face with her hands, feigning a frog in her throat.

"She was a pole dancer, Earl!" Merle corrected.

"Well, that's a stripper, ain't it?" he snapped back.

Leigh "coughed" violently.

"Point is," Merle went on, "some of those women were mighty 'righteous' about the whole thing, and you know what happens when people get all whipped up about sex and sin and punishment and hellfire... they turn into vigilantes, that's what. It's what everybody's been saying. Now, I never knew any of the women in charge of it myself — it's not like I went to any of the meetings. Somebody gives me a yard sign, and I take it, and that's that. But from what I heard, the woman who started the whole thing was crazy as a loon."

Merle leaned over and gave Leigh's hunched figure a thump on the back. "Are you okay, hun?" You're awfully red in the face. "You need a glass of water?"

"Maybe she needs that choking squeeze thing," Earl commented. "What's that called?"

Leigh forced her head up and breathed. "No Heimlich needed!" she squeaked. "I'm fine. Thanks. But I really should be going now. There's... a lot of work to be done inside still, getting ready for opening night, you know."

She rose abruptly and reattached Chewie's lead to his collar. "Will we see you at the show?" she asked, moving toward the steps.

"Oh, we'll be there!" Merle said cheerfully. "You tell Bess that!"

Leigh's arm pulled away from her body as she moved. She gave a tug on the lead, but Chewie wouldn't budge. He was too busy licking the concrete. She walked over to pick him up, then maneuvered her way back through the extra chairs to the porch steps. She blew a stray tuft of corgi fluff away from her mouth, bade farewell to Merle and Earl, and darted across the highway.

The front doors of the building, as well as the old signpost on the curb, were now decked out with striking show posters, courtesy of Cara. The advertisements showed a rather delicious-looking white wedding cake collapsing on one side, with the plastic bride and groom figures teetering perilously off the edge of the top layer. *See You in Bells,* the poster proclaimed, *brought to you by the North Boros Thespian Society*, would open Friday night and run through the weekend. Patrons were encouraged to support their new local theater; all tickets would be sold at the door.

Leigh felt another twinge of angst. The posters promised a delightful evening of fun and laughter, and for Bess's sake, she certainly hoped that's what would happen. But tacking such a jolly promise on the outside of this particular building seemed rather like advertising fresh-baked cookies outside a funeral home.

She put Chewie down and pulled on the front door. Naturally, it was locked. She banged on it impatiently, and eventually Gerardo appeared. He gave her another cheesy smile and swung upon the door, avoiding her eyes. *You are so busted,* she thought. But she said nothing. He closed the door behind her and followed her back into the sanctuary.

As she looked around the transformed room she thought for a moment that opening night had already arrived. Everyone working in the building seemed to have converged into the one room, and a few extras had been added for good measure. Up on the chancel, Camille was having a meeting with a dozen or so people Leigh assumed were actors in the show. A lighting guy was fussing with the lights. Ned and Chaz were still setting up and wiping off chairs, and the Pack were arguing over how to arrange them. Lydie was fixing a broken chair with Cara's help, and there were a line of others awaiting their attention. Frances was inspecting the chairs as the Pack placed them and then dragging half of them back to Ned and Chaz. And Bess was hurrying up to Leigh like the place was on fire.

"She's coming *here*. Again! Do you believe it?" Bess railed.

"She who?"

"That despicable Sonia Crane!" Bess answered. "And with Gordon's blessing! *Again!*"

"You mean she's meeting him here?" Leigh asked, intrigued. Perhaps Sonia was withdrawing her offer for the building. The lawyer would give some fabricated excuse, of course, but regardless, the timing would be suspicious. She should inform Maura...

"No, no," Bess replied. "Gordon isn't coming. But he did set it up, despite my protests. Sonia wants to talk to *us*, the Thespian Society. Me, Camille, and the actors, too. She wanted to talk to the board, but I told Gordon that was impossible — we just met last night and I'm not calling them all together again for that miserable woman's convenience!"

"But why does she want to do that?" Leigh asked, confused.

"Lord only knows," Bess responded, her voice agitated. "Gordon wouldn't say. That man is as stubborn as a mule!"

Leigh wondered if her Aunt Bess had any idea just how much she and Gordon Applegate had in common, but she decided to keep her mouth shut.

"So now we have to hold up the entire rehearsal for her," Bess continued to rage, "because Gordon made me promise to give her ten minutes of our time to say her piece! It's absolutely infuriating! Chewie is licking the chair leg."

Struck by the non sequitur, Leigh looked down to see her corgi splayed out full length on the hardwood, lapping with determination at the underside of a metal chair rung.

"Some more remnants of strawberry yogurt, no doubt!" Frances announced as she hustled forward. She picked up the chair, turned it upside down, and scowled. "As expected. How these two perfectly capable men continue to miss such egregious cases of food detritus adhered to metal I have no idea. Why would anyone have served something so drippy as yogurt in a place like this anyway? It hasn't been a banquet hall for ages. Ridiculous!" She folded up the chair and tucked it under her arm, then looked at the corgi critically. A rather frightening-looking smile spread across her face, and she reached out a hand for his lead. "You leave him with me for a while," she said smugly.

Leigh watched her dog happily toddle off with her mother and felt a wave of pity for Ned and Chaz. Chewie's food-particle location abilities were unparalleled; with both he and Frances on the case, the men would be wiping down seemingly clean chairs for the rest of their natural lives.

"There she is," Bess said in a low voice, her expression menacing.

Leigh turned toward the main doors to see Sonia Crane enter, survey the room, and make a hasty beeline for Camille — avoiding any eye contact with Bess.

"I didn't even have a chance to tell Gerardo I was expecting her," Bess groused. "He shouldn't have let her in. I was looking forward to taking my time getting to the door."

Sonia charged up to Camille and extended her usual rocklike hand. Camille responded by cradling Sonia's hand gently in her own limp ones. Leigh and Bess moved closer to listen in, but before they could hear anything, Camille turned abruptly to the assembled cast and raised her voice. "Meeting, everyone! Important meeting! Will you all please take seats in the first rows? You too, Elizabeth, dear!"

Bess grumbled under her breath and grabbed Leigh's arm. "You listen to this, too," she whispered, pulling them both forward. "I don't trust Sonia as far as I can throw her. Although right now, that might be farther than you'd think."

They stopped near the first row of folding chairs, but Bess refused to sit. "Let's get on with it," she said brusquely. "What do you want, Sonia?"

The lawyer didn't cast so much as a glance in Bess's direction, but handed each of the others a business card, then stepped up onto the chancel and began speaking as if she were making a business presentation. "Thank you all, so much, for allowing me to meet with you today. Your desire to bring the theater arts to this community is a noble one, and I applaud you. In fact, I'm here to help you."

"Ha!" Bess scoffed.

"I've come here today," Sonia continued as if she had heard nothing, "to present you with an exciting proposal. An opportunity I know you'll be anxious to pursue." She reached into her briefcase and withdrew a laminated photograph. She held it out in front of her and walked from one side of the assembled crowd to the other so that everyone could see it. Leigh craned forward, but could make out only the outline of a rectangular building, as Sonia seemed reluctant to move any closer to Bess.

"This," Sonia continued in her raspy voice, "is the future of your Thespian Society. *This* is what you've been waiting for. Nearly forty *thousand* square feet of theater space... with its very own huge paved parking lot!"

Sonia smiled a sickly fake smile, revealing cigarette stained teeth and a misplaced dab of dark red lipstick.

For a long moment, no one said anything. Then one of the male actors, a bearded middle-aged man with a booming voice, lifted a hand. "Correct me if I'm wrong, but don't we already have a building? Or am I actually sitting in the street?"

Sonia's forced laugh sounded like a seal barking. "This building? Oh, but you can't possibly be serious. This building is totally unsuitable."

"Says who?" Bess protested.

Leigh felt a sinking feeling in her gut. Sonia was *supposed* to be withdrawing her offer.

"Surely you all noticed as you walked in today how many ghoulish spectators this place has attracted?" Sonia forged on. "They are not here because they are waiting to buy tickets. They are here because this building is a crime scene. A community travesty. Do you not realize that two, count them, *two* murders have been committed here? The first, horribly wrapped up with devil worship and shades of satanism, and the second... well, who knows? The rumors I've heard flying are beyond ghastly. The reputation of this building as a wholesome location for community entertainment has been lost forever. It will never recover from this stigma. *Never.*"

"Oh, I don't know," said one of the actresses lightly, her brown curls bobbing as she gave a dramatic shrug. "I think a lot of people might come to the show just out of curiosity about the building."

"Hear, hear!" Bess agreed.

"That's just it!" Sonia said intently, her eyes bugging. "That's what I mean! Do you *want* to stir up that kind of interest, arouse that sleeping element of evil in our society?"

Camille gasped and put both hands over her mouth.

The actors gave snorts of derision.

"Evil!" Sonia insisted, her voice rising. "I'm talking about this building, the stain that's upon it, and how it will color everything you ever try to do here, ever again!" All at once, she lowered her voice with a smile. "Now this place, on the other hand," she said holding up the picture again, "is pure as the driven snow. Without blemish. A perfectly clean slate that you can write your own story on. And here's the exciting part. I'm offering it to you, for no rent whatsoever, for the entire first *year!"*

"It's a warehouse," the first actor said flatly.

"It's open space bursting with possibilities!" Sonia countered.

"Where is it?" another actress asked.

"Not far at all!" Sonia beamed. "Just a short drive away."

"How short a drive?"

"I've already discussed the particulars with Mr. Applegate," Sonia went on, "and I'm sure we can work out an amicable settlement. He and I will transport all your equipment to the other location, anything you'd like to take along — including the appliances! — *and* you can start remodeling the other space as soon as you want. No questions asked!"

"But where *is* it?" the curly haired actress insisted.

Sonia cleared her throat. "Beaver Falls."

The actors responded with a chorus of groans.

"Beaver Falls!" Bess cried. "That's a forty-five minute drive!"

Camille stood. "We are the *North Boros* Thespian Society, dear," she said to Sonia sweetly, removing the picture from the attorney's hands and setting it back on top of her briefcase. "So I'm afraid we shall have to decline. And we simply *must* get back to our rehearsal."

Sonia's eyes flashed with panic. "But... I have another building, too! In Butler County. And it's even bigger!"

The actors began to rise and take their places on the stage.

"But you *can't* stay here!" Sonia began to preach again, her deep voice rasping with near hysteria. "This building is *cursed*, I tell you. *Cursed!*"

Bess's eyes slid sideways over toward Leigh, who looked down at her shoes self-consciously. It did sound silly when someone else said it.

"The only way to root out the evil is just to level this place and start over!" Sonia continued to rail. "Don't you see? By moving out now you would be ridding this community not only of a blot on its past, but a magnet for future criminals! Think how much better off everyone would be if this monstrosity were razed, and a new shiny building built in its place! You *must* make it happen! It's your civic duty!"

Sonia was losing it. Flecks of spittle flew from her mouth, and everyone in the room — except the actors she was talking to — had stopped what they were doing to stare at her.

"My dear Ms. Crane," Camille said in a wispy, angelic voice as she floated over and put a hand on Sonia's arm. "You mustn't upset yourself. The society will be just fine, I promise you. In the words of Henry Wadsworth Longfellow, 'For after all, the best thing one can do when it is raining is let it rain.'"

Sonia frowned. "What the hell does that mean?"

"It means you're out of here," Bess said curtly, stepping up onto the stage. She made a series of exaggerated gestures to Gerardo, pointing first at Sonia, then at the door, and he smiled an obsequious smile and hastened forward.

"But I—" For a long moment, Sonia's eyes darted warily between Bess and the approaching bouncer. Then, with an indignant huff of breath, she grabbed her briefcase and stormed past Gerardo. Leigh expected a parting shot from the door, but was disappointed. Sonia continued straight out into the vestibule without looking back. Gerardo followed her, returning a few seconds later with a confirming nod to Bess.

"Good riddance," Bess muttered. "The nerve of that woman!"

"All right, everyone," Camille was saying to her actors onstage. "Exercises! Now, hands on hips! And bend, *slow-ly*. That's it! Now, breathe with me. *In. Out. In, out...*"

Leigh looked at Bess, who rolled her eyes. "Don't ask," Bess murmured.

"Aunt Bess?" Mathias called, hurrying up to them.

"Yes, kiddo?"

"You told us to make a center aisle, but the director lady, she said we needed to make zigzags. Something about having the chairs look like the outline of a flower from above? Then she started going off about orchid blossoms—"

"Oh, for the love of—" Bess cut herself off with a groan. "We need a large center aisle for the wedding scene, as I told you. Just ignore the director. Lord knows everyone else does."

Camille moved from the breathing exercise into a round of jumping jacks.

"Can we stay and watch the rehearsal when we're done?" Mathias asked them both.

"You may if you're excited by calisthenics and poetry recitations," Bess replied. "But that's all you're likely to see happen."

Mathias and Leigh both blinked at her. "But isn't the day after tomorrow opening night?" Leigh asked.

"Without question," Bess replied glibly. "But no one expects to make any progress while Camille's here. That will come later."

Leigh's brow furrowed. "You mean, the cast is going to practice *without* the director?"

"Why, of course," Bess said matter-of-factly. "We always make up one hush-hush schedule for the cast and another for Camille. We couldn't possibly let her direct otherwise."

Leigh cast a furtive glance back at the stage. The actors were now all crouched on the floor, their arms arched over their heads. "Acorns!" Camille crowed with delight, flitting about between them. "We are all acorns!" She stopped by the male actor who had been so outspoken earlier, and her face drew into a frown. "Oh, no," she chastised. "No, no, no. You must be more three-dimensional!"

"Um..." Mathias said dubiously, "*Yeah*. Maybe we'll finish the chairs and just take off, then."

"An excellent idea," Leigh agreed.

Mathias returned to the Pack, and Leigh watched as her aunt's face slowly reddened. "I can't believe Gordon subjected us all to such nonsense," Bess fumed. "Beaver Falls, indeed! He should have known better. Well, he'll get an earful from me next time I see him, that's for sure."

Uncomfortable thoughts swirled in Leigh's brain. "Sonia definitely still wants this place," she thought out loud. "And badly. I have to wonder what else she might do to get it. How far she'd go."

Bess harrumphed. "It will never happen. Gordon promised me. We make a success of this show — good crowds, positive reviews, excitement in the community, and the theater is ours. *No one* is knocking this place down to make some shiny new hamburger stand. Not while there's breath in my body!"

"Aunt Bess!" Leigh said sharply.

"What?" Bess asked with surprise.

The image her aunt's euphemistic words created in Leigh's fertile imagination could very well make an appearance in future nightmares.

"Nothing," Leigh answered quietly. "I just don't want anything to happen to you, that's all."

Bess's expression softened. "Don't you worry about me, kiddo," she said confidently. "If that pint-sized harpy sticks her nose in my business one more time, it's *her* that can do the worrying."

Chapter 11

When Leigh arrived in Avalon the next morning to visit Maura, she found her friend sitting up in bed surrounded by an even wider array of paperwork than before, plus a laptop and a printer.

"This doesn't look so relaxing," Leigh commented, entering the room with Allison behind her.

"It's just right," Maura replied, closing the file she'd been studying. "Technically I'm on modified duty, not disability, much to Gerry's annoyance. Hey, Allie."

"Hey, Aunt Mo," Allison said quietly, slipping into a chair.

"Where's the Chewmeister today?" Maura asked.

"He had a prior social obligation," Leigh replied. "Cara took the rest of the Pack to North Park this morning for a charity-sponsored dog walkathon."

Maura's eyebrows lifted in surprise. She turned to Allison. "You're not missing that just to come over here and babysit me, I hope?"

Allison smiled shyly and gave a shrug.

Leigh's teeth gritted. She had good reason to fear Allison's motives in asking to come, and the internal debate she'd waged over whether to ship the girl off to the park with the others had been fierce. She had relented in the end only because she knew that Allison's curiosity, once sparked, was impossible to quench, and that any attempt to thwart it only made the child more determined. And potentially, more devious.

It was Maura's fault the child was so fascinated by crime anyway, Leigh thought ruefully. Why not let the detective deal with it?

Maura studied mother and daughter a moment, then moved the files on her lap aside and picked up her notebook and pencil. "So," she said cheerfully. "Somebody catch me up. What's been going on at the theater lately?"

Some time passed before Maura received the complete rundown, perhaps because whatever details Leigh left out in the interest of sparing Allison, the girl herself made a point of supplying. The detective listened carefully, making occasional notes.

"So, I guess Sonia's out as my prime suspect for Marconi's murder," Leigh admitted. "Did you ever find a connection between the two of them?"

Maura shook her head. "She wasn't named as his attorney on any of the public records, anyway."

"Are you in charge of the case now, Aunt Mo?" Allison asked.

Maura grinned. "Well now, that's a more complicated question than you might think. Officially, no, Detective Stroth is heading up the investigation. Unofficially, well... assume what you will."

Allison grinned back. "Could I ask you a question? If you're not allowed to answer it, that's okay."

"Agreed," Maura replied. "Shoot."

"Do the police know yet exactly how Andrew Marconi was killed?"

Leigh got a familiar sick feeling in her stomach. *Why* would Allison need to know something like that?

"Yes," Maura answered. "The autopsy results just came in. What will become public knowledge soon, if it hasn't already, is that Marconi was most likely killed by a blow to the back of the head."

Allison's eyes widened. But she made no response.

Leigh hastened to change the topic. "What do you think about Bess's one hire pretending he can't speak English?"

Maura shrugged. "Could mean a lot of things. You have any reason to believe he has ties to the building or any of the people involved, aside from trying to make a few bucks doing manual labor?"

Leigh shook her head.

"Yes," Allison answered. "Maybe."

Both women turned to look at her. "What?" Leigh barked. Allison had already confessed that the Pack had suspected Gerardo's deceit from the beginning and had even gone so far as to confirm it. Evidently, he had underestimated their powers of observation — a costly error, always — and had been tricked into acting on several throwaway comments, like "Look at all this cash!" and even the classic "Quick, duck!" But the Pack, like Leigh at first, considered the deception a harmless enough secret. They all liked Gerardo, and Mathias and Ethan were convinced that he had begun the ruse just to shut Chaz up.

"What's the connection?" Maura asked.

Allison squirmed in her seat. "Well, yesterday I saw him talking to Gordon Applegate."

Leigh stiffened. "You saw Gerardo *talking* to him? I didn't think Mr. Applegate was even at the building yesterday!"

"Well he wasn't, exactly," Allison qualified. "And I can't be sure they were talking. It's just that while we were on the second floor putting away props, I saw Mr. Applegate's limousine out the window. Or at least another white one just like it. It didn't turn into the parking lot — it just pulled up on the curb by the entrance. And Gerardo was supposed to be guarding the door then, but he walked over to the car and talked to somebody in the back."

"You couldn't see who he was talking to?" Maura asked.

Allison shook her head. "No, the window was tinted and it was only rolled down partway. But it sure looked like Gerardo was talking in full sentences — not just gesturing for them to move along, you know."

"How long did they talk?" Leigh asked.

"Only, like, ten seconds," Allison replied. "Then Gerardo looked around and ran back to the door. I don't think he realized we could see him; you really can't see that spot from anywhere else in the building."

Leigh exhaled uncomfortably. "Well, I don't like the sound of *that*."

"Who's paying the men for their work?" Maura asked her. "Bess or Mr. Applegate?"

"I think the society is, but I'm not sure," Leigh replied. "Allison, why didn't you mention this earlier?"

Allison squirmed again. "I was going to. I just wanted to see what Aunt Mo thought about it, first."

Maura studied Allison. "You have a theory of your own. Don't you?"

The girl nodded self-consciously.

"Well?" Leigh demanded.

"I'm afraid it might upset Aunt Bess," Allison said mildly.

Maura smirked. "Oh, I'm sure it will. Spit it out, Allie."

Leigh looked from one to the other with annoyance. Was she missing something?

"I think Gerardo's a spy," Allison announced. "I think he's really working for Mr. Applegate."

Maura grinned broadly. "A brilliant deduction!" She looked up at Leigh. "See there? Police academy, here she—"

"Stop that!" Leigh ordered.

Maura chuckled. "Gordon Applegate does have a reputation for micromanagement. Which is to say, he's a grade-A control freak. Warren could have told you that." She looked back at Allison. "I think you'd better tell your Aunt Bess what you just told me. She's a big girl. She can take it from there."

"Okay," Allison agreed calmly.

"Back to the Marconi case," Leigh said, anxious to change the subject, lest she feel even stupider than she already did. "Is the detective you mentioned going to be questioning my mother, now? Should I be worried?"

"Absolutely," Maura answered. "But it's Detective Stroth you should be worried about."

Leigh chuckled. "Yeah, you got that right. Mom will *not* be pleased."

Maura smiled reassuringly. "Stroth knows my opinion of your mother, and your aunts, and he's sharp enough to value that opinion. But the neighbors' theory that somebody who opposed the strip club might have become unbalanced enough to do Marconi bodily harm isn't as far-fetched as it sounds. Your mother knows the people involved; I'm betting she could be helpful to the investigation."

"But what about the other murder?" Allison piped up.

Leigh's panic sensor started to flicker again.

"What other murder?" Maura asked. "You mean the one that happened in the same building? Back in the sixties?"

Allison nodded mutely.

Maura turned to the card table on the other side of her bed and picked up a folder. "What about it, Allie?"

Leigh stifled a sigh. It was, of course, too much wishful thinking to hope that the Pack hadn't heard every detail of the sordid "satanists sacrifice church custodian on altar" story by now. All it would take, after all, was five minutes of working in the same room as Chaz.

"I was just thinking," Allison began tentatively, "that there are some similarities between the two."

Leigh frowned. "Just because they happened in roughly the same location doesn't mean they're connected," she insisted.

"Maybe not," Allison agreed. "But the two men were killed the same way."

Leigh cast a glance at Maura. Her pulse increased. "Did you investigate that other murder? I mean, I know you weren't even born yet, but is it covered in the Marconi file?"

"Not well," Maura said thoughtfully, looking at Allison. "But I do know that the custodian was also killed with a blow to the head. That's true."

"Well, it's a common enough way to kill somebody," Leigh argued. She wasn't sure why it was so terribly important to her that the two murders had nothing to do with each other. But she *was* sure that she wanted Allison to stop thinking about it. "The two events happened fifty years apart, for heaven's sake! Half the people on the planet the first time were dead by the second."

"Mom," Allison said with maddening calmness, "you're including the time it took to find Marconi's body. The actual murders were only forty-something years apart."

Leigh's face reddened. "Be that as it may, the similarity is just a coincidence," she proclaimed.

Allison frowned and looked away. Her small voice was barely audible. "I don't *like* coincidences."

The bedroom door opened to reveal Maura's husband Gerry holding a telephone handset and looking extremely unhappy. "It's Stroth," he announced, with the same tone of doom and gloom he might have used to say, "It's an Ebola virus."

Maura's lips curved into a smile. "Well, are you going to let me talk to him?"

The Lieutenant's jaw muscles twitched. "I haven't decided yet."

"Gerry," Maura said heavily. "Whatever it is, it's not going to make me get up from this bed. I promise. I can think, and talk, in complete repose. Have I not behaved so far?"

"You're not supposed to get stressed."

"Work doesn't stress me," she assured. "Boredom does. Now give me the damn phone. Sweetheart."

Gerry's mouth twitched into a reluctant smile. He handed the handset to his wife, then kissed her on the lips. "I'm taking it back in five minutes, whether you're done or not. Deal with it." He gave a friendly nod to Leigh and Allison, then walked back out.

Leigh smiled, and Allison giggled. The two policemen had always been a bizarre pair, hardly seeming to be a couple at all most of the time, as they were both so reserved. But ever since they found out that Maura was pregnant, they'd been acting like lovesick teenagers.

"That man!" Maura sighed with an exaggerated simper. Then she made a gesture for her visitors to hang tight a moment, grabbed her notepad, and put the phone to her ear. "Yo, Stroth! What's up?"

As Maura's smile faded into a full-on frown of concentration, Leigh's anxiety grew.

"Where did it happen exactly?" Maura asked, scribbling madly. "Any witnesses?" The silence between her questions seemed to drag interminably. "What's the prognosis? I see. So you're going to— Right. I agree. No, that's good. I'll check out what I can from here. You keep me apprised, all right? Every hour, if you need to. No matter how Gerry barks at you. Right. Good work."

At long last, she hung up the phone. She said nothing for a moment, just continued catching up on her scribbles.

Finally, Leigh could stand no more. "Please tell me that call had nothing whatsoever to do with my Aunt Bess's building or the Marconi case."

Maura looked up and met her eyes, and Leigh's hopes sank. "Sorry, Koslow," the detective answered. "No can do."

"Oh, crap." Leigh, who had been standing up for the entirety of the visit so far, sank down onto the foot of Maura's bed. "What is it? What's happened now?" As much as she hated for Allison to overhear, she had to know. Allison would doubtless find out anyway. She always did.

"It's Sonia Crane," Maura explained. "She was assaulted as she went into work this morning. She's in the hospital."

"Assaulted?" Leigh repeated, horrified. "Why? How?"

"Too soon to tell," Maura answered. "All we know is that a passer-by found her unconscious outside the door to her office and called an ambulance."

"But..." Leigh stammered, still disbelieving. "There were security cameras, I hope?"

Maura shook her head. "If she worked for any of the firms

downtown, there would be. But Sonia Crane hung out her own shingle two years ago. Her new office is in Sewickley, just off the Boulevard. There weren't any cameras. Or any witnesses either, at least not that we know of. Yet."

"Is she going to be okay?" Allison asked.

Maura considered a moment. "I can only tell you what the press already knows. She's in fair condition."

Leigh's jaws clenched tightly. Musing over ancient crimes was one thing — dealing with current ones was another. Sonia was supposed to be a suspect, not a victim. *Nobody* was supposed to be a victim.

She straightened and cleared her throat. "Well, that's frightening to hear. I hope she's okay. But we have no reason to believe the assault had anything to do with her bid for the building. She could have scads of enemies out there. Other business deals gone sour. It could have been a random mugger. There's no reason to think it has anything to do with the theater or with any of us." She looked at Maura hopefully. "Right?"

"There's no obvious link, no," Maura replied.

Leigh found that answer less than comforting.

"Aunt Mo?" Allison asked, her voice a squeak. "Can you tell us what kind of assault—" She broke off awkwardly. "I mean, why she's unconscious, specifically?"

Maura drew in a measured breath. Her eyes flashed a warning note to Leigh, even as her gaze centered on Allison.

"She was struck on the back of the head."

Chapter 12

Leigh had promised herself, ardently, that she would keep the Pack out of the wretched building all day for at least one day. And yet here she was, driving herself and Allison straight back into the lion's den so that Allison could give Bess the scoop on Gerardo. Maura had thought it best they do it promptly, and Leigh had agreed.

But they were *not* sticking around.

Really. They weren't.

They arrived at the building to find Bess in as close to a tizzy as Bess ever got. Getting a private moment with her required following a moving target — she roamed through the building from end to end at a frenetic pace, directing the men to hurry, opening closet doors, switching lights on and off, flushing toilets, and peering into every nook and cranny for heaven only knew what. "The inspector is coming today," she explained. "We can't open the show unless he's happy — you have no idea how important this is!"

"It looks fabulous, Aunt Bess," Leigh said honestly. Although the majority of the annex was still a mess, the parts of the original building that made up the theater proper had undergone an amazing transformation. The auditorium was spotless, the hallways and bathrooms were beyond reproach, and Frances had worked wonders in the basement practically overnight. The men were still repainting the basement walls and the ancient tile floor desperately needed a good polish, but the clutter, dirt, and grime had been thoroughly vanquished. "Really," Leigh gushed. "I'm sure the inspector will be more than satisfied."

Bess stopped moving at last and huffed out a breath. "Well, he certainly should, shouldn't he? I only wish I knew when he was coming. All I know is 'sometime today.' And the rehearsal is going to begin shortly!"

"Wait," Leigh said, confused. "It isn't even noon yet. Isn't the dress rehearsal tonight?"

"Yes," Bess replied. "But Camille will be at that one. A couple of the actors are still struggling with their lines — they get to say them so infrequently at the regular rehearsals, you know — so everyone who could take a long lunch is coming for an emergency run-through." She looked down at Allison. "You had something you wanted to talk to me about, kiddo?"

Allison nodded and pulled Bess into one of the second-floor classrooms so they could talk privately, but just as Leigh began to follow, her phone rang. She stepped out in the hallway and answered it. "Hey, Warren. What's up?"

"I was just wondering if Allison had hit you up with her plan yet."

Leigh's heart beat faster. "Evidently not. What am I in for now?"

"I'll let her tell you," he said evasively. "But for what it's worth, I don't mind if you don't. Are you still at Mo's?"

Leigh slipped into another classroom across the hall and gave him a quick summary of the morning's revelations.

"I don't like it, either," he said worriedly. "Any of it. But if it makes you feel any better, I'd be surprised if Sonia Crane hasn't collected a fair number of enemies over the years. There's no reason to assume that what happened to her this morning has anything to do with Bess. And as for Gordon hiring a spy... well, that wouldn't surprise me in the least. I told you, the man is a master manipulator. He enjoys a good game. As uptight as he's been *pretending* to be about whether or not he should sell the theater, I really don't think he gives a flip about the money. Or his local reputation. The more I think about it, the more I think he's really just looking for a way to get to Bess."

The door across the hallway burst open and a red-faced Bess stormed out.

"Sorry, gotta go," Leigh said quickly.

"Okay, I'll be there soo—" Warren's voice cut off as Leigh stuffed the phone back in her pocket.

"Aunt Bess!" she said, lunging forward to stop Bess in her tracks. "Where are you going?"

"I am going to get in my car, go find Gordon Applegate, and then beat the man to within an inch of his miserably privileged life!" Bess replied hotly.

"Don't be ridiculous," Leigh chastised. "If you kill him, his heirs would sell the building."

Bess growled low in her throat. "You're right, dammit. But I can still maim him, can't I?"

"Only if you want to spend opening night in the Allegheny County jail."

Bess crossed her arms over her chest and let out a humph. "But he deserves it! The gall! As if him dropping in here himself practically every day wasn't keeping enough of an eye on me and his precious investment!" her eyes flashed fire. "I should have known something was up when the woman at the Outreach foisted Gerardo on me. He didn't have any prior work experience with them, but she kept insisting he came *highly* recommended... and now I know by whom! Gordon knew I was going to look for men through the Outreach; he paid them off!"

Light footsteps echoed down the hallway, and within a few seconds a paint-splashed Chaz came into view. "Hey, Ms. Bess. Just thought you might want to know, Mr. Applegate is waiting for you in the sanctuary. I know you told us not to let anybody in, but he used his own key and all, and although I *would* have tackled him if he was anybody else, he *does* own the building. And if the YBC ever gets itself together again, it'd be great to use this place for another haunted house, so I really didn't want to tick him off too bad. So that's why when he asked where you were I said —"

Bess roared something incomprehensible and pushed past him like a fighting bull. Leigh followed, fearing an imminent explosion, but when she and Allison caught up to Bess just inside the old sanctuary, they found her outwardly calm and smiling.

"Gordon, dear," Bess purred. "I wasn't expecting you today."

"Have you heard about Sonia?" he asked brusquely.

Leigh blinked. She had no idea how Bess could look so collected, when just the sprint across the building and down the stairs had left both her and Allison panting like dogs. As for Gordon, the man looked unrecognizable. His hair was barely combed, his face was pale, his shirt was only tucked partway in his trousers, and she was pretty sure his shoes didn't match.

"What about her?" Bess asked quickly.

Leigh felt a stab of guilt for not filling in her aunt herself, but they'd hardly had time.

"Somebody struck her on the head outside her office this morning," Gordon said slowly, his ice blue eyes watching Bess keenly. "I just heard about it on the news. I was... wondering if you were all right."

Bess digested the information a moment. "I'm perfectly fine. Why wouldn't I be?"

The two continued to stare at each other. "No reason," he replied.

"How bad is she?" Bess asked.

Gordon shook his head. "All they said was 'fair condition.'"

"Well, that's a shame," Bess said with sincerity, but as she looked around the room, her paled face began to redden all over again. Chaz, Gerardo, and Ned — all covered to various degrees with cream-colored paint — stood clustered at the doorway to the alcove, blatantly eavesdropping.

"Well, now that we have everyone's attention," Bess began, "I would like you to explain to me, Gordon, why exactly you planted a spy in our midst?"

Chaz gasped and covered his mouth with his hands. Ned looked confused. Gerardo remained expressionless. Gordon's eyes flickered with a sudden intensity, but he showed no other signs of alarm. "Excuse me?" he asked.

"You heard what I said," Bess insisted, planting both hands firmly on her hips. "I know that Gerardo speaks English, I know you bribed the director of the Outreach to recommend him to me, and I know you've been secretly meeting with him along the curb outside and God knows where else. I just thought maybe you'd like to fill me in on the rest of it."

The two locked gazes for another long moment. Everyone else in the room seemed afraid to breathe. Finally, Gordon straightened. He ran long, spindly fingers through his mussed fringe of hair and gave his shoulders a defiant shake. "Your lack of confidence wounds me, Bess," he said heavily. "You are correct in only one assumption. I have indeed conversed with Gerardo outside of this building. I drove by *my* property, as I often do, and when I saw him outside the door I called him over to ask him, in essence, what the hell he was doing here. I recognized him because I have seen him many times, at my estate. He happens to be one of my gardeners."

Bess showed no sign of being appeased. "He speaks English!" she accused.

"Well if he does, that's news to me," Gordon insisted.

"You spoke to him!" Bess protested.

"In Spanish!" Gordon fired back. "I spent almost three years in Argentina, I should think I can ask my own gardener why he's moonlighting!"

Leigh felt Allison shrink beside her. Seriously, they should have thought of that. But whether Gordon realized it or not, Gerardo *could* speak English. She was certain of it.

"Seems a bit too much of a coincidence for my tastes," Bess continued, unrelenting. "Why would an employee of yours go to the Outreach looking for extra work? And who would have recommended him?"

Gordon sighed. "As Gerardo explained to me, work for gardeners is understandably thin over the winter. He's been on part-time hours at my place for some time now, and my manager was trying to help him out. He's an excellent worker, as you should well know. He didn't realize I owned this building until I told him so myself. Are you happy now?"

Bess sniffed. "Marginally. Perhaps."

"Well, I hope you're mollified," Gordon continued with a superior tone, "because we need to talk about this business with the Marconi remains. I'm starting to get calls."

"Calls?"

"Yes, calls," he said shortly. "From people who think this building is a menace to the borough. Those blasted news articles mentioned that I owned it, and now the complaints are rolling in. 'The building's cursed. Two murders are enough. Tear it down!'"

"I don't believe it," Bess argued. "That's not what I'm hearing. People are intrigued, but they're hardly carrying pitchforks and torches!"

"It will only get worse when the news about Sonia Crane gets out."

"That's nonsense!" Bess protested. "Nobody outside the Society knows she had anything to do with the theater!"

"I'm telling you, Bess," Gordon continued, "I won't stand for owning a public nuisance! If there's one more *unpleasant* finding in, on, or around this place — or if anybody else associated with it gets hurt, I'll unload this box of bricks so fast it will make—"

"Oh, poo," Bess interrupted lightly, both her tone and manner softening as abruptly as if she'd flipped a switch. She took a step closer to him. "You're just looking for excuses to worry, Gordon. Opening night is tomorrow, we're right on schedule, and everything will be fine. I *promise*."

Their eyes met once more, and this time Gordon responded with a sly smile. At which point both of them seemed to remember that they were not alone.

Gordon turned sharply and flung a line of rapid Spanish at Gerardo. Gerardo returned a slightly longer speech, then whirled to descend the steps, delivering a solid smack to Chaz's shoulders as he went. Chaz, who had been looking from one man to the other in confusion, jumped to attention and followed. Ned, who was looking even more confused, did the same.

"He said he's sorry if his being here caused you any trouble, and he's going to get back to work," Gordon translated.

Bess harrumphed.

"Allison," Leigh said firmly, "we should be going now."

"But, Mom—"

The child's plea was interrupted by a sharp rapping on the building's front door.

"I wonder if that's the inspector," Bess said nervously. "Oh, I was hoping they could finish painting the basement first!"

Neither Bess nor Gordon moved, but instead looked expectantly at Leigh.

"We'll just get that on our way out," Leigh responded, crossing the room and heading into the vestibule. When she reached the door with no Allison behind her, she began to call for the girl over her shoulder, but the sight of the person she opened the door to snatched the words out of her mouth. She had never seen the man before, but she had seen enough like him to know what he was.

"Hello," he said pleasantly. "Detective Daniel Stroth of the Allegheny Police. I was wondering if I could speak with Ms. Bess Cogley?"

Bingo. Stroth, who appeared to be somewhere in his late thirties, was largely unremarkable in both physical appearance and manner. Real detectives, Leigh knew, did not strut around attracting attention like Steve McGarrett on Hawaii 5-0. They preferred to come across as ordinary and nonthreatening. What gave them away was that if you looked at them closely enough, it was obvious they were looking at *you* even closer.

Leigh summoned a pleasant expression. "Yes, of course. I'm her niece, Leigh. Bess is right inside."

"Ah. I've heard of you." His brown eyes danced with mischief.

"No doubt," Leigh returned. She gestured to Allison, who now hovered at the inside doorway. "My daughter and I were just leaving."

The detective gave a nod to them both, then moved around Allison and into the sanctuary. Leigh felt a sudden twinge in her middle. Was the detective following up on the Marconi case, or was he here because of Sonia? Bess had made no secret of her antipathy for the woman. The entire cast had seen it...

"Mom?"

As Allison's small voice interrupted her thoughts, Leigh's warning sensors raised another alarm. It was the child's best "parental schmoozing" tone, and it never boded well.

"No," Leigh answered preemptively. "I don't want you spending any more time here today. You shouldn't be here at all. I'm sure the detective is just covering all the bases where Sonia's assault is concerned — there's nothing to worry about."

"I wasn't worried about that. I just—"

"There's nothing more to be done here," Leigh continued. "I already told you. We'll all go see opening night together, but the rest of the prop inventory can wait until after the show."

"That's not what I was going to ask."

Leigh studied her daughter warily. "Then what?" She wasn't fooled. Allison was about to ask for something she desperately wanted and was afraid she wouldn't get.

"I just wondered if it would be okay if dad took me to the library."

Leigh's eyebrows lifted. It was an innocent enough request — coming from someone else's daughter. "*Which* library?"

"The Carnegie," Allison answered. "I already asked Dad. He was going to work from home all day, but he said he didn't mind taking me to Oakland and working on his laptop there in the library for a couple hours. If it's okay with you, that is. I told him I was sure it would be. After all, I'll be perfectly safe in a library." She smiled innocently.

Leigh wasn't buying it. "Why make him drive you all the way into town? Why not use our branch in McCandless?"

Allison's nose twitched. "Well, I like the main library better. It's bigger."

Leigh waited.

Allison sighed. "And they have old copies of the *Post-Gazette* on microfilm."

Aha! Leigh thought. "You want to research that first murder, don't you?"

The girl nodded solemnly. "But I'll be perfectly safe," she repeated.

Leigh studied her daughter, carefully contemplating the various risks. A couple hours in the library wouldn't violate the doctor's orders, at least. The swelling and redness around Allison's eye had resolved nicely, and up to now she'd been good about not straining her vision. As for her mind straying where it shouldn't — Leigh was certain that would happen regardless of where the girl was located. But the most critical point was that every moment Allison spent dwelling on events that happened in the sixties would be a moment she was *not* creating trouble for herself in the here and now.

"Are you sure you don't want to go to the skating rink with the others this afternoon?" Leigh asked, giving the more age-appropriate alternative one last chance. "Lenna will miss you, you know."

"No, she won't," Allison replied. "She's meeting her friend Megan."

Leigh gave up. "Okay, then. Fine."

Allison smiled brilliantly. "Thanks, Mom!"

The girl's unbridled excitement made Leigh question her decision. But it was too late now. According to her phone, Warren had texted twice since she'd hung up and was already on his way. "Apparently your dad was pretty sure I'd cave, because he's coming here to pick you up," she informed Allison, swinging the front door open again. "Until then, we can wait outside in the parking lot."

It was stupid, she knew. A hundred-year-old collection of bricks and mortar and wood and beams could not logically, in and of itself, conspire to endanger the wellbeing of her only daughter.

But she wasn't taking any chances.

Chapter 13

Leigh had just sent Allison off with Warren and unlocked the door of the van to drive herself home when her mother's Taurus rolled up beside her in the parking lot. After catching the look of righteous indignation on Frances's face, Leigh was seriously tempted to wave and make a run for it, but her sense of daughterly duty won out. That, and the fact that she was pretty sure that she herself wasn't the object of Frances' wrath — at least not at the moment. She steeled herself, relocked the van, and dragged her feet over to the Taurus's driver's side.

"What's up Mom?" she asked carefully.

Frances arose from the car in stages, first checking the seat and mirror positions (which most people did only when getting *in* a car), then switching off all applicable dashboard controls, and only then — in a predictable order which Leigh had memorized early in childhood — checking her lipstick, collecting her giant bag, retouching her lipstick, readjusting the mirror, smoothing her skirt or slacks, moving the giant bag to her shoulder, pulling the keys from the ignition, exiting the car, locking the car, then dropping the keys into the giant bag.

"What's up," Frances replied, her ears not visibly steaming, but glowing beet red nevertheless, "is that despite my stellar record of a lifetime of church and community service, I have just spent half the morning being subjected to interrogation by a county detective, and all over that miserable Mr. Marconi!"

"I'm sure they know you had nothing to do with it, Mom," Leigh soothed, feeling sympathetic. "It's no fun being treated like a suspect. Believe me, I know. But they have to ask the questions."

Frances' back went ramrod straight. "*Me*, a suspect? Why they wouldn't *dare* insinuate such a thing!"

"Um... no?" Leigh said uncertainly.

"Certainly not!" Frances declared. "It's bad enough that I'm expected to tell tales on our good friends and neighbors who respect decency and deplore moral turpitude! The very idea that one of

them could have become unhinged enough to commit murder...
Really! It's an insult to honest citizens everywhere! I told that
detective in no uncertain terms that he should be looking for
Marconi's murderer in the gutter, not a church pew. The man dealt
in a dirty business, and you know what they say, 'you lie down
with dogs, you get up with fleas!' Except not in any decent
household. Any competent wife is perfectly capable of keeping a
home free of fleas and other vermin, provided she has the proper—"

"Mom," Leigh interrupted quickly, "Detective Stroth is inside the
building right now."

Frances' eyebrows rose. "Why would he be?"

Leigh summarized the news about Sonia Crane, which Stroth
had evidently not yet known when he interviewed Frances earlier
in the morning. As far as Leigh could tell, Frances had spent every
minute since her interview personally warning every former
member of the Citizens Against Indecency and Moral Turpitude of
their risk of impending persecution.

Leigh was beginning to feel sorry for Detective Stroth.

"It's positively dreadful for a defenseless woman to be attacked
in broad daylight," Frances opined with regard to Sonia. "But I
daresay that particular woman has lain down with some dogs
herself. I doubt it has anything to do with the theater."

Leigh wished she could believe that.

"Still," Frances continued, "I think it's best if you and the
children remain at home for a few days. It's prime time for spring
cleaning, you know. Those curtains in your living—"

"I'm on my way home now, Mom," Leigh assured, pulling out
her keys. But in fact she found herself wavering. What was taking
Stroth so long? Was he interviewing the workmen as well as Bess?
All three of them (as well as Camille and the entire cast of the play)
had heard Bess berate Sonia for her interference with the theater.
Leigh could only hope that Bess had arrived at the building this
morning before the assault occurred — and that she had witnesses
to prove it.

"Are you staying or going?" Frances demanded when Leigh
hesitated.

"I—" Leigh did not have the chance to answer. Bess popped out
the side door of the building and held it open while gesturing
wildly in their direction. "Leigh!" she said urgently. "Don't go!

Come here!"

Leigh hastened to the door with Frances following. "What is it? What's wrong?"

"Nothing's *wrong*, kiddo," Bess said more mildly, shutting the door after them. "Not now that you're here, anyway."

"Me?" Leigh repeated. "Where's Detective Stroth?"

"Oh, he left a while ago." Bess gestured for the women to follow her toward the sanctuary. "And yes, *you*. I'm so glad I caught you in time. I told them you'd be perfect!"

Leigh tensed. "You told who what, now?"

"For heaven's sake, Bess," Frances broke in, "What did the detective say to you? Are you in danger of arrest? Should we call a family meeting?"

Bess whirled in her tracks, causing Leigh to bump into her and Frances to bump into Leigh. "Don't be ridiculous, Francie!" Bess protested. "I'm not in danger of anything, and neither is anybody else!"

"You have an alibi, then?" Leigh inquired, rubbing the heel that had just been clipped by the toe of Frances' sensible shoe.

"Not that I should need one!" Bess replied, pretending offense. "But as it happens, I stopped by the animal shelter on my way in this morning, which puts me safely up in Franklin Park at the time in question. Angie and Jackie can both vouch for me."

Leigh exhaled with relief. "That's good."

"Nevertheless, we should start collecting a bail fund just in case," Frances offered. She threw a sideways glance at Leigh. "You never know who in the family might need it."

Leigh's face reddened. She was offended, but she would be more offended if she hadn't had the same idea herself.

They walked into the sanctuary in single file to find assembled on the chancel most of the cast members Leigh had met the day before. While waiting with Allison in the parking lot, Leigh had seen Gordon leave and the actors arrive, but she had somehow missed Stroth's exit. She wondered if he had parked on the secondary street that ran down the building's other side.

"Leigh's your woman!" Bess called, giving her niece a shove in the direction of the chancel.

"Fabulous!" said a crisp, businesslike actress with a cell phone headset stuck over her ear. She thrust a playbook into Leigh's hands and pulled her by the elbow up toward the altar. "So here's the deal. I'm the spinster business tycoon, you're the free-spirited third-world missionary. We're sisters, and we've been fighting since we were toddlers. Our baby sister is getting married tomorrow, and we've both come to the wedding, but we haven't seen or talked to each other in years, because the last time we were together was at my wedding, which never happened because you seduced my fiancé at the altar. Got it?"

"Um..." Leigh stammered.

"So you just read all the lines that say 'Cat' and we'll take it from there, okay? Thanks!"

"Carol couldn't get off work," Bess explained, more to Frances than to Leigh. "So I told them Leigh fancied herself an actress and would be thrilled to stand in!"

Leigh frowned. *Fancied herself* an actress?

She tightened her grip on the playbook, cleared her throat, and smiled. She did love to act, but she'd had no time since high school to indulge herself by actually being in a show. For a thoroughly enjoyable, heady half hour, she faked her way through the role, becoming so absorbed that she temporarily forgot her reservations about their ill-fated venue.

Then she caught sight of Stroth.

A knock at the front door had been answered by one of the actors; seconds later Stroth entered the sanctuary and settled himself in an audience chair in the first row. The same actor disappeared out the door to the alcove, presumably on his way to fetch Bess — or somebody — from the basement.

"Cat?" Somebody was shouting at her. "Cat! Your line?"

Leigh jumped. "Oh, right. Sorry." She delivered the line mechanically while the majority of her brain sought an explanation for the detective's reappearance. He must have been around the building somewhere the whole time. Yet Bess was under the impression he had left. Where had he been? She was certain he had not walked through the parking lot. Could he have been outdoors on the other side of the annex?

A sudden image flashed in her mind of a certain pair of elderly people beckoning across the road with broad smiles. *Merle and Earl.*

Oh, dear.

"Cat? Your line again!"

"Sorry, sorry!" Leigh redoubled her efforts to pay attention, but failed miserably. Had Stroth got an earful from Merle and Earl about the "religious crazies?" If so, he might very well be back to continue grilling her mother. And what if they had told him about all the "bobbing lights" and other oddities that convinced them someone had been sneaking in and out of the building for years? It couldn't have been Marconi himself, so who was it? And would that whole line of speculation make Bess look more, or less, guilty of using foul play to acquire the building?

Leigh couldn't seem to think straight. It did not help matters when she noticed that Stroth's attention had been caught by something on the floor by his feet. He leaned down to pick it up.

"This is the part where you kiss me," informed a handsome actor in his mid-thirties.

Leigh snapped back to attention. "Say what?"

The man chuckled. "We can fake it if you want to. Just put your arms around my neck."

Leigh cast a quick glance at Stroth. He had dropped something into his pocket and was now searching around the nearby chairs. Before he could do so thoroughly, however, Bess and Frances appeared in the alcove doorway. He straightened and moved toward them.

Leigh drew in a breath, looked back at her script, and threw her arms around the actor as directed. "You're right," she cooed in a weak attempt at a seductive tone. "And for the record, I am jealous. *Very* jealous."

They remained clenched for only a second before the actress playing the business tycoon bounded onto the stage with a roar of indignation so real that Leigh forgot for one terrifying moment that the other woman was acting. Pandemonium ensued until at last the character of Cat was allowed to make an exit. Leigh slipped off the chancel and started toward the back of the sanctuary, where Stroth appeared to be in deep conversation with both Bess and Frances. Bess looked both frustrated and annoyed; Frances just looked worried. But Leigh had taken no more than two steps before "Cat" was summoned back up on stage again.

Holy crap, this actress has a lot of lines!

She plowed through the rest of the scene as best she could, keeping one eye on her script and the other on the detective. Bess appeared to become increasingly defensive as they talked, even as Frances became more contemplative... and more grave. Then Bess seemed to capitulate, stepping back from Stroth and gesturing him toward the stairs to the basement.

The hired men? Leigh thought curiously. Why would the detective want to interview them?

She had little opportunity to ponder the question as the play's action suddenly became nonstop. Everyone in the cast was coming and going like whack-a-moles except for Leigh's own character, who was apparently never allowed to leave the stage. By the time the third act had concluded and the cast decided to call it an afternoon, Leigh had lost track of both her mother and her aunt and hadn't seen Stroth in half an hour.

Her first action was to check out the area where Stroth had been sitting. What had he pocketed? Had someone spilled something? It seemed unlikely, with Frances in the building, that any spill would last long. Leigh saw nothing on the floor by Stroth's chair, but as she scouted around to either side, she did find something lying on top of another chair seat.

It was a business card. She snatched it up and read it.

Sonia J. Crane, Esquire. Crane Legal Services, LLC. Specializing in Real Estate and Property Law.

And under the title banner, the address of an office in Sewickley.

Leigh sank down onto the chair. Sonia had handed these out to the cast last night, and at least two people had discarded them immediately. There were probably several others lying around the building as well. But what of it? The information was all readily available online, if not in a printed phone book.

Still, Stroth's pocketing the card did not look good. Everyone present last night — including the entire cast, the hired men, the Pack, and virtually all Leigh's female relatives — had overheard Sonia's desperate spiel and witnessed her eviction.

So whom did Stroth suspect? And what was he up to now?

Leigh rose, headed for the basement staircase, and crept quietly down it. But if she hoped to eavesdrop on the detective as he conducted his interviews with the hired help, she was to be disappointed. Hearing no voice other than Bess's, Leigh push opened the door into the basement to see her aunt engaged in conversation with all three of the men and Stroth nowhere in sight.

"Don't look so miserable, Ned," Bess said comfortingly. "It doesn't mean a thing, truly, it doesn't. Detectives have to ask questions. That's their job."

"But it was the *type* of questions he asked," Chaz whined like a child. "What if he suspects *us* of something?"

"I'm sure he doesn't," Bess soothed, delivering a gentle pat to one of Ned's hunched shoulders. Bess was right — Ned did look miserable. Confusion and fear in equal proportion had turned his face to putty and dilated his pupils to twice their normal size. With his wild gray hair looking even wilder than normal — thanks to liberal flecking with cream-colored paint — the mere sight of the man made Leigh want to run screaming. If Stroth was looking for suspects based on cinematic resemblance to villains of low-budget slasher films, he could pack up his investigation now.

Fortunately for Ned, inherent creepiness seemed not to be an issue.

Diarrhea of the mouth, on the other hand, seemed to carry some risk.

"But how can you be sure?" Chaz continued to whine, shuffling his feet like a fifth grader. "I didn't know what he wanted at first, or I wouldn't have said so much! I just went on and on about what my grandma says about the devil worshippers — I don't even know if it's true, really; it's just what she said! But there were so many weird things that happened with the haunted houses — one guy brought in a devil statue and put it up on this platform, and the next morning it was on the ground and smashed to bits — now how could you *not* think that just maybe this place was haunted by devil worshippers after something like that? And my grandma, you know, she's just the kind of person who likes to talk, and sometimes we all get so tired of hearing it but you really can't shut her up, you know? And ever since we found the body in the attic she and her friends have come up with all these theories, about satanists worshipping in here at night, and a whole cult using this place for its sacrificial ceremonies—"

"That's all total bunk!" Bess said forcefully, stamping her foot. "And don't you say another word about it or we'll lose Ned altogether!"

Leigh didn't doubt the statement. Ned had lost whatever color he started with and was beginning to sway on his feet.

Without a word, Gerardo appeared with a folding chair and deposited it behind Ned's knees. Then he put his hands on the older man's trembling shoulders and shoved him none too kindly down onto it.

"There are no satanists here, nor have there ever been," Bess declared fiercely. "And I absolutely forbid any more discussion of the matter. Detective Stroth wasn't asking about that anyway — you're the one who brought it up!"

"He asked what we knew about Marconi's murder," Chaz insisted. "Some people *do* think the two are related, you know. I was only trying to be helpful!"

Bess rolled her eyes, then tossed her head in Gerardo's direction. "And the detective interviewed him in Spanish?" she asked, seeming to know the answer already.

Chaz nodded. "We don't know what they said. But it didn't seem to take too long."

"Well, that's one good thing," Bess replied tiredly. "Do you all have solid alibis for this morning?"

Chaz and Ned exchanged an uncomfortable glance. "Not really," Chaz said sheepishly. "We both just kind of woke up and came to work. We didn't talk to nobody."

"Your mother didn't see you leaving?" Bess asked.

Chaz shook his head. "She goes to work early. Besides, I live in the basement. She doesn't come down there much. Not since I got the third boa and started raising my own feeder mice. When I got the second boa, she said—"

"And you?" Bess asked Ned, cutting Chaz off. Did you ride the bus yesterday or did you walk?"

Ned's voice was a mumble. "I walked. I only take the bus if the weather's nasty."

"You didn't see anybody on the way?"

He shook his head gravely.

Bess exhaled. "Well, I'm sure that's the last we'll hear of it, regardless. I want all of you to stop worrying. Whatever happened to Ms. Crane, it had nothing to do with any of you or with my theater, and the detectives will realize that soon enough. Now!" She clapped her hands together briskly. "Let's get this painting done, shall we?"

As the men shuffled back to work without enthusiasm, Leigh

cornered her aunt by the stairs to the annex. "What was all that about?" she whispered. "Where did Mom go?"

"Stroth stepped on a paint can lid and tracked spots all the way to the parking lot," Bess explained.

"Oh, dear," Leigh commented. "Poor man."

"Indeed," Bess agreed.

"Does he really suspect that someone from here assaulted Sonia?" Leigh pressed.

"I doubt it," Bess said unconvincingly. "But something those two across the street told him made him want to talk to Chaz and Ned. They both live nearby and have worked in the building before, you know. He seemed to be pumping them about the local rumor mill, things people might have heard or seen around the time Marconi disappeared." She sighed. "I just hope Ned doesn't quit on me. He's been jumpy ever since you found the body, and Chaz's constant nattering about satanists and devil worship hasn't helped one bit — and then Stroth had to go and question them! I had hoped to keep one of the men on to clean the building for us, and Ned *was* willing, but if he runs for the hills now, I'll be out of luck. Chaz is worthless and I don't trust Gerardo — if Allison says he speaks English, he speaks English, even if he won't admit it. And I still think Gordon is hiding something!"

As Bess paused to take a breath, Leigh felt a wave of sympathy. As if Bess didn't have enough to worry about just getting the building ready for the show! "On the bright side," Leigh said cheerfully, "The play's going to be great. The actors are all really good, and so funny! Just think, a mere" — she looked at her watch — "twenty-nine hours from now, and your first audience will be rolling in the aisles!"

Bess let out a humph, but Leigh noted the usual sparkle creeping slowly back into her eyes. "Let's just hope they're falling out of their seats from laughter," she said drily, "and not carbon monoxide poisoning."

Chapter 14

"So," Maura said, sitting up in bed with her legal pad and pencil at the ready. "Lay it on me, Allie."

Leigh suppressed a sigh. She knew that her daughter, for whatever reason, loved both digging into the past and solving puzzles. It made sense that the mysteries of the theater building would hold strong appeal, particularly during a week off from school. It also made sense that as long as Allison was going to look up old newspaper articles *potentially* related to the Marconi case, she might as well make copies for Maura, who could not physically acquire them herself and who might otherwise have a long wait marshaling another of the already overworked county homicide squad for the task.

But still. No matter how one justified it, it certainly looked to Leigh's eyes like her eleven-year-old daughter was taking her role — however harmless and incidental — way too seriously. And Maura, who had always treated the Pack like small adults, could hardly be counted on to disabuse the child of her notions.

After a long discussion with Warren, Leigh had agreed to bring Allison to talk to Maura again this morning about murder and mayhem, but only on the condition that the girl would then go straight to the Koslow Animal Clinic and spend the rest of the day with her grandfather, immersed in the comparatively healthier realm of puppy dogs and kitty cats. Since Randall was scheduled to do first examinations today on both a giant litter of borzois and two different batches of kittens, the deal had been an easy sale.

But Leigh still wasn't looking forward to the first part.

Allison pulled a bunch of papers out of a very un-girl-like leather satchel and held them out in front of her. "Well," she began with poorly concealed excitement, "the first related story I found came on March 31st, 1961. That's when a man named Clyde Adams was reported missing by his family. He lived in West View, and the last anyone saw him was at a bar around six o'clock in the afternoon. He never came home. The article doesn't give any more details, it just says the police were investigating."

"Good, good," Maura encouraged. "What next?"

"The murder of the custodian was reported two weeks later, on April 14th. It doesn't give a lot of detail, either. It just says that the victim was a man named Bill Stokes, that he was thirty-six years old, and that he had been employed as custodian for the Saving Grace Free Gospel church for the past two years. It says that he was killed by a blow to the head, that his body was found inside the church by the pastor the next morning, that he was survived by a wife and two stepchildren, and that police were investigating."

Allison put down the papers and looked up at Maura. "That article doesn't link the two men at all. But Grandma Lydie told me that everyone in West View was talking about it from the minute the janitor showed up dead. She was only a teenager when it happened, but she still remembers it."

Leigh frowned. So Allison had been pumping Lydie for information, had she? Leigh had to give the girl credit. Frances would have refused to talk about the unseemly incident at all, and Bess hadn't spent much time in West View after she hit the age of consent and became the family wild child.

"The two men had some kind of feud going," Allison continued. "Grandma Lydie said that as best she can remember it, the janitor guy, Bill Stokes, wasn't very well liked. He had a prison record, and he was loud and rough. But he had gotten married to a woman in the church and settled down some, and the pastor gave him the job to help the family out. Grandma Lydie said that after Clyde Adams went missing, a lot of people started accusing Bill, because the two men had been seen arguing not too long before. Of course, none of that was in the papers."

Maura nodded. "What did Lydie say happened after Bill's body was found? What did people think then?"

"She said there were all kinds of theories. Some people thought that Clyde's wife killed him, like for revenge. She was a character — I'll tell you more about her in a minute. And some people started wild rumors that he'd been killed by the church members in some sort of ritual. Grandma Lydie said almost nobody really believed that, but everyone was talking about it just the same. And some people thought Bill's own wife killed him, because he was abusive and maybe she was having an affair with Clyde. But most people thought Clyde killed him. That maybe they'd fought earlier and Clyde was injured and went into hiding, but then came back and finished Bill off. Clyde never showed up in West View again, which made that theory seem more and more likely as time went on."

"Any more news articles?" Maura asked.

"Only two," Allison answered, looking at her papers again. "One was the obituary for Bill Stokes. It was really short. It just gave the same information as the first article, except that it said he had been in the navy and in the bricklayer's union, and then it gave his wife's first name as Millicent. It said that his murder was unsolved and that the police were still investigating."

Allison shuffled her papers and cleared her throat. "But two months later, there was a long article in the local section about Edna Adams, Clyde's wife. She was complaining that the police weren't doing enough to figure out what happened to her husband, and she was irate because she felt like they were treating her husband like a suspect instead of a victim. She gave a long list of all this great stuff her husband had done, trying to make him sound like the perfect man, you know. But Grandma Lydie said Edna was a nut and probably made up half of it. You can read it yourself if you want — it sounds pretty fake to me. But what was interesting about that article is what it says about Millie, Bill's wife. The reporter was careful how he phrased everything, but it's pretty clear that Edna thought Millie flipped out and killed her own husband because he was beating up on her and the kids. And Grandma Lydie admitted that's what she always thought, too. Millie and Bill were living in a tiny little house not far from the church, and the neighbors said there was always a lot of fighting and screaming going on. She could have ambushed him in the church and walked right home after."

Maura's eyebrows knit with concentration. "Did Lydie say anything about Bill's body being found sprawled on the altar? Was that mentioned in any of the news reports?"

Allison shook her head. "Grandma Lydie said she wasn't sure she believed that part."

Maura blew out a breath. "I wouldn't either, but it happens to be true. It's in the reports."

Allison deflated a bit. "Oh."

Maura looked at Leigh. "Would your dad remember this stuff?"

Leigh was about to answer that there was absolutely no chance of that — that her veterinarian father paid no attention to gossip that happened right under his nose, much less in the community at large, but she didn't get the chance.

"He doesn't remember anything," Allison supplied.

Leigh's teeth gritted. Who else had the girl pumped for information? She made a mental note to keep the child away from Merle and Earl.

Maura settled back in her pillows. "Days like this," she said wistfully, "I really wish Mom were still alive. Memories like hers don't come along every day."

Leigh smiled her agreement. Mary Polanski might have ended her days with Alzheimer's, but her brain, in its prime, had catalogued more information than most people could manage in three lifetimes.

"You've done excellent work, Allie," Maura praised, straightening back up and holding out her hands for the article copies. This is all very interesting."

"I *know* there's a link to Marconi's murder," the girl said with sudden passion, handing over the papers. "There just has to be! But there's still a missing piece, somewhere."

Maura looked at her thoughtfully. "It's possible," she agreed. "What's needed is a thorough background check on everyone involved with the building, and with Bess's theater efforts. If there's a link, we'll find it — eventually. Stroth and I have already started on the task, but there's only so much I can do from here, and he's swamped, particularly since the assault on Sonia."

She turned to Leigh. "Which has been ruled an attempted homicide, by the way. She took a glancing blow to the side of her skull, which usually means the victim ducked or turned at the last second. If she'd been hit straight on, the doctors say the blow would have been fatal."

Leigh felt a sinking feeling in her gut. "Is she still unconscious?"

Maura, oddly, made no response. Instead, she turned back to Allie. "Thanks again for sharing this. And now I believe you have some vaccinations to assist with?"

Allison smiled. "That's right." She leaned over to look at Leigh's watch, and her eyes widened. "We'd better go, Mom. I don't want to miss the borzois!"

Now it was Leigh's turn to smile. *This* was appropriate behavior for an eleven-year-old.

It lasted all of five minutes. Just as they were pulling up to the curb outside the vet clinic, which was only a few blocks from Maura's house, Allison dropped her next bombshell.

"Mom," she said heavily. "I think you should know that Matt and Ethan, and Lenna too... they're all pretty sure they know who killed Andrew Marconi."

Leigh shifted the van into park and tried not to get nauseous. "Oh, they do, do they?"

Allison nodded. "They already told Aunt Bess, but they wanted me to tell you, because... well... you know how upset you get."

Leigh's heart beat like a jackhammer. "I do not!"

"Anyway," Allison said smoothly, "They think it was Ned."

"Ned? You mean, just because of the way he looks?" Leigh asked. "And acts?" she added after a beat. She could hardly accuse the children of making an assumption based on Ned's physical appearance. He did act every bit as weird as he looked.

"I think his looks are a big part of it," Allison admitted. "But they've convinced themselves he's in love with Aunt Bess."

Leigh swallowed hard. "And they think this... why?"

Allison shrugged. "Just because he seems to like her, and he always jumps to do whatever she wants. I think they're wrong, though. I think he just likes her a lot because she's nice to him, and most people aren't."

"What does any of that have to do with Marconi?" Leigh asked.

Allison's eyes rolled. "Nothing, Mom. That's what I keep telling them! They think Ned killed Marconi and stuffed him in the attic because Aunt Bess wanted the building, never mind that Aunt Bess swears she never met Ned until a couple weeks ago! And they're convinced that Ned whacked Sonia just because Aunt Bess didn't like her. If you remember, she *did* make a pretty big production of throwing Sonia out, in front of the cast and everybody."

Leigh remembered.

Allison sighed. "I know it's weak, but there's no talking them out of it. So they made me promise I would warn you to stay away from Ned today, and to be sure *not* to tick off Aunt Bess when he's around. Okay?"

Leigh blinked. So the Pack was trying to protect *her?* That was rich. Touching, but rich.

"Well, that's thoughtful of you all," Leigh said sincerely. "But I'm not going to the building today. Not until we all go to the show together tonight."

Allison's dark eyes twinkled. She put a hand on the door handle. "Sure you won't, Mom. See you later."

And with that, the girl hopped out of the van and skipped across the street into the clinic.

I will not, Leigh thought.

Her phone rang exactly six seconds later.

It was Bess. "Leigh? Where are you, kiddo?"

"I'm outside the clinic," she answered warily. "Why?"

"Oh," Bess said, sounding disappointed. "I thought you and the kids were coming back this morning."

"No, you didn't."

Bess clucked her tongue. "Well, I *hoped* you would. I've run into a bit of a problem, you see. The men are AWOL."

"What?" Leigh replied, distressed. "You mean *all* of them?"

"Well, none of them are here," Bess said anxiously. "And there's so much work to be done today!"

"Like what?" Leigh asked, aware of a giant sucking sensation even as she asked. "Did they say they would come in today?"

"Of course!" Bess insisted. "The basement floor needs to be polished; Francie is going to supervise that right after lunch. But now that the weather's finally dried out a bit, I wanted them to spruce up the grounds — everything is so terribly overgrown, you know. And it needs to look nice, especially around the parking lot and the front entrance!"

Leigh bit her lip. Why would the men not come to work? That Ned would fail to show was not surprising, given how freaked out he had been by Stroth's interview yesterday. But Gerardo still seemed to have something to prove, and Chaz — well, who else could Chaz talk to all day? His boas?

"I just don't know what to do!" Bess fretted.

Leigh sighed. Her aunt was playing her, and she knew it. Bess could easily hire a lawn company on her own dime to take care of the grounds, and Frances could polish the floor herself in less time than it would take to supervise the men to do it "properly." But those facts only begged the question of why Bess really wanted

Leigh there. Could it be that, despite Bess's seemingly limitless bravado, she was less than comfortable working in the building alone?

If so, she would never admit it.

The giant sucking sensation concluded with a pop. "All right," Leigh capitulated. "I'll swing by on my way home. Maybe the men are just running late this morning."

When she reached the theater eight minutes later, her aunt met her in the parking lot. If Bess had not, Leigh might very well have circled the lot and headed right back out, seeing as how Ned, Chaz, and Gerardo were all plainly visible mowing grass, pulling weeds, and trimming shrubs, respectively.

"We had a little miscommunication," Bess said cheerily, opening Leigh's car door for her. "They thought I said an hour later than I thought I said! They all got here just as I hung up the phone with you. How funny is that?"

"Hilarious," Leigh said without humor. She considered not getting out of the car, but ultimately she relented. There was a reason Bess wanted her here, and she knew her aunt would come out with it sooner or later.

It had better be sooner.

"Since you're here," Bess prattled, noticeably more nervous than usual, "why don't we sit down in the annex kitchen and have some tea? I brought some of that huckleberry flavor you like so much."

Bess continued to talk of nothing until they were both seated with steaming cups in their hands. Then her gaze drifted suddenly into space, and her worry lines deepened.

"Aunt Bess," Leigh prompted gently. "What is it?"

Bess's lips pursed. "That Detective Stroth came by here again this morning."

Leigh set down her tea. "Oh?"

Bess nodded. "Sonia Crane has regained consciousness."

Leigh felt her own worry lines deepen. No wonder Maura had avoided the question. Stroth would want to witness Bess's reaction to the news firsthand; Maura couldn't take a chance on Leigh or Allison tipping Bess off. How awkward.

"What is Sonia saying?" Leigh asked hesitantly.

Bess made a growling noise low in her throat. "She's not completely with it, yet. She's just sort of babbling... like she's delirious. But according to Stroth, there are two things she keeps saying over and over."

Leigh took a sip of tea and waited for it, her heart thudding in her chest.

"*My* name," Bess said heavily, "and *black magic.*"

The tea spewed. "Sorry," Leigh apologized, wiping up the drops with a paper napkin. "I wasn't expecting... I mean... *what?*"

Bess let out a long, dramatic sigh. "Little known fact about Sonia Crane, kiddo. She may look all tough and businesslike, but underneath that lizard skin, she's as superstitious as they come. I heard it first from a lawyer friend of mine who used to work with her at a firm downtown. But Cara said the same thing just a couple days ago. Even back in college, Sonia was reading tarot cards and running séances, pretending to be a medium... and a wiccan, and a voodoo priestess, and a psychic. Lord only knows what else. You name it, if it's not provable by science and a little bit twisted, Sonia Crane is into it."

Leigh recalled with sudden clarity how Sonia had tried to warn her and Cara away from the building the first day they met. She had mentioned the human sacrifice rumors, and she had blamed it all on *black magic.*

"Oh, my," Leigh murmured. She looked her aunt square in the eye. "Sonia Crane is scared to death of you."

Bess's shoulders lifted with the tiniest of shrugs. "It would seem so, wouldn't it?"

Leigh gasped with sudden understanding. "The bathroom at the sheriff's sale! Aunt Bess, what did you do to her?"

Bess hid her face behind her teacup. "A little harmless opposition research, that's all. I knew she was determined to outbid Gordon. I found out she had a thing about the occult. And what can I say? One can order just about anything on Amazon. Is it my fault that the woman had an unnaturally strong reaction to ten dollars' worth of cardboard pentagrams and a bloody rubber rooster?"

Leigh banged her forehead on the tabletop. "Aunt Bess!"

"Well?" Bess defended hotly. "It worked, didn't it? She took off out of that building like her pants were on fire! And as I said before, I never touched her. She did connect me with the incident somehow, however."

"Clearly," Leigh said heavily, lifting her head. "And what you're telling me is that now, for whatever reason, Sonia's delirious brain has decided that *you* were to blame for the assault as well?"

Bess's lips pursed again. "That would be about the size of it. Me and my 'black magic.'"

Leigh exhaled roughly. "Then she didn't see who actually assaulted her."

"Evidently not."

"Did you tell Stroth the truth? About everything?"

Bess threw her chest out indignantly. "Of course I did! You know I never lie unless it's absolutely necessary!"

Leigh decided not to go there. "Do you think he believed you?"

"I don't know," she said uncertainly. "But your friend Maura will. Won't she?"

Leigh considered. "I think that under the circumstances, your past history with Detective Polanski will weigh in your favor." *As a relatively harmless crackpot,* she refrained from adding.

Bess's smile, for the first time that morning, seemed genuine. "Well, that's a relief. Thanks, kiddo. I knew you could cheer me up."

Leigh smiled back. "No problem."

Chapter 15

Leigh was on her way back to her van when she caught a glimpse of Gerardo carrying a pair of pruning shears around the rear of the building. Bess had said she didn't completely trust him, yet she had made no move to fire him. Nor, as far as Leigh knew, had Bess specifically confronted him about the language question. On the surface, that seemed odd. But with Bess, odd behavior was relative. If Leigh had to guess why her aunt continued to tolerate Gerardo's presence in the building, she would say that Bess still believed Allison's theory that he was a spy for Gordon, and she was keeping him around to play with him like a cat with a mouse.

In fact, Leigh was sure of it. And she was feeling rather feline herself at the moment.

She put her keys back into her pocket and walked across the lot and around to the rear of the building. The annex had been built to within ten feet of the property line, leaving a narrow alleyway of grass between the building and a neighbor's overgrown hedge and detached garage. Leigh walked past a concrete stairwell that led down to a metal fire door and window on the lower floor of the annex. She paused a moment. The metal door was scratched up and dented; the window was an opaque casement type that had clearly seen better days. She walked down the steps for a closer look.

The fact that the building had been easy to break into at various points in its history was a foregone conclusion. Churches and fraternal orders always had numerous keys floating about. The banquet halls and dance studio might have kept a tighter grip, but there were double-hung windows on the second floor of the annex that would be vulnerable to anyone with a short ladder who could pick a lock. The first floor, which was half underground at its rear because of the upward slope of the block, had only casement windows. Also easily picked, but inherently safer because the opening would be too small for an adult to crawl through.

Leigh studied the metal door. It had a new one-way locking mechanism, with no knob on the outside. She knew that it also had a sliding deadbolt on the inside, because she had checked it herself a few times when they were working in the evenings. According to Bess, Gordon had hired a company to replace all the locks as soon as he bought the building, and the only keys at the moment belonged to her and to him. The double-hung windows within easy reach had also had been outfitted with sash pins, so the building certainly *should* be secure now, even without the expensive monitoring system Bess hoped to purchase for the theater down the road.

Of course, no building was ever 100% secure. Glass and doors could be broken; bombs could explode. But there were no obvious holes in the building's current armor, either.

Feeling slightly mollified, Leigh climbed back up the steps and walked around the other rear corner of the building to the side opposite the parking lot. Here, the building fronted a narrow secondary street which ran uphill into a residential neighborhood. Between the crumbling sidewalk and the brick wall were a few small trees and any number of seriously overgrown bushes and shrubs, one of which Gerardo was now pruning with a vengeance.

Inspiration struck.

"What are you doing?!" Leigh cried with alarm, running toward him. "That's a *diffelostra*, for crying out loud!" He stopped in surprise, and when she reached him she pretended great interest in what was left of the bush. "You have to cut them back in the fall, not the spring! If you cut them back in the spring, they won't bloom all season, possibly two! Everybody knows you can't prune *diffelostra* in the spring!" She faced him straight on, her tone and eyes accusing. "Most especially *professional gardeners!*"

He stared back at her, calculating and a little defiant.

She stared straight back.

"Give it up, Gerardo," she cajoled. "You know you want to."

They stood staring at each other for another long moment before his brown eyes suddenly twinkled.

"I do *not* want to," he responded, with no trace of any accent besides well-educated middle-American. "But it doesn't look like I have any choice. I underestimated you and those kids from the beginning."

"Uh huh," Leigh agreed. "But don't feel bad. It's a common error."

He dropped the pruning shears at his feet and wiped the sheen of sweat off his brow with a sleeve.

"The question is," Leigh pressed, "Why?"

Gerardo's dark eyes flashed with sudden insight, making Leigh all but certain she was about to be lied to.

"Mr. Applegate is worried about his investment here. He wants somebody on the inside, watching how Bess is handling things, making sure all is well. I've been working for him for years, basically as a glorified gofer, so he put me on it. The no-English thing was his idea. He figured I could find out more that way — that people would leave their guards down around me."

"A very smart and devious man, that Mr. Applegate."

A grin played at his lips. "You have no idea."

Leigh's bravado faltered suddenly. And what, exactly, was she going to do now? She was not afraid of Gerardo, although rationally speaking, she should be. All ancient-history murders aside, *somebody* had knocked Sonia Crane unconscious, and she couldn't be sure that somebody wasn't him. She couldn't be sure of anything.

He surprised her by addressing her next question before she asked it. "If you're feeling obligated to go spill everything to Detective Stroth, be my guest. Mr. Applegate and I spoke with him together last night. He's fully aware of my... employment situation."

Leigh frowned. "But Bess is not."

Gerardo shook his head. "Oh, I wouldn't say that. She knows I can speak English, even though she pretends she doesn't. She knows I work for Mr. Applegate. She could fire me anytime she wanted to. Why she doesn't — what she guesses his motives to be, I have no idea." His eyes caught Leigh's with another flash of insight, but this time Leigh construed his words as genuine. "I'm not convinced even Mr. Applegate knows exactly why he put me here. But whatever reasons he gives *her* are his business. I can promise you I'm not here to make trouble, just feed information to a very rich, inquisitive, and libidinous old man with too much time and money on his hands. I hope you can believe that. And if it ever gets back to him that I said those last few words, I will deny it with my dying breath, which it definitely would be."

Leigh considered. "And if I tell Bess—"

"Tell her anything you want — aside from the libidinous part.

Mr. Applegate won't be shocked that you've found me out. But I have a feeling not much will change. Those two seem to like playing games with each other, if you haven't noticed."

Leigh chuckled. "Oh, I've noticed."

"I do have one request," he began tentatively, "One plea."

Leigh took in his expression, which was notably more distressed than at any other point in their conversation, and her mouth curved into a smirk. "You don't want Chaz to know you speak English?"

"God, no," he said heavily. "I'd lose my mind. I have no idea how long Bess will want to keep us on after the opening, or how long Mr. Applegate will want to keep his charade up. Have mercy, please?"

Leigh smiled. She didn't trust Gerardo, but she couldn't help liking him, either. As Allison and the Pack had also perceived, his intelligence and sense of humor were evident even without speech.

"I won't tell Chaz," she bargained, "if you'll dish on him and Ned."

He smirked. "What do you want to know?"

"Are they really what they appear to be?"

His eyebrows tented. "You mean a lazy idiot and a hardworking oddball?"

Leigh nodded.

"As far as I know. But for obvious reasons, they don't confide in me."

She sighed. "Well, keep an eye out, will you? For anything... even more strange than usual?"

He grinned at her shamelessly. "That's why I get the big bucks."

Leigh stepped away from him and had just started down the sidewalk when he called to her with a stage whisper. "Hey! What other bushes am I not supposed to be hacking, here? What kind did you say this was?"

Leigh smirked and gave a shrug. "Damned if I know. Looks like a weed to me."

Leigh knew the risks when she decided to walk back around the front side of the building. Subconsciously or otherwise, she had wanted it to happen.

"Yoo-hoo! Miss Leigh! Come on over!"

Don't mind if I do.

Leigh crossed the traffic and joined Merle and Earl on their front porch, which had been divested of its dining room chairs but still offered two extra lawn chairs and a bean bag. She sat down in one of the original deck chairs next to Earl, who beamed at her. "Had a detective come over here yesterday," he said proudly.

"Did you?" Leigh encouraged.

"Yes, ma'am," Merle agreed, sitting on Leigh's opposite side. "Fine young fellow. Works for the county police. In *homicide*, you know."

"I met him, too," Leigh admitted. "What did he come over here for?"

"His name was Toth," Earl informed.

"It was Struth," Merle corrected.

"It was *what?*" Earl demanded.

"Smith! His name was Smith!" Merle snapped, rolling her eyes. She hid her mouth behind her hand and spoke to Leigh in a whisper as loud as her regular voice. "He can't hear worth a damn, you know."

"Can too!" Earl protested.

"What did the detective ask you about?" Leigh inquired, intervening.

"Oh, the same thing everybody asks us about," Merle answered. "What we see happening from over here. Who goes in and out of the building, and when."

"His name was Toth."

"He also asked us about what everybody else was saying way back when," Merle continued. "You know, what the people around here thought when Marconi went missing. He wanted to know which of the neighbors had lived here since then besides us."

"David Toth."

"Of course, there's not all that many long-timers around here anymore. It's all rentals on this side, and the houses across the way have a lot of younger families. They come and go pretty quick, you know. But I gave him a few names of people who've been here even longer than we have."

"Was it David or Raymond?"

"Not that many of them can see what goes on in the building, though," Merle informed. "We've got the only view of the front, besides those next door. We can't see the parking lot or around back, but nobody living over there can either, really, because of that hedge being so overgrown. Easy as pie to slip in and out one of those doors without being seen, that's what I told Mr. Struth."

"I think it was Raymond," Earl concluded.

Leigh was beginning to get dizzy from whipping her head around.

"He was plenty interested in everything we've seen happen since Mr. Marconi came around," Merle boasted. "I told him about those awful haunted houses. Did you know the borough turned on the power and water for a month every year just to suit those crazy hoodlums? No mystery how all that happened — one of them was the son of a councilman, you know. Our tax dollars going for that nonsense! Come November, they'd shut everything off again. But Earl and I, we saw lights over there all year round. Flashlights I imagine, but lights."

Leigh's pulse quickened. She had heard the claim before, but now it seemed more than idle fancy. If someone, obviously not Marconi himself, had regularly been visiting the building at night, what was their purpose? They had done no obvious damage. They could have stolen things they didn't steal. No single item in the basement had any great value in terms of pawning, but a decent amount of it taken together would have *some* value. Why break into an abandoned building with a flashlight just to sit in the dark and the cold?

A flash of inspiration struck. Were they *looking* for something?

"Did Detective Stroth tell you why he wanted to know?" she asked anxiously.

"Stroth!" Earl shouted triumphantly, raising a pointed finger in the air. "I told you it was Stroth!"

"He didn't say much," Merle answered. "He just asked questions. That's how they do, you know."

"Was it Raymond Stroth?" Earl questioned.

"I expect he'll be calling us back any time now, though, and I might just ask him then," Merle mused. "What all he thinks is up. We saw them lights again last night, you know. That's what I plan to tell him. But he didn't answer his phone, so I just left my number."

"It was David," Earl proclaimed. "David Stroth."

"It's Daniel," Leigh supplied, then swiveled in her seat to fully face Merle. "Wait, when last night? You know they had the dress rehearsal — I'm sure it went pretty late."

Merle shook her head. "Oh no, I mean after that. It was all quiet over there by midnight, but then I got up again around three because Earl was snoring—"

"*You* were snoring!"

"And I saw a little light bobbing over there again, down low like, in the basement. We can see those windows all up the side, you know."

"I saw them too," Earl insisted. "Her snoring had me up at five. The detective told us to keep an eye out, so I did."

Leigh's mouth seemed to have gone dry. She swallowed painfully. "You're saying you saw lights in the building just last night, after the actors had all left?"

And since Gordon Applegate had all the locks changed?

"That's what we're saying," Merle confirmed.

Earl nodded his head along with her.

Leigh felt the color drain from her face. "But you couldn't have," she protested. "There's... no way to get in the building. Not anymore."

Merle chuckled. "Oh, there's always a way. When somebody puts their mind to it."

"Damn hippies," Earl added.

Leigh rose. "I'm sorry, but I need to go. I need to tell my Aunt Bess about this."

"Oh, we already did," Merle offered pleasantly. "She popped over again earlier this morning, all excited to tell us that the inspection came through and that it was official — tonight's the night!"

"I'm wearing a tie," Earl said with a smile.

"I may have to break out the panty hose myself," Merle added. "Much as I hate the damn things."

"Don't bother," Leigh said absently. "I'll be there tonight, and I haven't worn them since the nineties."

"Women used to wear garters, you know," Earl informed.

"I really do have to go," Leigh said, moving toward the steps. "But thanks for catching me up on everything."

"You think Lori Ann ever wore garters?" Earl asked.

"Not the kind you mean," Merle answered.

"Bye! See you tonight!" Leigh said quickly, hastening down the steps and across the street. Assuming Bess was in the sanctuary, she headed for the front door and banged on it. There was no response. With frustration, she turned around to try the door in the parking lot. But she had only moved a few steps before she heard the door creaking open behind her.

"Hey, kiddo," Bess said curiously. "I thought you left already."

Leigh swung around again and moved through the open door and into the vestibule. "I leave several times daily," she answered, planting her hands on her hips. "Why didn't you tell me that Merle and Earl saw lights over here last night? Did you tell Detective Stroth that when he was here?"

A look of vague discomfort flitted across Bess's face, but she dismissed the idea with a wave of her hand. "Oh, bosh. Why would I bother the detective with that nonsense? Or you either, for that matter? Merle and Earl are lovely people, but their imaginations are a little too vivid. I'm sure they were just confusing the times — the rehearsal went quite late, you know."

Bess walked past Leigh and on into the sanctuary.

Leigh followed. "They seemed quite specific about the times, and they both saw the same thing," she countered. "You can't just dismiss this, Aunt Bess."

"Can't I?"

"No," Leigh insisted. "You told me that you and Gordon have the only keys. Are you sure he couldn't have loaned his out to someone without telling you? Or did you loan one out? To Camille, maybe?"

"Heavens, no," Bess retorted. "She'd be the last person I'd allow in this building unsupervised. No one has had access to my key. As for Gordon," she looked suddenly contemplative. "Well, it's possible. I really don't know *what* that man is up to."

Leigh gave a summary of her conversation with Gerardo, minus his potentially inflammatory comments about his employer. The omission gave Leigh no qualms, as her aunt was obviously well aware of the state of Gordon's libido.

"Yes, yes," Bess replied rather impatiently. "Gerardo is a spy for Gordon and he's reporting back everything I'm doing, yada yada yada. That's all yesterday's news. The man is conniving and manipulative, yes, but that's just Gordon. It's part of his charm, if you consider such things charming. But if you're insinuating that he had anything to do with the assault on Sonia, you're barking up the wrong tree. I *know* Gordon. He may be a high-handed little tyrant, but underneath all that bluster, he's a lamb in wolf's clothing. And you'll just have to trust me on that one.

"Now, what was I doing?" Bess asked herself. "Oh, right. The water." She began walking toward the stairs to the basement.

Leigh followed. "So you're not just the teeniest bit curious why Gordon — or Gerardo — might be wandering around this building with a flashlight in the wee hours of the morning?"

"Of course I am," Bess replied as she hurried down the stairs. "But can we theorize about it later? I have a thousand things to do before the show, and I just found out there's no hot water in the ladies' room, never mind that it was perfectly fine yesterday! And God forbid, if it's anything Lydie can't handle, I'll have to call—"

She broke off as she opened the door into the basement. She held it open for Leigh, then shut it behind them.

"Do you smell that?" she asked, sniffing.

Leigh sniffed, too. "Gas."

Bess's lips pursed with annoyance. "Well, I suppose that's good news," she said without enthusiasm. "Probably just means the pilot light on the hot water heater went out, right?"

Leigh nodded. The odor, although distinct, was still faint. "Where *is* the hot water heater?"

"The boiler room," Bess answered, moving toward a door along the front wall of the basement. "Well now, how did this get here?" she said irritably, running the toe of her shoe through a streak of dust on the floor. "You could have licked these tiles after Francie finished with them yesterday. Even the inspector was impressed..."

Bess's voice trailed off as she opened the door and disappeared inside the gloomy looking space. Leigh hung back, further examining the dirty floor. The streak of dust was an odd whitish color, and it started at the boiler room door and angled away toward the stairs to the annex. Smaller patches of dust lay ahead along the same trajectory. She frowned.

She walked to the open door and peered into the boiler room. It was every bit as charming as she had imagined, complete with dimness, a low ceiling, variously sized pipes and ducts running everywhere, and multiple outdated-looking metal appliances. The one surprise was that despite its inherent dinginess, the space was amazingly free of dust and cobwebs. Which could only mean that it had recently been visited by one Frances Koslow.

Bess emerged from the back side of a particularly mysterious looking appliance with a sigh of exasperation. "Well, the pilot's out all right," she informed. "The tank's cold. But darned if I can figure out how to light it. Doesn't look like any hot water heater I've ever seen."

Bess moved toward the door, but almost tripped over something on the floor. "What the—" She leaned down to take a closer look. "Oh for heaven's sake, when did this happen? Francie cleaned in here! It looked perfectly fine for the inspector!"

She made her way back to the doorway and let out a gruff exhale. "I'll go fetch Ned. I bet he's dealt with this dinosaur before. I'll have him clean up the mess, too. Honestly, it's like a truck ran into the outside of the building or something! Be right back, kiddo. Of all the..."

Still muttering to herself, Bess crossed the basement and headed towards the annex and the exit to the parking lot.

Leigh remained in the doorway of the boiler room. Her body tensed. Someone had been snooping around down here last night, and whatever they had been doing, they had managed to leave a trail of dust across the floor as a result of it. What was it that Bess had nearly tripped over?

She pulled out her phone and turned on the flashlight app. The one bulb in the room's ceiling was beyond pathetic, and the ductwork blocked most of its light from shining where Bess had stumbled. As Leigh moved forward, she could see a rectangular opening in the original brick wall facing Perry Highway. Black soot stained the bricks all around the hole, which looked at first glance like a fireplace, but which was several feet off the floor. Leigh noticed the wooden frame bordering it and realized that it must be an old coal chute. With the original sanctuary being built in the early 1900s, the outside wall would have had an opening to the street with a wooden or metal hatch, through which the coal truck would have made its delivery. Inside, the chute would open to a coal bin.

Leigh looked at the area more closely. All the surrounding bricks were still black with coal ash, but the bin itself was long gone. The only thing beneath the opening now was a pile of broken bricks and chunks of mortar. It was this debris that Bess had tripped over. A mess that couldn't possibly have been present when Frances cleaned yesterday.

Leigh's brow furrowed. When coal furnaces went the way of horse-drawn buggies, the chute openings on both ends must have been bricked in. The rough remnants of a line of mortar were still obvious along the inside frame, where the debris on the floor must have come from. She picked up a broken chunk of brick left just inside the chute, and noted that unlike those in the wall around it, it bore no stains of coal ash. Yet even the newer bricks must have been placed a very long time ago. Why would they fall out now? She leaned over the pile and shone her flashlight up the chute. The bricks at the other end were still intact.

That was weird.

She turned her light back toward the door to the basement. Enough of the boiler room for her. It bore entirely too much resemblance to the attic.

"Hey, Ms. Leigh," Ned said politely, filling the doorway in front of her. "Don't you worry about that hot water heater. I've lit that pilot before. I worked for the banquet hall, did you know? It was always going out."

Leigh stepped back out of his way, but remained close to the exit. "I thought you worked for the dance studio," she said absently, remembering the Pack's warning about not being alone with him. She still believed they were judging the man too much on his appearance, but still — no way was she getting stuck in a boiler room with anyone whose tee shirt read "Magic Man."

Ned smiled sheepishly and moved away from her and on into the room. "Oh, I did them, too. I expect I've cleaned half of West View at one time or other. I've done the water treatment plant and the chocolate factory — I used to work summers at West View Park, too. Cleaning up trash. Your mum likes to clean, just like me. She's a good, moral lady and she says being a cleaner is important work."

"Here, Ned," Bess said, entering behind him with a giant flashlight. "You want me to hold the light for you?"

"That'd be fine, Ms. Bess." Ned dropped to his hands and knees beside the hot water heater, and Bess aimed the light in his direction. "Yep, it's out," he announced. "I'll have it lit in a jiffy."

Leigh had been primed for escape, but now she couldn't step out without both dislodging her aunt and disrupting Ned's light. "What do you think happened to these bricks, Aunt Bess?" she asked instead.

"Oh, Lord only knows," Bess answered. "I'm just glad they waited to fall out until after the inspector left."

"Would anyone in the cast have come down here last night during the rehearsal?"

"A few of them do have to walk through the basement for entrances and exits," Bess explained. "But I can't imagine why they would come in here, no."

Leigh considered the implications of the timing, and a growing chill began to gnaw at her insides. If the bricks had fallen out by themselves, how had a trail of mortar dust come to cross the basement on the other side of the door? Someone *must* have been snooping around down here, both inside and outside the boiler room, after both the inspector and Frances had left for the day.

But who? And why?

She shone her flashlight beam back onto the floor under the coal chute. Had someone busted out the bricks intentionally? There were enough on the ground to fill up the hole; if someone had taken a sledgehammer to the false front of the chute, they obviously hadn't done it to steal the bricks. She stepped forward and pushed a few of the pieces around with a toe. Her gaze fell on what looked like a thick cigarette, and she reached down and picked it up.

The object was roughly a cylinder, about an inch and a half long. But its ends were wider than its middle. And as the significance of their curved smoothness hit her already confused brain, she felt suddenly weak in the knees.

She held the object between her thumb and index finger, and her hand began to shake. Slowly, she moved her opposite hand holding the phone light up beside it.

It couldn't be. It really, *really* couldn't be.

Her own hands had enough finger bones, thank you very much.

By no stretch of the imagination did she need a spare.

Chapter 16

"Aunt Bess?" Leigh said with a squeak. "What does this look like to you?"

Bess craned her neck, but couldn't move without depriving Ned of his work light. "Can't see that far, kiddo. Bring it over here."

Leigh stepped over on shaky knees. Pretty much all of her was shaky.

Bess lowered her spectacles and squinted a moment. "Chicken bone," she pronounced.

"Chicken?" Leigh asked weakly. "In a coal chute?"

Bess waved a dismissive hand — a hand which, it occurred to Leigh, had been doing a lot of dismissive waving lately. "A pigeon, then," Bess conceded. "What of it? Lord knows how many bat bones are in the attic!"

"Bird bones are hollow," Leigh stated. "This one isn't."

"So, a rat then," Bess persisted. "Or a squirrel. What does it matter?"

Leigh could hear her own pulse pounding in her ears. Maybe she was thinking crazy. Maybe it was just an animal bone. If she'd swept it out from behind the furnace, she wouldn't give it a second thought. But the facts were this. *Somebody* had been in the basement last night. That somebody had gone into the boiler room, broken apart the bricks blocking the lower end of the coal chute, left the bricks, and trailed mortar dust back out. Why leave a trail of dust... unless you were carrying something dusty?

Why bother at all, unless the object you were after was very, very important?

"Aunt Bess," Leigh said more firmly. "Somebody was in here last night, and you know it. I don't believe those bricks just fell out of the wall, and I don't believe whoever did this was looking for squirrel bones. I think..." She swallowed hard. "I think this bone might be human."

A loud thump made both women jump. At the word "human," Ned had scrambled up from the floor and bonked his head on an air duct. Unfazed, at least by the air duct, he stood stock still for a good five seconds, staring at the object in Leigh's hands with his eyes bugged and his mouth agape.

Then he pushed past Aunt Bess and ran out the door.

"Oh, now look at what you've done!" Bess said irritably. "Why did you have to say it like that? You'll have the poor man hiding under the desk in the office again! And I need him to stay on here. We'll never find anyone else willing to clean this place so cheaply!"

Leigh blinked in disbelief. Bess thought *her* behavior inappropriate? With Ned running and hiding under a desk... *again?*

"Aunt Bess!" she said even more firmly. "I'm no expert on bones, but you can't just ignore the possibilities, here!"

Bess let out a harrumph. "I most certainly can."

"You can't deny that it *could* be human," Leigh argued.

"But what are the odds?" Bess countered. "People find little bones here and there every day!"

Leigh raised one eyebrow. "Well, *people* didn't find this one, did they? *I* did!"

Bess's left eyelid twitched. Her determined facade began to falter. "Well, hell." She plopped herself down on the edge of the furnace.

"We have to tell Stroth," Leigh pushed.

"Oh, no, we don't!" Bess argued, jumping back up. She glanced about with desperation. "Why don't we just put it back where you found it? Nobody knows about it except us and Ned, and he won't say anything if I tell him not to. We'll just close the door behind us and go our merry way, and then first thing Monday morning—"

"No," Leigh declared.

"But it's obviously an *old* bone! Surely—"

"No!"

Bess crossed her arms over her chest and pouted. "Oh, I suppose you're right. But I just know they'll throw us out of the building again! And what if we can't get back in by tonight? The box office opens at six!"

Leigh sighed. Realizing she was still holding what could very well be something she didn't want to touch, she crossed to the chute and laid the object down just inside the remaining rim of mortar. Then she took her aunt by the hand, pulled her out of the room, and closed the door behind them. "Look, the sooner we call him, the sooner this will get resolved," she reasoned.

Bess nibbled on a fingernail. "But if the neighbors see anything... if the press gets wind of it before tonight..."

Leigh considered. "We'll call Stroth directly and tell him we want to show him something. Maybe he'll just put it in a bag and that will be that. There won't be any need for sirens and a coroner's van... not for one bone, and not when we don't even know whether it's human or not. Right?"

Bess looked faintly hopeful. "They'll have to do testing or some such thing. Surely that will take some time!"

"Almost certainly," Leigh agreed. "It could be days before anything at all gets reported by the media." She wasn't terribly confident about the last part, but as determined as her aunt was to open the show *tonight* — come hell, high water, or an apparently unlimited number of corpses — she felt justified in telling one white lie. They had not yet set up the bail fund, after all.

"All right," Bess said evenly, "I'll go call Stroth right now. My phone is... in the office."

Leigh's eyes narrowed with skepticism. "No, that's okay," she insisted. "I've got my cell phone right here. I'll call him."

Bess's lips puckered with annoyance. "Well, in that case, I'll go tend to Ned." And with a flounce, she headed toward the stairs.

Leigh pulled out her phone, quickly talked her way through the county police's switchboard — a process she was unfortunately familiar with — and left an urgent voicemail on Stroth's private line. Bess did not return immediately, and after standing around alone in the empty basement for several minutes, Leigh began to get antsy. A part of her felt she should stay and guard the boiler room door until the detective's arrival. But a stronger part of her couldn't stand the thought of it — not when she had no idea when he might arrive. It could be hours.

She thought a moment, then was inspired. She sprinted up the stairs into the annex and opened a closet where she knew Bess had stashed some basic office supplies. Then she pulled out a clear tape dispenser and returned to the basement. After sticking about forty different pieces of tape from the door across to the frame at a variety of angles, as well as from the knob to the door, she declared herself satisfied. No one could possibly turn the knob and open the door and get all the tape back in the same configuration afterwards, including her Aunt Bess, whom she had no doubt was the most likely person to try it.

Leigh pocketed the dispenser, took a series of photographs of the tape on the door with her phone, then texted one of them to Bess with the caption, "Don't even think about it." Then she turned her attention to the dust trail.

There was little to go on in the far half of the room, but it was clear to Leigh that whoever was dribbling mortar dust had been headed for the stairs. Another small splash of powder midway up the steps confirmed it. But she saw nothing more in the hallways on either route leading to an exit. Nothing except fresh grass clippings, which Ned had obviously just trailed in. She could hear Bess talking to him in the office, insisting that her "overwrought niece" had merely been imagining things.

Leigh gritted her teeth and tried to concentrate. If someone had intentionally hidden something in the coal chute, and she was doing her best not to dwell on *what*, how long must it have been there? Surely coal furnaces would have been obsolete by the fifties, at the latest. The chute could have been bricked up at the same time the furnace was removed, or it could have sat idle for a while, or been boarded over temporarily. For a congregation without much money — which all the former occupants appeared to be, considering the history of default — prettying up the entrance to a coal chute wouldn't seem a high priority. *Unless...*

Allison's voice popped into her head, rattling off information from the newspaper archives. Leigh hastened to the rear fire door, slid back the bolt, and started up the crumbling concrete steps. One... no, two spots of distinctive gray-white powder were visible on the otherwise dirty pavement. She stepped carefully over them, into the alley, and around the corner to the secondary street side of the building. The brick on the annex, she noticed now, was different from the original brick on the sanctuary. Both were red, but the new brick was slightly darker and more uniform. It was easy to tell where the original building ended and the annex began.

Leigh continued around to the front corner of the building, where the coal chute would have opened to the street. She found the spot without difficulty, although she would never have noticed it had she not been looking. A square section, several feet off the ground. The brick in the square didn't match the brick around it.

But it did match the annex.

Leigh stood back and looked from one to the other. It wasn't her imagination. The bricks were a match. And why wouldn't the church go ahead and fill in the coal chute when they were already paying for a batch of new bricks? And who better to grab a few and take on that odd job, if those bricks happened to be around at just the right time?

She dashed around the front of the building, hoping Merle and Earl weren't currently watching. Since they didn't call out to her, she assumed they were not. She made her way to the parking lot and the main entrance to the annex. If what she was looking for existed, it would be there.

It was. Leigh halted in her steps and stared a moment. The cornerstone was right in front of her face, and she read it out loud, feeling equal parts victorious and nauseated. *Educational Building 1961.*

Bill Stokes the custodian had been murdered in 1961. Murdered a matter of weeks after the disappearance of another man... a man who had never returned.

And Bill Stokes, Leigh remembered her daughter reporting, had once been in the navy.

He had also been in the bricklayer's union.

"They've been in there forever," Bess fretted, pacing back and forth along the aisles in the sanctuary. "You'd think they'd at least let us get started on the floor!"

"You're lucky they let us stay in the building at all," Leigh reminded. "Now sit down and eat your pierogies." She patted the seat of a chair beside her. "I got those potato, bacon, and blue cheese ones that you love so much. Eat up!"

Bess grumbled, but sat. "The men had better come back," she said worriedly.

"They will," Leigh assured. "I'm sure they're delighted to have an unexpectedly long lunch break. They needed to change clothes anyway. Mom would have a fit if they all paraded back in here covered with grass clippings. There would be green specks stuck in the floor polish for months."

"They'll suspect something," Bess fussed. "What if they're afraid to come back?"

"All Gerardo and Chaz know is that Mom doesn't need them until two-thirty. But even if they did know what was going on, they would still come back. Chaz loves the macabre and Gerardo is getting paid twice. As for Ned, whatever you said seemed to calm him down just fine. He finished sweeping the clippings off the sidewalk, didn't he?"

Bess nodded and took a bite of pierogie. "Umm, these are good," she mumbled.

Leigh allowed herself a smile. It was the first she had managed in hours.

Stroth had shown up within twenty minutes of her voicemail, looked around inside the boiler room, traced the same path Leigh had followed through the hallways and out the back door, then called for backup. Much to Bess's relief, however, that backup had come in an unmarked car with no flashing lights or uniforms in sight.

Stroth's questions had been predictable; his comments few. Leigh knew he would soon be reporting everything that had happened to Maura, and she hated the thought of the expectant mother worrying over the implications. She didn't want to worry, herself. But it was hard not to.

If the bone she had found *was* human, it almost certainly had not been the only bone in the boiler room twenty-four hours ago. It had probably been bricked up in that coal chute with a full complement of its skeletal cohorts for the last fifty-plus years. That it had been put there by the murdered-soon-after janitor, she had little doubt. That it belonged to the man who went missing just before then, Clyde Adams, seemed equally likely.

What made no sense was how anyone else could know about it. And why, if someone did know and had known about it all along, they had suddenly been possessed by an overwhelming desire to disturb Clyde's final resting place *last night.*

"We're all done for today, Ms. Cogley," Stroth announced from the alcove, startling them both. "You can return to the basement and clean up the mess if you'd like. We've taken some samples and the scene has been thoroughly photographed."

"Was it human or not?" Bess demanded, rising.

Stroth's face gave no clue. He was a sober man who talked little and showed emotion less, and Leigh found him difficult to read. But because Maura seemed to trust his judgment, Leigh did also. "We'll have to wait for the lab to tell us that," he answered simply. "But you should know one thing before I go. The door at the rear of the building — it looks like you recently had a new mechanism installed?"

"Yes," Bess answered, her tone almost defensive. "Gordon — I mean, Mr. Applegate, the owner, hired a locksmith to change all the locks. I believe the old knob on that door was broken altogether."

Stroth nodded. "Well, it's broken again."

Bess's face paled. "It's what?"

"Either the part was faulty, or it was intentionally tampered with," Stroth explained. "It's a one-way mechanism — designed to hold the door closed and locked unless the inside knob is turned. But it doesn't lock at all. Anyone could pry it open from the outside, at any time. There is a separate sliding bolt on that door which does work; have you been using it?"

Both women nodded. "I check it every night!" Bess protested.

Stroth looked thoughtful. "The casement window beside that door has a broken lock as well."

"Detective Stroth!" A male voice shouted from the front entrance. "I need to speak with you!"

They turned to see a livid Gordon marching down the aisle, an unusually large and burly man following one pace behind him like a dog at heel.

"Mr. Applegate," Detective Stroth said mildly. "There are some things I need to discuss with you as well."

Bess made a small sound rather like a whimper.

"Well, you can start by continuing what you were about to say," Gordon instructed as he reached them. "What's this about a broken lock?"

"The detective was just telling us about a few minor security matters that need to be attended to," Bess soothed. "Nothing to worry about, though. Everything with the show is right on schedule!"

Leigh suppressed a snort.

"I believe we've been playing phone tag," Stroth said to Gordon apologetically. "But I'd like to update you on the matter of the break-in last night."

Gordon's already fiery eyes turned to Bess. "The *what?!*"

"It's nothing!" Bess protested. "Nothing at all, really. There was no harm done. Just a little banging around in the boiler room. That's all we really know for sure at this point, *isn't it*, detective?"

Bess turned the full force of her pitiful, pleading eyes on Stroth, and it was all Leigh could do not to groan out loud.

Stroth, thankfully, was unaffected. He launched into a summary of his recent findings in the building that was thorough, concise, and completely devoid of any embellishment or drama whatsoever. Leigh was so impressed she wanted to applaud.

Bess was less amused. "I'm sure the detective is making way too much of this," she insisted to Gordon, taking his arm. "There's no reason whatsoever for you to be bothered, dear. Where old squirrels go to die is hardly our concern! We'll simply fix the door and the theater will go on as planned. No worries!"

Gordon stared back at her with unbridled skepticism.

"As I was about to say when you came in, Mr. Applegate," Stroth continued. "I believe that another security check of the building, by a professional locksmith, would be advised. I noticed that the lock in the window by the back door was broken as well, even though the latch appeared to have been recently replaced, just like the doorknob."

"Oh, bother," Bess said lightly. "Nobody could crawl through a hole that size anyway, could they?"

"Crawl through, no," Stroth said heavily. "But any burglar worth his salt could fashion a rod to slip through it and pull back the deadbolt."

Bess's face paled again. She opened her mouth to say something, but reconsidered and shut it.

Leigh watched curiously as Gordon slid a proprietary hand over the small of Bess's back.

"This is what I came here to discuss with you," he said to Stroth in a low voice. "I don't know what's going on with old bones in boiler rooms, but I believe there is a very real threat to this theater project of Ms. Cogley's — and to her personally. And after everything you've just said, I am more certain than ever that it's coming from the *inside*."

Chapter 17

"The *inside?*" Bess protested, twisting away from Gordon's protective hand. "And what exactly do you mean by that?"

Gordon frowned at her. "You've had an army of people in and out of this building the past week. Any one of them could have slipped off downstairs and tampered with the locks, making sure they could access the building at any time."

"But why on earth would anyone associated with *my* theater want to do that?" Bess protested again.

"Damned if I know!" Gordon countered hotly. "But I refuse to take chances where your safety is concerned!"

Bess's eyes widened with alarm, but Leigh knew that alarm had nothing to do with Bess's fears for her own safety. She was afraid that Gordon was about to pull the proverbial plug.

"My..." Bess sputtered. "But that's ridiculous! I'm not in any danger!"

"I'd wager Sonia Crane didn't think she was, either," Gordon said heavily.

"What happened to Sonia has absolutely nothing to do with me or this theater!" Bess insisted.

Gordon huffed out a breath and pulled an envelope from a suit pocket. "We'll let the detective decide about that." He withdrew a note-sized slip of paper from the envelope and held it out towards Stroth. "I received this at my business address this morning. One of my secretaries brought it to my attention, but I'm afraid she did so only after it had been handled by quite a few of my staff. It's bound to be crawling with extraneous fingerprints."

Stroth took hold of the letter with a handkerchief. He examined it for a long moment before asking to see the envelope as well. Gordon handed it over wordlessly.

"Well, don't keep us all in suspense!" Bess cried. "What does it say?"

Stroth cleared his throat. "It says just five words. *Don't sell...*" he studied Bess's face as he spoke, "*or Bess dies.*"

Leigh felt a sharp prickle of horror, and she could tell from her aunt's rigid stance and rapid loss of color that the words affected her similarly. Only in Bess's case, the effect did not last long.

"That's preposterous," Bess announced. "Absolutely preposterous! I certainly don't want this building sold! Why threaten me?" She turned to Gordon indignantly. "*You're* the one who keeps threatening to close down this theater. Why not kill you?"

Leigh could swear she saw the hint of a smile twitch at Gordon's mouth. "I am touched by your concern," he said evenly. "But whether it makes logical sense or not is hardly the point. The most dangerous people are often illogical."

Bess sniffed and turned to Stroth. "When was the letter mailed?"

"Yesterday," the detective said thoughtfully, watching both her and Gordon. "From this zip code."

Leigh's discomfort ratcheted up another notch. What was Stroth thinking? Surely he didn't believe that Bess had sent the note herself. Not that such a stunt would necessarily be out of character...

Leigh frowned. The note did make little sense otherwise. What if Bess, as a knee-jerk reaction to Sonia's attack, wanted to keep Gordon in line but was loathe to make false threats to anyone but herself?

Please, no.

Leigh simply *had* to get to work on that bail fund.

"I believe that someone in your acting troupe is taking this project of yours far too seriously," Gordon declared. "It's the only semi-rational explanation, since artistic people are well known for being irrational."

Bess's cheeks flared with color again. "I *beg* your pardon!"

Gordon ignored her and turned to Stroth. "I have no idea what this note has to do with the break-in last night, or whether they're even connected. But regardless, I believe that security in this building is unacceptably lax, and I intend to rectify that situation immediately."

He turned and gestured to the hulking man who had followed him in, whose presence Leigh had forgotten. "This is Jenkins," Gordon informed Bess sternly. "He's going to be your new best friend. He's staying here at the building and he's not letting you out of his sight until we figure out who's behind all these shenanigans. I have two more guards coming in a matter of hours, and from then until this damnable show closes on Sunday, there will be security watching this building 24/7. Is that understood?"

Bess blinked. Her eyes grew suddenly moist. "You mean, you'll let the show go on?"

For the briefest of moments, Leigh believed she saw Gordon's eyes soften to mush. But just as quickly they flashed with blue fire again.

"Well, I promised, didn't I?" he spat back gruffly. "An Applegate never reneges on his promises. But the original bargain still stands. If this show doesn't cut the mustard, if this theater doesn't prove itself an instant cultural asset to the community, I'll pull the rug out from under it in a trice and won't lose a minute's sleep over it, either! Do we understand each other?"

The fierceness of his tone, particularly when directed toward a woman, caused Leigh and even Stroth to wince a bit. But it had no effect whatsoever on Bess.

"Perfectly," she said sweetly, stopping just short of a wink.

Leigh stifled a sigh of frustration. As well as she knew her aunt, the woman was such a good actress — and such a shameless schmooze — even Leigh couldn't always be sure where reality ended and illusion began. All she could tell for certain was that Bess, at least at this particular moment, was getting what she wanted.

What the detective had made of the bizarre exchange, God only knew.

"I'll need to keep this letter," Stroth informed, dropping it into his own pocket. "And I'm glad you plan to improve security, Mr. Applegate. I think that's well advised. Now, if you'll all excuse me, I have quite a bit of work to do."

Bess jumped to walk the detective out, and as she moved toward the front door, Jenkins the giant wordlessly detached himself from his employer and followed her, leaving Leigh and Gordon alone to stare at each other awkwardly.

"Your husband's been a big help to me," Gordon said finally.

The change of subject took Leigh aback. "I'm glad to hear it," she responded.

"Keep an eye on her for me, will you?" he said, his blue eyes focused on Leigh a little too keenly for comfort.

She didn't need to ask who he was talking about. She also didn't need to ask why he'd brought up Warren.

Her eyes narrowed. The man might be cute sometimes, but "master manipulators" were not to her taste. Particularly ones who juxtaposed statements about her husband's employment next to demands for personal favors.

"I'll watch her, all right," Leigh said evenly, staring back at him. "But I won't be doing it for you."

Leigh sank into a chair in the front row of the empty theater and fingered the car keys in her pocket. She should probably try to leave. Again. Maybe she would actually succeed this time. She did have other things to do today, didn't she?

Truthfully, she did not. Allison had requested to stay with her grandfather at the clinic until the show tonight, which was the best news Leigh could possibly imagine. She was sorry for the litter of newborn mongrels that had been brought into the clinic after having been abandoned near the elementary school, but if the task of tube-feeding puppies was what it took to distract Allison from thoughts of murder and corpses, Leigh would not argue with providence. Ethan was spending the afternoon with a friend, and Cara had taken her two out shopping somewhere. Warren was meeting with a client in Fox Chapel; Mao Tse never rose from her afternoon nap before four. Leigh could not even use Chewie as an excuse, because Lydie had taken both him and Cara's spaniel Maggie to the dog park for some kind of social outing. (A mystery in itself, as Lydie frequently disappeared for social outings which she refused to explain, leading Cara to believe that her mother was secretly dating either a priest or a mafioso.)

Leigh thought of Maura and sighed. By now her friend would have heard the whole story from Stroth, and Leigh itched to go see her and hash things out. But she resisted the urge. This situation no longer qualified as the kind of low-stress cold case that Maura and Gerry had agreed was safe fare for an expectant mother on bed rest. If Sonia's assault had warmed the case up, last night's bone-hunting expedition had set it on fire, and Leigh was *not* going to be responsible for raising her friend's blood pressure any further. If Maura needed anything from her, she would call.

Leigh closed her eyes and tried to concentrate. There were entirely too many pieces of disconnected information floating about in her head. Exactly when had the question of who killed Andrew Marconi and stashed his body in the attic become secondary? Did that event have any relation to the murder — or possibly *murders* — in 1961? A connection had always seemed unlikely, if for no other reason than the length of time between them. But if someone who was alive and well *right now* could know about the bones in the coal chute, that pretty much shot the whole time-interval argument to heck. And what of Sonia's attack, and the threatening note sent to Gordon? Were they related too, or were they just red herrings unrelated even to each other?

Leigh's jaws clenched. She could not swear that her aunt hadn't written that note herself. There was no question that Bess didn't completely trust Gordon when it came to selling the building. He was too wishy-washy, his motives too suspect. Which was why Leigh also couldn't be sure that Gordon hadn't written the note himself. Maybe he wanted to unsettle Bess a bit, paint himself as her savior. Stranger mind games had been played between lovers. If, in fact, the two of them—

Leigh gave her head a shake. Some things, she didn't want to know.

As little as she liked to think that the note had been faked by either Bess or Gordon, that thought was better than the alternative. If someone wanted to prevent Gordon from selling the building badly enough to make threats, that same person could have been responsible for the assault on Sonia. Had the attorney not announced to an entire roomful of people, the very night before she was struck, that she wanted to buy the building from Gordon and sell it to some company that would tear it down?

There it is, Leigh thought grimly. If Gordon sold the building to Sonia, it would be torn down. The bones in the coal chute would be discovered. They had been discovered anyway, but not for lack of somebody's best efforts to remove them first. Marconi's body had already been discovered, and if—

Holy crap! She stood up with a start; her stomach heaved. Were there *other* bodies, too?

How many more could there possibly be?

"Hey, Leigh!" Chaz called pleasantly, strolling in from the annex.

"Your aunt said you were around here somewhere, so your mother sent me to find you. She said that as long as you were in the building 'idling about' and she was teaching me and Ned how to 'properly' polish a floor, you might as well listen in. Your mother has a pretty specific way she likes things done, you know. She's a real class-A clean freak. My grandma's like that, too, but my mum, she's a slob like me, so whenever Grandma comes over, she —"

"Chaz, why on earth are you wearing that thing?" Leigh interrupted, pointing at the banged-up yellow construction worker's hardhat that obscured the top half of his skull.

His face turned first defensive, then sheepish. "Just a precaution, that's all."

"Against what?" Leigh pressed, her heart pounding. She was being paranoid. There were no more bodies. She needed to forget she ever thought that. She took a breath and regrouped. "My mother is a slave driver, yes, but she prefers psychological manipulation."

Chaz offered a goofy grin. "Well, it's kind of silly, I know. But I was thinking over lunch about those guys that got whacked here, and how both of them got hit on the head, you know? And then that lawyer woman, she got hit on the head, too. And then I started thinking — we did have some people get hurt during the haunted houses. Nobody died, but one guy did get a concussion. He was standing on a ladder and fell off, and everybody thought he hit his head when he fell, but what if something hit *him* on the head *before* he fell? And there was a woman, too, she passed out in the bathroom. Nobody found her for a while, but when they did they called an ambulance, and it turned out she was all right, but we never did find out what was wrong with her. What if something conked her on the head, too? Huh? What if?"

"Something like what?" Leigh asked.

"Like I don't know!" Chaz defended. "Like maybe this building really *is* haunted, did you ever think of that? And maybe stuff just kind of falls on people and kills them sometimes. How cool a movie would that make?"

Leigh groaned. "Chaz," she said with all the patience she could muster. "Would you please go tell my mother that I am otherwise occupied?"

He studied her with skepticism. "Okay. But just between you

and me, I don't think she's going to buy it. When I told my grandma I wasn't cleaning out the mouse cages because I was working too many hours and besides, the smell would help keep the boas downstairs so they wouldn't want to crawl up into the bathroom again, she said—"

"Chaz," Leigh said more firmly. "If you wait any longer, my mother is going to think that *you're* the one 'idling about,' and seeing as how you're going to be spending the rest of the afternoon at her mercy—"

Chaz grimaced and took off toward the basement.

Leigh's fingers found her keys again. She could leave whenever she wanted to. Unfortunately, whether she was in the building or out of it, the macabre nature of her thoughts was not going to improve. Something was very, *very* wrong around here, and whatever it was, Bess had not only landed right smack in the middle of it, she was wholly committed to ignoring it. No matter what.

The show must go on.

Leigh let out a mirthless laugh. How many million times had thespians the world over said exactly the same thing in relation to their own troubled opening nights? She frowned. It was rather disturbing, if one thought about it, that theatrical events attracted so much mayhem they rated their own cliché.

Still undecided about what, if anything, she could do to keep her Aunt Bess out of harm's way, she postponed the decision of staying or going by heading for the bathroom. Once in the annex, she took a short detour halfway down the basement steps to see how the hired men were faring. Chaz had mentioned only himself and Ned — did that mean that Gerardo had not returned? A quick glance around the basement indicated that he had not.

Leigh crept silently back up the stairs and into the women's restroom. Gerardo had been irregular with his hours all along — an issue easily explained by the fact that he was also in Gordon's full-time employ. But why would he skip out now? Perhaps Gordon felt that with the new security guard sticking to Bess like glue, Gerardo's spying was no longer necessary.

Leigh took her time in the quiet, still-spotless bathroom, musing over Gordon Applegate and his potential motivations and getting nowhere. He was as difficult to read as her Aunt Bess, and at least as much of a schemer. As Leigh washed her hands at the sink she noticed a fresh coat of paint around the windowsill, and remembered her Aunt Lydie saying that a spot around the window needed to be smoothed over after an ice damage repair.

Leigh stared at her aunt's paint job, mildly bothered and uncertain as to why. After a moment, she realized that what seemed odd was not that the building had some weather damage, but that it didn't have *more* damage. Marconi's disappearance had left the place abandoned for nearly a decade, used only by a bunch of rowdy twenty-somethings for nefarious purposes at Halloween. Yet all that time, the borough had somehow managed not only to keep it structurally sound, but — with the exception of some peeling paint and accumulated dust and grime — in pretty darn good shape.

Why bother?

Maybe the ghouls were protecting their own.

"Shut up!" Leigh told herself out loud, drying her hands and hastening out of the bathroom. Her overactive imagination — which had now endowed the building with dead bodies wedged behind every sheet of drywall and under every floorboard, complete with a legion of devil-worshipping ghouls who fixed ice damage and scared off threatening real estate attorneys — had to be stopped.

It was just a building. And there had never been any devil worshippers in it. Period.

By day, they take the form of bats...

"All right, that's it!" Leigh ordered herself. "You're getting out of here and going for a walk in the park. Maybe you'll catch Aunt Lydie with her mystery man."

She headed out into the hall and turned the corner toward the exit, resolute. But she didn't make it far. Frances caught her at the door to the parking lot.

"Leigh Eleanor!" Frances spouted. "Don't you dare leave this building until you've explained to me who that hulking man is who's been following your Aunt Bess about. She says he's a private security guard hired by Gordon."

"He's a private security guard hired by Gordon."

Frances sniffed. "So, it's true then. About the threatening note mailed to him?"

Leigh nodded. Evidently Bess had come clean with her sister... at least partly. "It is rather worrying."

Frances' lips pursed. "I find it more suspicious, myself. I wouldn't be a bit surprised if it came from one of the actors trying to preserve the theater — they're such a *dramatic* lot, you know. Or for that matter, Gordon might have written it himself, just to give another of his men an excuse to keep an eye on Bess. I told her she shouldn't trust that man's minions any more than she trusts him. Lord only knows what he's after this time around!"

Leigh blinked. "*This* time around?"

"Well, of course!" Frances responded. "He and Bess have done this dance before. I distinctly remember his serving as 'rebound man' after husband number three, but there have been other equally debaucherous episodes. Never mind that Gordon is a confirmed bachelor and Bess herself has sworn never to marry again. The two of them have no respect for the institution of marriage, for the commitment that is necessary to forge morally acceptable liaisons—"

"But, Mom," Leigh broke in, feeling left in the dark, "if Bess has known Gordon that long, shouldn't she know by now if he's trustworthy?"

Frances frowned. "Your Aunt Bess sees what she wants to see, as you well know. What's different this time is that she has been foolish enough to allow herself to become indebted to him. She *needed* him to make this theater happen, and now she's made her bed. So to speak."

Leigh's stomach did a flip-flop. Was Bess tolerating Gordon's overbearing behavior — and his goons — because deep down, she trusted him? Or did she want the theater so badly she was taking a calculated risk?

Chaz's voice drifted up from the stairwell. "Um... Ms. Frances? I think my mop's broken. The squishy part fell off."

Frances's eyes rolled. She turned toward the basement, but spoke to Leigh over her shoulder. "If you have nothing constructive to do here, perhaps you should get home and start that spring cleaning."

"Never mind!" Chaz called again. "Ned fixed it!"

"Small miracles," Frances drawled. "Bess is lucky that at least one of these three has some cleaning sense. Ned can sweep a floor and disinfect a bathroom, at least. But you mark my words, she won't find any minimum-wage worker who will take it upon himself to keep the ductwork in that furnace room shining!"

"Seems unlikely," Leigh agreed. Frances was obviously still unaware of the bone in the coal chute. Bess had been adamant that there was no point in worrying anyone else until — and unless — the bone was found to be human. And as much as the grim discovery was currently messing with Leigh's own mind, she was inclined to agree.

"I should think so," Frances huffed. "Now, off you go. Those curtains in your living room won't wash themselves."

Leigh pulled her keys out of her pocket. "I'm going."

Frances headed back down the stairs, but almost immediately Bess popped out into the hallway, the silent guard following two paces behind her. "Oh, there you are, kiddo! I'm so glad you're still here. Would you mind running upstairs and opening the front door for Camille? She texted that she's waiting up there, but I'm positively buried getting ready to open the box office, and Lurch here" — she smiled flirtatiously in the guard's direction — "refuses to go anywhere without me. Isn't that sweet?"

"I can do that," Leigh agreed, stealing a glance at the guard, whose face remained stony. Now that Bess mentioned it, he did look a great deal like the spooky butler on *The Addams Family*. If Pittsburgh ever held a cartoon celebrity look-alike contest, he and Ned should definitely enter.

"Aunt Bess," Leigh added, lowering her voice to a whisper. "Do you want me to stick around? At least until the rest of the theater people start coming?"

"No need, kiddo," Bess said cheerfully. "Gordon has promised to let us press on, everything is on schedule, and really — what else could possibly *happen*, anyway?"

Leigh promptly envisioned a ceiling tile falling out and two corpses spilling into the hallway.

Stop that!

"Aunt Bess," Leigh tried again, her voice still low. "You are going to watch your back, aren't you? You're not going to pretend that nothing's happened today? That there's no possible chance of a threat here?"

Bess blinked at her innocently.

Leigh sighed, long and slow.

She put her keys back into her pocket.

Chapter 18

If there were safety in numbers, Leigh's angst over her aunt's well-being should have been put to rest a half hour ago. Three women from the Thespian Society had arrived to help set up the box office, the lighting guy and his assistant were buzzing about the back of the theater switching switches, two more security guards had been installed at the doors, two men in black tee shirts rearranged things on the stage, ushers in bright red vests settled into "the house," and half-dressed actors and actresses continually flitted about the annex between the dressing rooms and the makeup tables. Ned and Chaz had finished polishing the basement floor and left, visibly excited about returning later to see the show. Camille had carried two huge plastic bins into one of the spare annex classrooms and closed the door behind her. The locksmith had come and gone. A catered meal for cast and crew had been delivered to the annex kitchen, and Frances had gone home to feed her husband and granddaughter. Neither Gordon nor Gerardo had reappeared, but "Lurch" refused to stir from Bess's side. The only person in the building with no clear function was Leigh.

She had considered going home and then returning with Warren and Ethan, but it was too late now and her house too far away to do much except turn around and drive right back. Besides, despite her lingering qualms about the building, the current atmosphere of anticipation and excitement was pleasantly contagious. Deciding to partake of a little food herself — her aunt had offered, after all — she left the vestibule where Bess had stationed the "box office" and headed for the annex kitchen. She walked past the make-up room, which emitted the distinctive smell of hot curling irons and hair spray, and watched as one actress swore at a fake eyelash while an actor insisted he did *not* need eyeliner. The room rocked with laughter, and Leigh felt a pang of jealousy at the cast's easy camaraderie. Maybe she could get back into acting herself... someday.

The next two classrooms had their glass windows covered over and bore paper signs that read — in Bess's neatly flowery script — *Men's Dressing Room* and *Women's Dressing Room*. The signs had been up since the afternoon before the dress rehearsal, when the Pack had helped to hang them. But the pink sign on the third door down was new, and Leigh stopped to examine it.

The Blessing Room.

Her eyebrows rose. No one else in the hallway seemed to have noticed the sign yet. But she recognized this as the room into which Camille and her mysterious bins had disappeared earlier. Tentatively, she knocked.

"Who's there?" came a sing-song soprano voice.

"It's Leigh," she answered. "Can I come in?"

"Yes, you may," the voice sang back.

Leigh slowly pushed open the door, then sucked in a breath. On a card table in front of her sat a single candle, a china bowl full of water, a dish of chocolates, and a rose. Behind the table stood Camille, radiant in a full-length cobalt blue gown, her silver hair shining and her face beaming. All around her, posed in a semicircle, was a veritable forest of stuffed animals, including a reclining tiger and a four-foot giraffe.

Camille giggled at Leigh's reaction and clapped her hands. "It's adorable, isn't it? My own idea! The time before a show can be so stressful, you know. So I thought, what better to calm one's nerves than cute, fluffy toys and the well wishes of a loving friend and compatriot? And of course, chocolate is good for *everything*. I have herbal tea brewing over in the corner, too!"

Leigh struggled for words. "It's very... creative."

"I know!" Camille agreed. "Can I practice on you? I'm just about to invite the actors in!"

"Um..." Though Leigh's first instinct was to turn and run, she had to admit she was curious. "Sure."

Camille giggled again. "All right. First I welcome you, then the blessing of peace!" She picked up the rose, dipped it in the water, and touched it to Leigh's forehead. "This is water from the Ohio River. Very pure and natural."

Leigh fought back a chuckle. She couldn't remember ever hearing the words "pure and natural" in the same sentence as "Ohio River" before.

"Now at this point," Camille explained, "I'll tell the actors how special they all are to me, and what a great job they're doing. But of course I don't know you, so we'll just skip that part, okay? Then I offer you a chocolate and tea and we spend some time chatting, and then I do an exit blessing and the next person comes in. What do you think?"

Leigh wondered if she was actually being offered the chocolate. She decided that she was and took a piece. It was shaped like a rose. "I think it's very creative and caring," she praised, trying not to let the stuffed animals creep her out. Camille seemed to mean well; it wasn't her fault that Leigh was a little touchy lately on the subject of bizarre rituals.

"Thanks for the chocolate," Leigh said, meaning it. She turned to leave.

"Would you invite one of the actors in, please?" Camille called after her. "Just give me a second to grab the tea and then I'll be ready. Tell them I'd like to see them all, one at a time!"

"Will do," Leigh agreed.

"Oh, wait! I need to see Elizabeth, too. *Especially* her. She's seemed so terribly stressed lately, and she's worked so hard for the society to make all this happen. Would you let her know?"

Elizabeth again, Leigh thought curiously. No one called Bess that, at least not since Leigh's grandmother had died. And Grandma Morton only used the name when she was angry. Leigh wondered if Camille's refusal to use nicknames was universal, or if she was trying to needle Bess, subconsciously or otherwise.

Leigh nodded and opened the door.

"Thank you, Leanna!" Camille called merrily. "Or is it Coralee? Or Alicia?"

"Just Leigh," she replied, her curiosity satisfied. She stepped out, shut the door behind her, and crossed into the kitchen. Then she grabbed half a sub, put it on a paper plate, and returned to the makeup room. "Camille wants to see all of you in the 'Blessing Room' down the hall," she reported. "One at a time, she says."

To her surprise, the cast members showed no surprise at all. "Is the giraffe there?" the bearded actor quipped as he smoothed foundation into his hairline. "I swear I won't go if there's no giraffe."

The others laughed good-naturedly. "Be nice," one of the actresses chastised. She looked at Leigh. "Did she bring the homemade chocolates? The little rose ones?"

Leigh nodded.

The group cheered its approval, and the actress who had asked the question scooted back her chair and rose with a flourish. "All right, I'm in. Make a note that I went first this year. Write that down, Sam."

She smacked the shoulder of a younger man who was wiping off some ill-placed rouge, and he responded without looking up. "*See You in Bells*, first victim: Carolyn. Got it."

Leigh backed out of the room. Clearly, everyone in the Thespian Society was well aware of, and not unduly bothered by, Camille's quirks. Perhaps Leigh shouldn't be, either.

Still carrying the plate with her sub, she went off to look for Bess. She didn't want to eat alone. In this building, she didn't want to *be* alone.

She found her aunt in the sanctuary, busily instructing a small army of ushers, crewmen, and anyone else handy in the art of constructing the programs. Evidently Bess had produced the handouts on the cheap, because the pages were all in separate boxes and not yet stapled together. Ned and Chaz had both been recruited upon their return, and Leigh couldn't help but smile at the men's attempts at formal wear. Chaz wore jeans and a striped shirt and tie in contrasting shades of purple, while Ned wore tired-looking workpants, a white button-down shirt with no tie, and a crumpled sports jacket. As soon as Bess seemed content that she had a functional assembly line going, she stepped away toward Leigh. As always, the guard stepped with her.

"We're in the home stretch now, kiddo!" she beamed. "How's the cast? Everyone all right over there?"

"Peachy," Leigh responded, swallowing her last bite of sandwich. "I'm supposed to tell you that Camille wants to see you in the Blessing Room."

Bess's eyes rolled. "Please tell me she didn't set up those giant tiki torches again!"

The bite of sandwich went down the wrong way. Leigh coughed. "Um... I only saw one candle," she reported.

"Well, thank God for small favors," Bess retorted, her face anxious again. "When she directed *One Foot in Heaven* at Harvest Presbyterian she nearly burned the place down! I know she means well, but with everything else going on tonight I do wish the woman would just disappear — at least until intermission! Her nonsense is so distracting for the actors and I can't run interference for them and run the house at the same—"

She broke off in mid thought as she noticed the frazzled usher who had appeared at her elbow, followed closely by a nearly unrecognizable Merle and Earl. Merle was wearing a tight dress of plum-colored silk, a wig in an unnatural shade of red, worn black flats, and uneven patches of brown on her legs that Leigh was pretty sure marked a spray tan. Earl was spiffed up in a suit with baby-blue suspenders and a bolo tie, and his walker was decked out with a blue bandana. The couple looked from Bess to Leigh and grinned from ear to ear.

"We made it!" Merle enthused.

"Where are we sitting?" Earl asked.

The usher frowned at Bess. "They insist they're supposed to get in for free. I told them okay if you said so, but the box office isn't open yet, much less the house. And they—"

"Well, that's perfectly all right! They're my special guests, of course," Bess said with a smile. She turned to Merle and Earl. "You just take a seat anywhere that's comfortable. The magic won't begin for a while now, but if you'd like to see how the preparations go, feel free!"

"We'd like that very much," Merle said eagerly.

"We'll just be flies on the wall," Earl agreed.

Leigh felt a vibration in her pocket, accompanied by the muted sound of a siren.

"But Bess," the usher dared argue. "Didn't you tell us that absolutely nobody—"

"Well, I changed my mind," Bess commanded, flashing a parting smile at the older couple as she hustled the usher away.

Leigh stepped to the side and pulled out her phone. The siren ringtone meant a call from Maura.

Her summons had come.

"Thanks for this," Maura said gratefully, taking a gigantic bite out of the chipped ham sandwich Leigh had just delivered. "Gerry left me something, but I had a hankering for Isaly's."

"No problem," Leigh said, dropping into the chair at the detective's bedside. "But I can't stay long. Aunt Bess would never forgive me if I was late for the big opening. Where is Gerry, anyway? I'm surprised he left you alone."

"I'm not alone," Maura mumbled with her mouth full. She swallowed and pointed to the cell phone on her nightstand. "The neighbors are home and on full alert. Plus, thanks to your thoughtful daughter, I have these guys."

Maura pointed to a small cardboard box sitting on the table on the other side of her bed. Leigh walked around and peered into it. Two tiny black pups, with closed eyes and fur like velvet, slept peacefully in a huddle amidst a nest of towels heated by a circulating water blanket.

"Allison brought the puppies *here?*" Leigh asked incredulously. "Why?"

"She said, 'nothing makes you feel more calm and peaceful than watching a newborn sleep,'" Maura quoted, smiling. "She's right, you know. Every time I think about you and Bess rattling around that old church playing Hercule Poirot, I just take one look at these guys, and the old ticker slows right down."

"We are *not* playing—" Leigh shut herself up with a frown. "I mean, I'm sorry the situation is stressing you out."

Maura's expression turned serious. "Yeah, so am I. Listen, Koslow. I don't like what I've been hearing today. I don't like it at all."

Leigh returned to her chair and slouched down. "You and me both."

"About tonight," Maura began. "Stroth was hoping to hang around the theater and see what else he could pick up, but he got stuck with another homicide this afternoon. It's making me crazy — I *know* these background checks would give us what we need, but I can't access the information from here, and my being laid up so long has got the department so shorthanded I can't get anybody else to do it, either."

Leigh winced to see the familiar worry lines returning to her friend's brow. "Maybe you should take another look at those puppies."

Maura leaned over and peered into the box. She put in one finger to stroke a pup, then smiled. "Yeah, that does help."

"Is there anything else I can do?" Leigh asked. "At the building, or... you're not supposed to feed them, are you?"

Maura shook her head. "Nope. Your dad is sending one of the techs over to do that. All I have to do is babysit them until after the show." She turned to Leigh. "And I *don't* want you to do anything about this case, either. But there is something I need to tell you. Actually, two things."

Leigh braced herself.

"First off, a little good news. Sonia Crane is much better. She's alert and clear headed, and she's not accusing Bess of anything."

Leigh released a breath. "That's good. Does she know who hit her?"

Maura shook her head. "It's pretty clear she never saw them. It's also pretty clear that she still wants the building. And she wants it bad."

"Are you kidding me?" Leigh asked. "Still? What's she been saying?"

Maura didn't answer the question. "You want the specifics on that, you'll have to ask Gordon Applegate. But I can tell you this. No one in the department has told Sonia Crane — or anyone else — about your little adventure with the coal chute this morning. So unless Gordon or one of you told her, she still doesn't know."

Leigh slouched further down in her chair. "I see."

"Who else knows about it?"

"Nobody," Leigh answered. "At least, Bess and I haven't told anyone. Ned was there, and he could have said something, but Bess told him it was a squirrel bone and I'm pretty sure he believed her. I don't know about Gordon, but I can't see why he would tell anyone, as much as he hates bad publicity. Not even Allison knows — although I can say that with certainty *only* because she wasn't physically in the building at the time. Give her five minutes inside the doors tonight and she'll pick it up by sheer osmosis."

Leigh looked up at Maura with a miserable expression. "I was kind of hoping this would be the part where you tell me I'm overreacting and that what I found was nothing but a petrified candy cigarette."

Maura shook her head slowly. "Sorry, Koslow. No can do."

Crap. "You got the lab results back?"

"No," Maura answered calmly. "But what you found wasn't the

only thing left behind in the rubble."

Leigh sank even further into her chair. "Tell me," she moaned.

"Three more very small bones, most likely fingers or toes," Maura answered. "And part of a vertebra."

"A vertebra?" Leigh asked weakly. "How big —"

"Let's just say it'd make one damned scary squirrel."

Double crap. Leigh sighed. "You think it's Clyde Adams, don't you?"

Maura nodded slowly. "Makes sense. That's why I don't like this, Koslow. You've got way too many people down there with access to that building, and way too many of them have longstanding ties to West View. These murders may have happened a long time ago, but it's not impossible that some of the principals could still be alive and kicking. It's even possible they could have relatives acting on their behalf. *Somebody* tried to keep us from finding those bones in the coal chute, and that same somebody could have tried to keep Gordon from selling the building to Sonia Crane, because she made no secret of the fact that she would tear it down. That same someone could be behind the threat to Bess."

Leigh nodded grimly.

"There's a link somewhere, Koslow," Maura said determinedly. "And we're going to find it. Or rather, my loving husband is."

Leigh sat up a little. "Gerry? But he's not —"

"On the county payroll? Um, no. And please don't remind him. But he knows me, and when Stroth got pulled to the other homicide and no one else was available to finish these checks, Gerry knew I was going to lose it, so he grabbed my notebooks and took off. Believe me, if there's a connection between anyone working with Bess's theater now and the murders of Andrew Marconi, Bill Stokes, and possibly Clyde Adams, he's *going* to find it."

Leigh pictured the city police lieutenant pounding away at a keyboard or buried behind stacks of documents — however the police actually did such things. He would be poring through the files with such intensity his brow would moisten, all the while swearing any number of profanities against whatever perp *dared* to put little Gerry or Maura junior at risk.

Leigh managed a weak smile. "I believe he will."

Chapter 19

Warren met Leigh at the door to the parking lot, as arranged, and handed her the bag she'd requested. "Thanks," she said gratefully. "I'd better get changed pronto. What time do you have?"

"Eight minutes till curtain," he answered, not bothering to look at his watch. The man's brain was as good as any timepiece. "Now you want to tell me why you've stuck around here all day?" he asked. His voice was even, but Leigh, picking up on the ever-so-slightly wounded edge to his tone, looked up at him with chagrin. He made a handsome picture, as he always did in his perfectly tailored business suits, and she stood on tiptoe and kissed him. "Sorry," she apologized. "But I'm afraid that whole story would take way longer than eight minutes. Intermission, maybe?"

He grumbled under his breath. "All right. But I consider that a firm commitment."

"Agreed." She started to walk away toward the dressing room, but he stopped her.

"Just answer this much, then. Is that a security guard I see following Bess around?"

"Yep."

"Did she hire him, or did Gordon?"

"Gordon."

Warren's eyes studied hers. "Interesting."

"Is Allison here yet?" Leigh asked, starting away again.

"Not yet," Warren answered, following her down the hall and stationing himself outside the dressing room door. "But I expect her and your parents any minute. Ethan is with Matt and Lenna upstairs. They said something about keeping an eye on 'the suspect.' That would worry me, but Cara's on it — she swore she wouldn't let them out of her sight."

"Good to know. Be back in a jiff." Leigh slipped inside the now-unoccupied women's dressing room and changed from her jeans, cotton top, and sneakers into the slightly better-looking khaki slacks, dress blouse, and loafers she had requested. She could stop worrying about three-fourths of the Pack, at least, if all they planned to do was stare at Ned as he watched the show. But as for her daughter, it was only a matter of time —

"Hi, Mom," Allison's small voice greeted as she slipped inside the dressing room. "Dad said you were in here. What did you find in the boiler room?"

Leigh sighed heavily. "How could —" her words broke off as she stared at the girl in front of her, who had become as unrecognizable as Merle and Earl. She was dressed in a frilly, baby pink concoction of lace and ruffles not seen on any fifth grader since the days of Shirley Temple — with the exception of some thirty-odd years ago when Leigh had been forced to wear a similar abomination herself, compliments of one Frances Koslow.

"Yeah, I know," Allison said blandly, "It's bad. But Grandma wouldn't let me wear what I had on, and she'd already bought this as an Easter present. I told her Dad could bring me something to change into, but she seemed so excited about it, and you know how, when Grandma's really, *really* happy about something, she's more likely to —"

Run her mouth. "Talk," Leigh finished. "Yeah, I know." How many times, as a child, had she herself pretended an interest in sewing or cleaned already-clean household items in a quest for crucial information?

"I don't mind, really," Allison insisted. "It's not like anyone import— I mean, anyone from school will be here." She stepped closer and lowered her voice. "Was it Clyde Adams?"

"Wait a minute," Leigh protested, suppressing the shudder she always got when her only daughter spoke of corpses. "Are you saying that *Grandma* told you I found something in the boiler room?"

Allison shook her head, then winced. The folds of her dress were so starched that the slightest movement made a crinkling sound. "No, I overhead Aunt Bess talking to Mr. Applegate on the phone about that just now. I asked Grandma about the Stokes and the Adams."

Leigh considered. Her eight minutes were slipping away fast, and getting more information out of Allison than one gave to her — intentionally or otherwise — was always a challenge. "There's a possibility that... *human remains* were sealed up in the coal chute," she admitted. "But we don't know for sure yet."

Allison's dark eyes studied her intently. "What's a coal chute? Could it have been there long enough to—"

"Hard to say," Leigh evaded. "Now tell me what you learned from Grandma. And talk fast or we'll miss the opening. If it's important, I can—"

"Oh, I already called Aunt Mo," Allison replied. "She said Uncle Gerry's working on it."

A knock sounded on the door. "Three minutes!" Warren called.

"*Talk*, Allie," Leigh commanded. "What do you know about all this that I don't?"

"Nothing much," Allison insisted. "Grandma never knew any of the people personally. West View's pretty small, but they were in different social groups, kind of."

Leigh could imagine. Her Grandma and Grandpa Morton had worked hard to scratch out a place for themselves in the middle of the middle class, and they'd been proud of it.

"Most of what she said was the same as what Grandma Lydie already told me. That everyone thought that Bill Stokes was a really horrible person who beat up his wife and stepkids and probably did something to Clyde Adams. But there's one thing the two of them remember differently. Grandma Lydie thought that Clyde was no good either — that he was probably having an affair with Bill's wife. But Grandma remembers feeling sorry for Clyde, because she heard that he was actually trying to *protect* Bill's wife and kids. That Clyde knew what was going on and tried to step in, and that's why the men were fighting."

"You've got thirty seconds," Warren called through the door, "and then I'm coming in!"

Leigh guided Allison ahead of her and towards the door. "Anything else?"

Allison shook her head. "Just that neither of the widows are still in West View. They lived here for a while after, but Grandma's pretty sure they both got remarried and left later on. They could have come back, but if they did, they'd have different last names."

Leigh opened the door.

"Let's go!" Warren urged. He was smiling, but his voice was tense. He hated being late.

The annex had emptied out; as they approached the stage doors to the theater, the only person they passed was one of the actresses, who stood in a quiet corner wearing earbuds and mumbling lines to herself. Most of the cast, Leigh knew, was hanging out in the "green room," the old choir room off the upstairs curved hallway. The room wasn't green, but it was the closest space to the stage entrances.

"Ethan is saving our seats," Warren explained, rushing them along. "At least I hope he is."

They reached the door to the sanctuary and Warren swung it open for Leigh and Allison to enter. Leigh's mouth dropped open with surprise. The theoretical audience her Aunt Bess dreamed of had miraculously appeared. The house was packed. Almost every seat was occupied, and the ushers were scrambling to add extras in the back. A loud buzz of excited chatter filled the room, and the air was thick with anticipation. Leigh shut her mouth, smiled broadly, and began to move forward, but a hand restrained her.

"Hang on, kiddo," Bess whispered. "Can I talk to you a minute?"

Leigh stepped back. She studied her aunt's face and didn't care for the unusual creases of worry around Bess's ordinarily bright eyes. "You two go on in," Leigh insisted, throwing an apologetic glance at Warren. "I'll join you before curtain if I can; otherwise I'll watch the first act from the back or something."

Both Warren and Allison returned disgruntled looks, albeit for different reasons. Warren because his flighty wife was forever standing him up at such events, and Allison because she wanted to stay and overhear the conversation. But they both walked on into the theater without her and without comment.

"What's wrong?" Leigh asked as soon as the door had closed behind them.

Bess hesitated a moment, fidgeting with her hands. "Hopefully nothing," she replied. "But I am getting just a teeny bit concerned. Have you seen Camille lately?"

Leigh shook her head. "Not since I got back from Maura's. Why?"

"Well, she did that blessing nonsense on most of the cast, but when Chuck went in to see her, she wasn't there. She left the candle burning, so he stuck around a while, but she didn't come back. They all figured maybe she just ran out of time and was getting ready for her big moment — she always sings an aria for the cast right before she calls places — but it's time now and she's not up there."

Bess continued to wring her hands together. "I didn't want to worry the cast, so I gave them a little pep talk myself and then I told them... well, I sort of *implied* that I had seen Camille and that she wasn't feeling well."

"But you haven't seen her and you have no idea where she is," Leigh supplied.

Bess shook her head slowly. "I wish I could tell you that it was perfectly in character for her to disappear before a show, but as loopy as the woman is, I truly can't see her missing her own opening night. Why, she lives for this!"

Leigh looked over Bess's shoulder at the security guard, whose face remained as impassive as ever. "Who else have you told?" Leigh asked. "Have you looked for her? Is her car still in the parking lot?"

"Nobody, a little, and yes," Bess answered. "Her car's still here, and she couldn't drive off now if she tried. The parking attendants blocked in all the cast cars to make more room. I've looked around a little, but it's a big building and I've had so many other things to do..."

"Well, we'll look now. Maybe she really is sick and just went to some quiet corner to rest," Leigh suggested, not believing it for a minute. "Can the guards help us?"

Bess scowled. "They absolutely refuse to leave the posts Gordon assigned them. And Gordon won't tell them otherwise — he thinks guarding the doors is more important. I don't even know where the man is — he was supposed to be here already, to watch the show!"

Chaz tore around the corner and nearly ran into them. He stopped himself short and then, with a sheepish look, removed his hardhat. "Had to run to the bathroom," he explained. "You can't be too careful in this building, you know. I didn't miss anything, did I? Has it started yet?"

His question was answered by a chorus of chuckles drifting through the door.

"Aw, no!" he said, disappointed. "Can I still go in this way?"

"No, you may not," Bess replied, turning him around. "You should have used the basement bathroom and come in through the back. As of now, this door is a stage entrance only!"

As if to prove the point, one of the actresses walked down the stairs from the green room and planted herself by the door, obviously preparing for her entrance. She looked over the assembled group with a frown. "Is something wrong?"

"Absolutely not," Bess lied, pushing both Chaz and Leigh back toward the annex. "Break a leg," she called to the actress. "The audience is loving it already!"

Once they were out into the main hallway, Bess turned to Chaz. "You might as well put that hardhat back on," she instructed. "I have a job for you."

Chaz's face fell. "What? But I thought I'd get to see the show!"

"You can watch it Saturday and Sunday both," Bess responded. "I'll get you a seat front-row center. But tonight we need your help. Don't we, Leigh?"

Leigh hesitated. Did they? *Somebody* needed to search for Camille, but the *who* part was tricky. She didn't trust Chaz. She had no reason to trust any of the hired men, or any of Gordon's guards, or even Gordon himself, for that matter. The only people she trusted were family, and they were all inside already watching the show, where she wanted them to stay.

Her first instinct was to pull out her phone and call Maura, but what could the detective do besides send over some uniformed officers, which Leigh could just as easily call for herself? And was that drastic a step really warranted? Camille couldn't have been missing for more than half an hour, and Bess hadn't even checked all the rooms yet.

"Let's do this," Leigh decided. "We'll search in pairs, and move through the building top to bottom, checking in with each other as we go."

"Ooh!" Chaz enthused, his chagrin forgotten. "Sounds fun. What are we searching for?"

"Camille," Bess answered. "She seems to have not been feeling well; we need to make sure she hasn't... passed out or something."

Chaz blinked at her a moment. Then he put his hardhat back on. "I'll stick with this dude," he announced, sidling closer to the security guard.

The guard didn't move, but as he looked down at Chaz, his lip curled ever so slightly up on one side.

Chaz stepped away again.

"Mr. Jenkins will go with me," Bess declared. "Why don't we

start on the second floor of the annex? You two take one side of the hallway and we'll take the other."

The teams began their search in earnest, checking one room at a time and meeting in the hallway after to compare notes. The upstairs classrooms were full of props and other theater gear, cluttered throughout and with their closets full to bursting. Leigh's heart pounded even as she tried to appear calm to Chaz, who responded to anxiety the same way he responded to excitement — by prattling nonstop.

By the time they had moved downstairs and reached the "blessing room," Leigh found herself considering the judicious use of duct tape. She was surprised when, three steps into the room, Chaz stopped short. The assembly of cute and fuzzy animals had done what nothing else could do — it had rendered him momentarily speechless.

"Wow," he said finally, his blue eyes bugged. "This is *so* unbelievably twisted."

Leigh arched an eyebrow. The man had been practically gleeful when talking about the scorched corpse in "the execution room," but stuffed animals and chocolate roses were twisted? "How do you figure?" she demanded.

Tiny drops of moisture beaded up on the narrow strip of brow visible below Chaz's hard hat. "Grandma kept saying it must be devil worship!"

Leigh resisted giving the man a shake. "This isn't devil worship! It's a nice older woman trying to create a peaceful environment for the cast to relax in, to calm their nerves." *Or some crazy thing like that*, she added wordlessly. "How do you get 'devil worship' out of a bunch of cute animals and one lousy candle?"

Chaz swallowed. "You say cute, I say creepy. Look at that giraffe! He's no innocent. He's *thinking things.*"

Leigh tried mentally to count to ten, but being an impatient person, she only got to four. "Don't be ridiculous," she chastised, looking quickly around the room for any potentially hidden spots. Camille wasn't there. "This room is clean. Let's move on." She started out the door.

"Grandma says that the janitor's wife was the head of it, you know."

Leigh's feet stopped moving. "The head of what?"

"The coven, of course," Chaz explained. "She was married to the janitor, but she had the hots for this other guy, so she got the coven to sacrifice her husband on the altar. They were all in on it, see —"

"Because getting the entire congregation of an otherwise respectable church to agree to cover up a cold-blooded murder was *so* much easier than getting a divorce?" Leigh challenged.

Chaz frowned. "Well, maybe they needed a human sacrifice, and he was convenient, you know?"

Leigh's patience was lost. "There were never any devil worshippers here!" she scolded, wincing even as she spoke. God help her, she sounded exactly like her mother.

"If you say so," Chaz said sulkily.

Leigh attempted to regroup. "Did your grandmother actually know the janitor or his wife?"

Chaz considered a moment, then shrugged. "I don't know. It's kind of hard to tell with Grandma. She says she hitchhiked to Cleveland in 1955 to see Elvis in a jamboree before he was really famous and that she did it with him in his car after but my mom says no way would Grandma ever have hitchhiked all the way to Cleveland because she gets really carsick and besides her brother my great uncle always said she made it up and that she had a thing about pretending she knew celebrities and that she used to say she'd petted the real Lassie too back when —"

"Chaz!" Leigh interrupted. "Can we focus, please?"

"Sorry," he offered. "But, like, those animals are seriously creeping me out, you know? Can I go watch the show now?"

"As soon as we find Camille," Leigh assured, following Chaz out into the hall and closing the door behind them. "She must be around here somewhere."

"Unless she got bonked on the head," Chaz muttered, adjusting his hard hat.

"Nothing in either of the dressing rooms," Bess reported as they convened in the hall. "Why don't you two check the restrooms, and we'll do the office and then start on the hallway behind the stage?"

"Then what?" Chaz asked nervously.

"Then we'll check the upstairs curved hall, the attic, and the basement," Bess replied, her worry lines deepening again. "I don't know where else she could be. The guards insist she isn't outside."

"We'll find her, Aunt Bess," Leigh assured, despite the pit of fear that was digging ever deeper in her gut.

Bess nodded, and she and the guard headed off in the direction of the sanctuary.

"Have a look around the men's room, will you?" Leigh directed, opening the door to the women's. "Make sure no one is in the stalls."

Chaz didn't move. "What if Camille doesn't *want* to be found?" he blurted, fidgeting with his hardhat again. "What if she's waiting somewhere with a sledge hammer to bonk all of *us* on the head? Huh?"

"Then you alone will survive," Leigh quipped, showing a bravado she didn't feel. "Just check out the bathroom, will you? Weren't you just in there a few minutes ago?"

"Well, yeah, but... Okay, fine!" he said anxiously.

Chaz slipped inside the door to the men's room and Leigh did the same with the women's. "Hello?" she called. It was possible that a patron could be inside, despite the plea in the program that any necessary exits during the show take place at the rear of the theater and make use of the basement bathroom. Chaz obviously hadn't read it; others might not either.

Leigh heard no response. She opened the stall doors and looked around the entirety of the small space. It was empty.

She returned to the hall and waited for Chaz. With Bess and the guard gone, the annex had become eerily silent. She couldn't help repeating Chaz's question to herself. What if Camille didn't want to be found?

And if not... why not?

The discomfort in her stomach had graduated to a full-blown ache. Chaz was taking too long. "Chaz?" she called, knocking on the men's room door.

He didn't answer. Leigh looked nervously up and down the hall. Then she kicked the door open a bit with her foot. "Chaz? Is anyone else in there?"

Silence. She took a breath and swung the door open fully. It met no resistance. One glance from the doorway showed her there was no one at the urinals or sinks. She reached out and pushed quickly against the one and only stall door, then jumped back out of the way.

The door swung in and banged against the corner of the toilet.

She could see enough of the space inside to answer her question. There was no one in the bathroom, including Chaz.

Gutless wimp had given her the slip.

Leigh moved back out into the hallway and heard the door to the parking lot swing open and shut. Heavy footsteps headed her way.

Calm down! she ordered herself. There were over two hundred people inside the building right now, with guards outside the doors. What could happen?

She stood still in the center of the hall, waiting for the person in question to round the corner. But she had never been very good at waiting.

"Who's there?" she called out, embarrassed at the fear in her voice.

A man appeared. He smiled at her tentatively and moved forward. "It's just me. Are you okay?"

Leigh stared at Gerardo blankly, her response to him cycling rapidly from relief to wariness and back again. "I'm fine. What... why are you here?" she stammered.

"Mr. Applegate sent me," he replied evenly. "He said Bess was upset about Camille going missing. Have you found her yet?"

Leigh tried to calm her frayed nerves with a deep breath. His claim was perfectly plausible. "No, we haven't," she answered. "But we haven't finished searching yet."

Gerardo squared his shoulders. "All right. Where would you like me to look?"

Leigh considered, long and hard. She did not trust Gerardo any more than she trusted Chaz, and she was not at all sure that wandering around the building with either of them was any safer than searching on her own. But it hardly mattered, because she had no intention of doing either anymore.

"Let's ask Bess," she deferred, slipping past him and heading toward the hallway behind the stage. She had not walked six feet before she collided with Ned coming the opposite direction up the basement stairs.

"I'm sorry, Ms. Leigh!" He apologized nervously. Despite the relatively nicer clothes, his hair was wilder than usual and his pale skin was beaded with sweat. "Are you okay? Chaz said it wasn't safe in here, that you and Ms. Bess both were gonna get conked on the head!"

Before Leigh could answer, Bess appeared around the corner. "What's this?" she asked, looking from Ned to Gerardo. "Why aren't you watching the show, Ned? And where's Chaz?"

"Chaz bailed on me," Leigh tried to explain. "He's scared. He told Ned—"

"Nobody's going to bonk you on the head, Ms. Bess!" Ned declared, pulling himself to his full height and making a lame attempt to suck in his substantial gut. "Not in my building! I won't let 'em, no way!"

Bess smiled sweetly at him, and Leigh wondered for a moment if the Pack wasn't onto something with their Ned-in-love theory. He certainly wouldn't be her first victim.

"I know you wouldn't, Ned," Bess said soothingly. "Thank you. But I assure you I'm in no danger. Why don't you go back on in and watch the show? And if you see Chaz again, tell him to do the same." She threw a calculating glance at Gerardo. "I'm sure everything here is perfectly under control."

Ned looked from Gerardo to the guard for a long moment, distrust written plainly across his pasty face. But with a single nod toward Bess, he turned around and went back the way he had come.

"Mr. Jenkins has agreed to carry the ladder for me," Bess explained to Leigh. "Camille isn't anywhere behind the stage, and she's not out in the audience, either. She also isn't in the basement, at least not in the main part of it. Hank and Ralph have both made that loop getting to their entrances at the back of the house, and Hank said she wasn't in the bathroom down there, either. There's simply nowhere else to look besides—"

Leigh groaned inwardly. She knew what was coming before the words left her aunt's mouth.

"The attic and the boiler room."

Chapter 20

"I don't see how anyone could have gotten up into the attic space in the last hour without someone seeing the ladder," Bess admitted, talking more to herself than anyone else. "But I simply won't forgive myself if we don't look everywhere."

"You want me to check the boiler room?" Gerardo offered.

Bess threw him a sharp look. "My, you've learned English quickly, young man."

Gerardo smiled back at her, unabashed. "I was always good with languages."

"Be my guest," Bess answered his original question, her tone still wary. "But don't think I won't have a look myself, as well."

Gerardo gave a nod and headed down the stairs.

Bess started toward the office and motioned for the guard to follow her. "The ladder's in here."

"Aunt Bess," Leigh began soberly, following them both. "I think it's time to call Detective Stroth. We've checked all the understandable places Camille could have gone, but there is no good reason for her to be in either the attic or the boiler room! Let's let him decide if the police should come out."

Bess paused in the office doorway, pointed the guard toward the ladder, and nibbled a fingernail. "I suppose you're right, kiddo. She's an adult with a mind of her own, certainly, but under the circumstances..."

"Exactly!" Leigh finished awkwardly.

"Hang on a minute, Jenkins," Bess said as he bent over to pick up the ladder. "I have a call to make first."

Leigh listened in as Bess got herself patched straight through to the detective. Bess explained the situation, then returned the phone to her pocket and looked mildly ill. "He's sending somebody out," she said weakly. "He didn't say who. But they'll come to the parking lot entrance without sirens or anything."

"You've done the right thing, Aunt Bess," Leigh praised. "I'm sure if we don't find Camille, they will."

"Let's go, Jenkins," Bess ordered, moving toward the steps to the upstairs hallway. "Thanks for helping me search, kiddo," she said to Leigh. "But the men and I can take it from here. Why don't you go sneak in the back and join the family? I'm sorry you missed so much of the show already. You will come back and see the next one, won't you?"

Leigh felt an unexpected pang. She was being dismissed. She need have no more personal involvement in the evening's mayhem. How great was that?

"Of course I want to see it," she mumbled. As they moved closer to the stage doors, the sound of rumbling laughter met their ears. The audience was indeed loving it.

If they only knew...

"I'm not sure I can enjoy the rest of the show tonight, though," Leigh said honestly. "Not until we know that Camille's all right."

"And if I know your husband," Bess said wryly, "he won't be able to enjoy the show either until he knows that *you're* all right."

Leigh bit her lip. "Good point."

"Go on in, kiddo," Bess said with a smile. "You can still catch part of the second act. I insist."

Leigh debated. A large part of her did not want to let her aunt out of her sight. But she also knew that as a bodyguard, her own worth was negligible. "All right," she said finally. "But will you at least stay where there are" — she avoided eye contact with the guard — "several other people? Stay backstage with the cast. Let the boiler room wait until the police come."

Bess waved her away. "Fine, fine. Now *go*. Enjoy."

Leigh turned and headed for the stairs down to the basement. Second thoughts pummeled her conscience with every step. Maybe she *should* stay with Bess, at least until the police came. Then again, as long as Bess didn't allow herself to be alone in a secluded place with anyone — *including* Gordon's hires — she really should be fine. The building was, after all, full of people.

As if to reinforce the thought, an actor appeared suddenly at the bottom of the basement steps and sprinted up them two at time. "Sorry!" he apologized, brushing past her. "Wardrobe emergency! Making this next entrance is going to be killer—" He rushed on in the direction of the green room, most likely in search of safety pins, and Leigh continued to the bottom of the stairs.

The basement lights were off, but Leigh could see well enough with the light that spilled through the glass door at the bottom of the ramp. She was hastening across the large, open space — wondering why the lights were turned off in the first place and resolving to turn them back on as soon as she reached the other side — when she heard the sound.

A high-pitched lilting sound. Faint and strangely muffled, yet still recognizable.

"I'm called Little Buttercup..."

Leigh froze. She knew that voice.

It was Camille. And she was singing.

Leigh looked immediately toward the closed door to the boiler room. The audience's laughter rumbled down through the ceiling from the theater overhead, drowning out the lone female voice. But when the audience quieted again, Leigh spun in her tracks. The singing wasn't coming from the boiler room. It was coming from the old kitchen.

She had practically forgotten the room's existence, as they had been using the newer kitchen in the annex. But the space next to and underneath the stairs, which had been stripped of all its appliances except for a couple giant WWII-era stoves, had originally been packed with junk like the rest of the basement, and was now as empty and clean as the rest of it.

Why would Camille go in there to sing?

Leigh frowned in confusion. Then again, why did Camille do anything?

She took another wary look around the open basement, then moved toward the kitchen door. "Camille?" she called from outside of it. "Camille!"

The singing continued. Given its current glass-shattering pitch, Leigh doubted the woman could hear her. She threw another paranoid look over her shoulder, then turned the handle and pushed the door in, being careful to stay outside of the opening. "Camille?" she called once more. "Are you all right?"

The singing stopped. "Yes, dear!" came Camille's familiar voice.

Leigh's shoulders slumped with relief. She pushed the door open wider, reached one hand through the doorway, and felt along the wall for a light switch. "Why are you singing in here in the dark?" she asked. "We were worried about you!"

"How sweet!" Camille returned, her voice sounding oddly muffled.

Leigh's fingers found the light switch. She flipped it. Nothing happened.

"Is it intermission yet?" Camille called.

Leigh pulled out her phone and turned on her flashlight app. The stage lights must have blown a circuit. "Not quite," she answered, shining her light through the doorway. Her view was limited. She could see the island in the center of the room, and the door to the pantry beyond it. "Camille," she said with frustration, stretching out her arm to shine the light a little farther into the room. "Why are you in there, and where exactly are you?"

In a split second, a hand reached out of the darkness and clamped down on Leigh's wrist, yanking her forward. Her shoulder pushed the door the rest of the way open and she stumbled inside as her cell phone flew out of her hand and dashed to the floor with a clatter. The hand released her wrist as quickly as it had grabbed it, and Leigh ducked, shuffled away, and threw her hands upward in an instinctual effort to ward off a blow.

None came. The door slammed shut behind her, and the room became pitch dark.

Leigh froze in place for a long moment, afraid to breathe. She wanted, quite badly, to believe that whoever had pulled her into the room was now on the opposite side of the door. But as she held her own breath and listened, she heard what she was hoping not to.

Heavy breathing. Just a few feet away.

Well, hell. Now what?

Leigh crept slowly backward, away from the sound. She could see absolutely nothing. From what she remembered of the layout of the kitchen, she was somewhere between the island and the counter along the wall. If she moved far enough quietly enough, maybe she could put the island between herself and the mystery lungs.

She continued inching backward, listening intently. She had not moved far when a new and even more disturbing sound met her ears.

Someone else was also breathing. And that sound was coming from behind her.

Leigh stole a choice word from Maura's repertoire and swore internally. *Now* where could she go?

She listened harder. The second set of breathing sounds wasn't coming from head level. It was coming from somewhere near her feet.

Very tentatively, she stretched one foot behind her. Her toe nudged something. Something that responded with an almost inaudible grunt.

She picked another word.

"Leigh, dear," came Camille's motherly soprano. "Are you all right?"

Leigh's head spun. The voice wasn't coming from the floor. It wasn't coming from the doorway, either, where the heavy breathing continued. It was coming from another place altogether. And given the fact that it was still muffled, she guessed it was coming from the pantry.

"Yes," Leigh answered, fully aware of the absurdity of the conversation. "Are you?"

The response came after a beat. "I'll be fine. It's almost intermission." And with that, Camille began to sing again.

Leigh was running out of swear words. She could not move forward; she could not move back. Speaking to Camille at all had given away her position, and with a muffled aria in her ear, she could no longer hear the breathing.

She reached out her arms and felt aimlessly along the counter and island countertops to either side. She had no weapon, and nothing to use as one. She wasn't likely to find anything either, as the kitchen had been emptied even before Frances sterilized it. She didn't know whether to be more afraid of a head bashing from the front or an ankle grab from the rear, and was contemplating a swift kick to the latter when a particular low-pitched sound fought its way through Camille's high-pitched tones to reach her ear.

It was a groan.

Oh, no.

Leigh made a quick decision. She lifted her feet high and stepped over the figure she presumed to be lying on the floor, putting herself on the opposite side from the heavy breather. Or at least, she thought with chagrin, where the heavy breather had been. He could have moved anywhere by now. Her eyes weren't adjusting to the light; there wasn't any light to adjust to.

Another surge of laughter echoed down through the ceiling, and

Leigh gritted her teeth at the irony. Warren, the kids, and a good chunk of her extended family were within feet of her this very minute — for all the good that did any of them. Pushing the thought from her mind, she leaned down and felt for the recumbent figure with a hand. Her fingers made contact first with what felt like a hip, then, as her hand traveled sideways, with a ribcage, and a shoulder. It was a man. A large man.

Her hand began to tremble as she felt for his neck, and a pulse. She found one easily under the open collar — slow, but steady and reasonably strong. Her fingers moved up the curve of his jaw to feel soft waves of short hair, and her suspicions were confirmed.

It was Gerardo.

More laughter, this time even louder. The play seemed to be reaching some kind of crescendo.

Leigh's hands felt gently around the top of Gerardo's head, and she found what she feared. A wet, sticky spot. And a large, misshapen lump.

Conked on the head.

She had not been the first person to enter this kitchen in search of Camille.

A sudden flash of light cut through the darkness, accompanied by the unmistakable sound of a siren. Her phone!

Leigh could see the cell phone where it had come to rest just under the counter about six feet away, screen down, edges glowing. She made a mad dive forward over Gerardo's prone body, but before she even got close, another hand closed down upon the phone, and the light was quenched.

She swore once more, this time out loud. The phone had received a text from Maura.

Had Gerry's background checks panned out?

The heavy breathing got even heavier — loud enough to be heard over Camille's continued caterwauling. Leigh scuttled hastily backwards, over Gerardo and to the opposite side of the counter. The siren sounded again, and the dimmest glow shimmered from the area behind the door. Heavy-breath had stuffed her phone in his pocket. He still had not moved. Or spoken a word.

Think, Leigh. Think!

Why was all this happening?

Camille had hidden herself in a closet and started singing once before. She had done it because she, like Lenna, was frightened of the bats. It only stood to reason that, despite the relative cheerfulness of Camille's voice, she was equally frightened now. When most people got scared, they trembled and/or ran. When Camille got scared, she sang herself to la-la land.

So Camille had encountered something that scared her. *One thing explained.*

Gerardo had heard her singing, come in to investigate, and gotten bonked on the head, as per the MO of this accursed building for more than half a century. *Two down.*

She herself had followed the sound of Camille's singing, just like Gerardo, but her head had been mercifully spared. Why?

Heavy-breath wasn't talking. The siren sounded yet again, and Leigh winced. She always answered Maura's texts. The good news was that her silence would ensure the arrival of the police within a matter of minutes. The bad news was that, deep in a nearby duplex in Avalon, it would also make the detective's blood pressure skyrocket.

Leigh had to do something besides stand still in the dark with her heart pounding. And she had never been able to sing opera.

Think!

She took a deep breath and tried to clear her mind. *I don't like coincidences*, Allison had muttered, long before Leigh found the bone in the coal chute. Despite the time lapse, the murders had to be connected. The love triangle — or whatever — that had sparked such violence in 1961 must also have caused someone to murder Andrew Marconi over forty years later. But why? Marconi didn't want to tear the building down. He only wanted to open a strip club. What threat did he pose?

More laughter from the ceiling. This time, loud guffaws.

Leigh fought to stay focused. This was not about Andrew Marconi, was it? If the murders were connected, it was about the building itself.

Merle and Earl had seen lights in the building at night as long as they had lived across the street. Lights when no one should have been there. People claimed the place was haunted; even vandals bent on destruction were scared away. Rumors of devil worship flew, despite a complete lack of evidence for anything of the sort, except for the placement of the janitor's body. Laid out on the altar...

a sacrifice. A sacrifice to... or *for*... whom?

The building stopped being a church shortly afterward, and was never a church again. It was a meeting hall, a banquet hall, a dance studio. None of those businesses thrived, but they were not plagued with employee concussions, either. Not until Andrew Marconi made public his plans to put a strip club in the building. And then when Sonia Crane announced her plans to tear it down.

Leigh's teeth clenched with frustration. It made no sense! What made the strip club any more of a threat than the haunted houses? Despite Chaz's suspicions of foul play, one guy falling off a ladder and one woman passing out in a bathroom had had no effect on the chain of events — the haunted houses proceeded anyway, with their fake chain saws and rubber rats and...

Chaz's words sprang back into Leigh's mind, along with a vivid image.

One guy brought in a devil statue and put it up on this platform, and the next morning it was on the ground and smashed to bits...

No devil worship. No strip club.

Not in my building.

Leigh felt suddenly numb.

A little song, a little dance. Parties with meals. Maybe even a few harmless spook shows. Certainly, a nice theater with a friendly proprietor — whatever it took to make that happen was well worth the cost. But no devil worship. And no sexual debauchery.

She's a good, moral lady.

And by the way, no ice damage, either.

Not in my building.

Leigh's pulse raced. Camille had stopped singing; Leigh didn't know when. Occasional laughter continued to drift through the ceiling. The room was black as pitch; heavy breaths still heaved by the door.

She didn't get it all. Not hardly. But she figured she was close enough. She straightened where she stood and cleared her throat. She tried her best to make her voice sound nonthreatening and pleasant. Then she aimed it at the figure behind the door.

"Ned?"

Chapter 21

"Yes, Ms. Leigh?" he answered quietly, almost meekly.

"Why is Camille in the closet?" she asked gently.

"Cause she wouldn't stop singing."

Leigh puzzled for a moment, but gave up. "Would it be okay if I let her out now? It must be pretty cramped in there."

"I can't let you do that, Ms. Leigh. Please don't try."

Leigh drew in a steadying breath. "All right, I won't. But why not?"

"She has to stay there till intermission."

The words came back to Leigh like heat lightning flashing in a distant corner of her brain. Bess spouting off in the sanctuary, while the ushers — and Ned and Chaz — folded the programs.

I do wish the woman would just disappear — at least until intermission!

Leigh let out the breath she'd been holding with a whoosh.

Holy crap. The Pack was right.

"You did this for Bess?" Leigh asked.

There was no response. Leigh suspected he was nodding.

"Ms. Bess is a good lady," Ned said after a beat. "She's going to keep this building a theater. A nice theater. I can work here again for real. And she won't let nobody tear it down, neither. *Ever.* She said."

At least, the Pack was partly right.

"You think of it as your building, don't you Ned?" Leigh asked softly.

No response. Probably more nodding.

"Have you taken care of it for a long time, now?"

"Ever since I was ten," he said proudly. "I know this place better than anybody!"

Ten years old? Leigh did some quick math in her head. Ned's age was hard to guess, but he appeared to be younger than Leigh's mother and aunts. In 1961, he would have been a young teenager or tween.

Survived by a wife and two stepchildren.

Leigh felt a clammy wave of cold pass through her body. "You worked here with your stepdad?" she squeaked.

"I don't want to talk about him!" Ned practically shouted.

"I'm sorry," Leigh said quickly. "I didn't mean to—"

"He was a bad man and he did terrible things!" Ned went on. "He made me do them, too!"

"We won't talk about him anymore," Leigh said hurriedly. Where the hell were the police? For all Ned's mild mannerisms most of the time, he was obviously on a hair-trigger. She paused a second to regroup, forcing herself to acknowledge that although it felt like she had been trapped in complete blackness with two nutjobs and an unconscious person for at least seven hours — in reality, only a few short minutes had passed.

"Leigh?" Camille called pleasantly from inside the closet.

"Yes?"

"You're okay out there with Ned, aren't you?"

"Just peachy," she answered, feeling like a psych nurse. "How about you?"

"I'm a little cramped, but it can't be much longer now. Don't worry about me!"

"Okay, I won't," Leigh lied. Did Camille even realize what had happened to Gerardo? If he had entered the kitchen without calling out first, she might not. A dull thud, his body slumping to the floor — neither sound would be recognizable through the closed pantry door, especially with Camille's own voice rattling around her skull.

Which would explain why she didn't seem overly concerned about Leigh's coming in.

"I'm thinking... *Tosca*," Camille mused.

Footsteps sounded in the basement outside, and Leigh sensed, rather than heard, Ned's body tense. A shuffling noise made her certain he was retreating farther behind the door.

Getting into position?

She pushed back a swell of panic. Why Ned hadn't hit her when she walked in, she didn't know, but Gerardo's unconscious presence was more than enough evidence that the next person to try it was taking their life into their hands. She didn't know what Ned had hit Gerardo with, but the swelling on his skull was massive... and Ned apparently had plenty of practice in the art. If Camille started singing again, anyone could be the next victim. It could even be Warren, leaving early to check on her...

"No, Camille!" Leigh whispered sharply. "You can't sing anymore! We have to stay quiet!"

"Why is that, dear?"

"Because..." Leigh's mind turned somersaults. The footsteps had gone away — probably one of the actors racing to make another entrance. But eventually, Bess herself would come downstairs. Not until the police were with her, though, *if* Bess kept her promise to Leigh. How much longer could it possibly take?

"Just stay in the closet and be quiet, okay?" Leigh called.

Gerardo groaned. Leigh heard Ned move forward a step, then stop. If he went all the way to Gerardo, she might be able to make a break for the door. She placed herself carefully on the opposite side of the island.

"He's not dead," Ned said without emotion.

"No, he's not," Leigh agreed. "That's a good thing, don't you think?"

"No," he answered. "He could tell somebody."

"I'm sure he won't," Leigh said quickly. "He doesn't speak English."

Crap, that was lame!

"I don't trust him," Ned drawled. "He works for Mr. Applegate. He wants to sell the building to that Crane woman."

"Gordon won't sell the building," Leigh assured. "He teases and threatens, but he won't. I'm sure of it."

"I'm not. I wish you hadn't come in here, Ms. Leigh."

More laughter from above. Would this infernal act never be over? And was she hearing other footsteps outside, or was it just her imagination?

"I have to finish him now, or he'll tell everybody. Then I gotta put him somewhere."

Leigh had no response to that. Her pulse was pounding in her ears. Ned had taken another step closer to the figure on the floor. A part of her itched to start moving away — to escape. If she ran, would he come after her — or would he stay and finish off Gerardo?

"I don't like bodies."

You and me both, Nedster.

"I wish you hadn't come in here, Ms. Leigh." Ned repeated. He stopped moving directly across the island from her. She could smell something garlicky on his breath.

Screams and shrieks sounded from above, along with a cascade of heavy thuds. Leigh's whole body tensed, even as she remembered, with sudden clarity, exactly what the sound represented.

The cast was pretending that the stage had collapsed. It was the end of the second act.

"Uh oh," Ned said worriedly. "I'd better do it quick."

Leigh heard a rustle of cloth — an arm rising in the air? — and screamed at the top of her lungs. "No, Ned! *Stop!*"

The kitchen door flew open; beams from multiple flashlights flooded in. Two uniformed police officers burst through the doorway and had Ned under control almost instantly. Leigh looked across at him, and her heart fell into her shoes.

He had been holding a broken brick.

She skirted the island and dropped down to Gerardo. His head and face were covered with blood, but as she checked his pulse again, his eyelids fluttered.

He muttered one of the exact same words she'd used earlier.

"You are such a fraud!" she teased, nearly laughing with relief. "No one swears in their *second* language!"

Another officer stepped forward to tend to Gerardo, and Leigh stood up just as Bess rushed over to meet her, with Gordon close behind.

Her aunt wrapped her in a bear hug, her eyes brimming with tears. "Oh, thank God, thank God," Bess gushed. "We knew you had to be in here, but they wouldn't let us—"

"I know, Aunt Bess," she exclaimed. "I'm all right."

"Is this yours, Ma'am?" an officer asked, extending Leigh's phone. Ned had already been led out of the kitchen; he had not said a word.

"Yes, thank you," Leigh took the phone in a trembling hand and looked at the text from Maura.

It's Ned. Stay the hell away from him!

Leigh knew it wasn't funny, but she must have been near hysterical, because she couldn't stop chuckling. Upstairs, above her head, the audience roared with applause.

"Better not be at all than not be noble!" shouted the forgotten

Camille, bursting from the closet with a flourish. "It's *intermission!*"

Chapter 22

"We *told* you it was Ned," Ethan repeated for the fortieth time. "We told everybody!"

"Yes, but you were only guessing," Allison protested, moving away from her brother and toward the box of puppies on the floor beside Maura.

The puppies, fortuitously, had been instrumental in keeping the detective reasonably calm in the tense moments after her husband relayed his critical information and before Leigh had answered her phone. As soon as Gerry returned to Avalon, Maura had moved to the couch in her living room and demanded the Harmon family stop by on their way home from the theater. Though Stroth had been keeping her updated as best he could, she still had a million questions. And so did Leigh, whom Stroth had told absolutely nothing.

"We *knew*," Ethan insisted, uncharacteristically holding his ground. "No dude that weird isn't hiding something. He was old enough to have been around for the first murders, he lived close enough to the building to walk there every day, and he totally had the hots for Aunt Bess. It was—"

"Ethan!" Leigh chastised.

"Sorry, mom," he apologized, his reddened cheeks nearly matching his hair. "But it was *so* obvious. He would have done anything for her! And he was twisted enough to believe he was helping her, you know? I'm just saying, it was *obvious*."

Allison's eyes rolled. Leigh wished he would stop using that particular word, herself.

"It's true that he didn't cover his tracks particularly well," Maura offered. "He barely covered them at all. It's just that until recently, no one had any reason to connect the dots, much less connect them to him."

"Has he lived in West View his whole life?" Leigh asked.

Maura shook her head. "Actually, no. When his mother remarried she moved the kids with her into the city, and then he got drafted and sent to Vietnam. He was discharged after ten months for nebulous reasons — in retrospect, probably pre-existing mental health issues — and he moved around the country a while, working minimum wage jobs and spending a fair amount of time in homeless shelters. By the time he was thirty, he had no family; his mother died of cancer and his younger sister had committed suicide. Eventually he came back to West View and started taking janitorial jobs wherever he could get them."

"And nobody who hired him ever connected him with Bill Stokes?" Leigh asked.

"No reason to," Maura explained. "He was just a kid when he left, and his last name wasn't Stokes. He kept to himself and didn't talk about his background. There just wasn't anything there."

"But didn't the people who owned the building think it was weird how he always wanted to work at that building?" Ethan asked.

Maura shrugged. "They might if they knew the whole story. But the owners didn't talk to each other; they came and went. And Ned worked at a lot of other buildings, too, which masked his obsession with the one. It's not like he carried around a written resume, you know. He would approach a business and give them the last place he worked as a reference. His references were always good because he kept his head down, did competent work for very little money, and didn't complain."

"You'd think Merle and Earl would have seen him coming and going over the years," Leigh protested.

"Not if he was slipping in and out the fire exit in the back at night," Maura pointed out. "Which he could easily do, by the way. He often had keys, but even when he didn't, he knew exactly where the building was vulnerable, and he was handy with locks. But as far as his being seen, when he was reporting to work he would have walked around the back to the parking lot entrance, which wasn't visible from Merle and Earl's porch. Even if they did see him outside the building now and then, there was nothing in particular to be suspicious of."

"Oh yes, there was!" Ethan argued.

Allison exhaled loudly. "Looking creepy is *not* what made him guilty!" She turned to Maura. "He killed his stepfather, didn't he? After Bill killed Clyde Adams."

Maura's expression didn't change, but her eyes twinkled with admiration. "A very reasonable theory. In fact, that *might* be exactly what Ned himself told Detective Stroth just a short while ago. Ironically enough, for a man who doesn't talk much, Ned is surprisingly willing to answer direct questions, as long as he's asked politely."

Allison stopped caressing the puppies in the box and straightened. "Here's what I think happened. Ned hated Bill Stokes because he grew up being abused by him, and because Bill beat up on his mother, too. But Ned really liked Clyde Adams. Maybe Clyde liked Ned's mother and was nice to Ned because of it, or maybe Clyde was just nice, period. But when Bill Stokes killed Clyde, in a jealous rage or whatever, I bet Ned was there and saw it happen. Maybe Bill even made Ned help him brick up Clyde's body in the coal chute. A couple weeks later, Ned snapped, and he hit his stepfather over the head and killed him."

"It does fit," Leigh agreed, squirming with discomfort to hear her daughter talking of murder *again*. Tomorrow, they would have to bake cookies. Or make a craft. Or some girly thing. She sighed loudly, then put forth her own theory. "Ned was young at the time, so it makes sense that he couldn't have fought Bill outright. But he was big enough to swing a rock from behind. I can picture him deciding to heave the body up onto the altar, making a show of "good" conquering over evil. It was like he was making a sacrifice, for his mother and sister, maybe even for Clyde. He probably wasn't even thinking about what would happen to him afterward. It was all about 'justice' for his stepfather."

Maura nodded. "My thoughts, exactly. Why Ned wasn't suspected at the time, though, I couldn't tell you. Maybe he was, off the record, but there was no proof. Or maybe the investigators were familiar with Bill's abuse and decided to look the other way. It happens."

"And he was never convicted of anything else, either?" Warren questioned, an edge to his voice. He had been none too pleased to look for his wife at intermission and run into an ambulance and a bevy of police officers instead. Leigh had reassured him as soon as she could, but he was obviously still smarting. "He had no criminal record?"

Maura shook her head. "None. Bess had no reason to suspect he was up to anything, and neither did anyone else."

"Yes she did! It was ob—"

"Ethan!" Leigh and Warren chastised simultaneously.

The boy folded his arms over his chest, refusing to be cowed. "I'm just saying."

"When Ned came back to the building after all those years, it probably set him off again somehow," Allison continued to theorize. "He got possessive of it and everything. He had ideas about what it should and shouldn't be used for, and when he felt like it was threatened, *he* felt threatened."

"Again," Maura praised. "A very reasonable theory. From all we know, I'd say Ned's understanding of the world seems to be fairly black and white, with a morality of his own invention. He also takes nearly everything he hears literally, and when you start doing that, it's easy to feel threatened."

Leigh remembered Gordon's shouted words of the morning before — that if *one more unpleasant finding* occurred at the building, he would *unload this box of bricks*. Ned had been listening then. No wonder he had chosen that night to try and remove Clyde Adams' bones from the coal chute. And no wonder he'd been so upset to find out he'd left some behind. He had caused the very problem he was trying to avoid.

I don't like bodies.

"A twisted sense of morality can be very convenient," Leigh said. "If only Ned considered knocking people unconscious to be as bad as pole dancing."

"Criminal minds often create their own rules," Gerry offered. He was leaning against the doorway to the kitchen, watching over his wife protectively even as he looked tired enough to fall asleep on his feet. "He seems to have deputized Bess as an accessory savior for the building, which was fortunate for her. He trusted whomever she trusted, and he was suspicious of anyone she appeared not to like. I believe he spared you, Leigh, because he knew that Bess was fond of you. But that kind of logic only goes so far. If he became convinced that anyone — including Bess — was a threat to *his* building, he could and would have hurt her, too."

"Fabulous," Warren muttered under his breath.

"What I still don't get," Maura asked Leigh, "Is how Camille wound up in the closet. Did Ned force her down there with threats of some kind?"

Leigh shook her head. "Not exactly. She told me he came up with some lame story about how Bess wanted to see her down in the kitchen. But he didn't lead her straight down there — I guess he was smart enough to realize that if anyone saw where she went, they might go and fetch her. So he led her up to the second floor and across, then snuck her down the stairs. Camille said she thought they were being secretive because Bess had some surprise planned for the cast..." Leigh shook her head. "I don't know. The woman is a loon. But she followed him down there, and then he shut the door behind them and flipped the circuit for the basement to keep himself hidden while he guarded her. She still thought it was some kind of surprise party, and she wasn't afraid of Ned. But—" Leigh smiled a little, despite herself. "It turns out she's absolutely terrified of the dark. And when she's scared—"

"She *sings*," Ethan, Allison, and Warren all chorused.

"Bingo," Leigh confirmed. "Well, that flipped Ned out, because he didn't want anyone to hear her and come looking for her. He clearly believed that her 'disappearing' until intermission was crucial to the success of the show, which was crucial to Bess's keeping her theater, which was crucial to his protecting the building and his dream job. So he told Camille to either stop singing or go in the closet. She chose option B."

"Surely she realized he wasn't right in the head when he made her go in the closet?" Warren asked.

Leigh shook her head. "I don't know. I think in her mind, bizarre behavior is relative. And it's not in her nature to assume the worst of anyone. She told me that she was upset about not finishing the blessings and not being able to sing for the cast before the show, but she really did believe Ned when he told her that Aunt Bess wanted her to stay in the basement. And she assumed Bess had her reasons. She was only trying to be cooperative."

"She had no idea that Ned had struck Gerardo?" Maura asked.

Leigh shook her head. "She had no idea Gerardo was even there. When she saw him on the floor with his head all bloody, she passed out. She would have hit her own head on the counter going down if Gordon hadn't caught her."

Warren rubbed his face in his hands. "I'm glad Gordon hired the guards when he did, but his mind games certainly muddied the waters, didn't they? You might have zoned in on Ned a lot quicker if Gordon hadn't been sending in spies and threatening to shut the place down every other minute."

"That didn't help, no," Maura agreed. "At least not from Bess's and Leigh's perspectives. But Applegate did let the police know that Gerardo was in his employ, presumably to keep an eye on his property and make sure Bess was running everything right."

Leigh scoffed. "You mean because he wanted to know what she was doing every second because he's an infatuated control freak?"

"That too," Maura agreed. "Turns out this gig isn't the only espionage Gerardo's done on Applegate's dime. He's made a career out of posing as an employee in Applegate's own businesses to see what's happening on the ground. Gerardo has an interesting history — his parents immigrated from Costa Rica when he was three, and he's fluent in both languages. He went to Penn on a full scholarship and got a business degree, which is why Applegate hired him originally, but with his talents at subterfuge, he was soon put to other uses."

"We knew he was a fake, too!" Ethan said proudly. He turned to his mother. "He's going to be all right, isn't he?"

Leigh nodded. "He got a nasty cut and a concussion, but he was awake and alert when they loaded him in the ambulance, and the EMTs seemed to think his injuries weren't critical." She looked at Maura. "And how is Sonia? It was Gordon's threatening to sell the building to her that made Ned go after her, wasn't it?"

Maura nodded. "Ned heard her say she wanted to tear it down. Whether she stood any realistic chance of buying the building from Applegate didn't matter. She was a threat, and she had to go."

Warren sighed. "She never did have a shot at buying the building. Gordon told me tonight he was only using her offer to up the tension with Bess. He felt bad about Sonia's getting hurt, though. In fact, he was late to the show because he was at the hospital — admitting to her that he had no intention of selling, ever."

"But why does she want the building so badly, if she wasn't involved with Marconi and had nothing to do with the other murders, either?" Leigh asked.

"She's on the brink of bankruptcy," Warren answered. "Sonia is a very good lawyer — but she's a lousy speculator. She invested in several real estate ventures that proved to be total blunders. She had a line on a major corporate buyer for the theater building, and she hoped to shore up her finances by making a quick buck on the turnaround. But it had to be quick, because she's got a balloon payment coming due in a matter of days that she knew would finish her."

"So Gordon gave her a final 'no' just before the show, and now she's going to go bankrupt?" Leigh asked.

Warren cracked a wry smile. "She would if Gordon took my advice, but he tends not to, you know. He was vague with me about the details, but I'm pretty sure he agreed to help bail her out somehow. The man does have a conscience, you know. And a heart."

"Applegate does seem sincere in his concern for Bess," Maura commented. "I believe even Ned could see that — which is why he threatened Bess, rather than Applegate himself, in the note he mailed. It worked, too. Stroth says Applegate's been driving him nuts, first worrying that Bess would be a suspect in Sonia's assault, then worrying about the note and the break-in. When Bess called Applegate earlier tonight and told him that Camille was missing, he was in town at the hospital still, but he immediately called Stroth and demanded that he personally go down and check it out."

Leigh's eyebrows rose. "He did? But Bess called — "

"By then, Stroth had already dispatched the nearest unit," Maura answered. "And a good thing, too."

"Bess didn't seem too appreciative of Gordon's efforts when I saw her," Warren noted.

Leigh remembered the "colorful" scene all too well. "Well, as my mother put it," she said with a chuckle, "*it's a dance they do.*" She gave her head a shake. She would never completely understand Gordon Applegate, but she supposed she didn't have to, so long as her Aunt Bess did. If the two of them wanted to liven up their golden years by playing incomprehensible high-stakes mind games with each other, well... she guessed it beat watching cable.

"What about the theater?" Maura asked. "I never even asked how all the chaos went over with the audience. I guess the rest of the show was cancelled?"

The room was quiet for a moment. Then Leigh, Ethan, Allison, and Warren all burst out laughing.

"Have you *met* my Aunt Bess?" Leigh teased. "The woman did everything but stand on her head to distract the audience from what was going on. As soon as she knew that Camille and I were all right and that Gerardo was being taken care of, she raced up the stairs to the auditorium and announced that everything was fine — that one of the theater employees had had an 'accident' in the kitchen, and that an ambulance had been called, but that he was going to be fine, and that no one need be upset by the army of police cars outside because... get this... it was clearly a slow news night in West View!"

Maura laughed out loud. "Damn, she's good."

Gerry joined in. "Sure she's not looking for a job in PR? The city force could use her."

"I believe she'll be fully occupied for some time," Leigh answered. "The show was, despite all odds, a rousing success. If Merle and Earl follow through with their promise to personally recommend the production to everyone they've ever met, the next two shows are definitely going to be sellouts."

"And if Mr. Applegate follows through on his promise to Aunt Bess, the North Boros Thespian Society will be able to use the theater as long as they want," Allison added, stroking the pups again. "By the way, Mom, Aunt Bess says they're doing *Wizard of Oz* over the summer. Can I try out for a munchkin?"

"Hey!" Ethan enthused. "We can train Chewie to play Toto!"

"Sounds good to me," Leigh responded, delighted with the thought of Allison doing something silly and fun... and *bright*. "But ixnay on the Toto thing. Chewie's too big for a basket, and anyway, he would eat his way out of it long before Oz."

"You could try out too, Mom," Allison encouraged. "You said you wanted to get back into acting."

"I did," Leigh confessed. "But *Wizard of Oz* is a musical, and I can't sing."

"The wicked witch of the West doesn't sing," Gerry offered, smiling sardonically.

Leigh caught his eye and grinned. True, the man had once locked her up for a murder she didn't commit. But they were past that, now.

And she always appreciated a good sense of humor.

Everyone else in the room watched as she stretched her arms lazily, cuddled into her husband's side, then let out a loud, spine-tingling cackle.

The show must go on.

About the Author

See You in Bells is a real play, which Edie wrote and acted in herself as the character of "Cat." The script is published by Samuel French (Baker's Play imprint) and is available for production.

Edie Claire enjoys creating works of mystery, romantic suspense, YA romance, stage comedy, and women's fiction. She has worked as a veterinarian, a childbirth educator, and a medical/technical writer; when she is not writing novels, she may be found doing volunteer work, raising her three children, or cleaning up after an undisclosed number of pets.

To find out more about her books and plays, please visit her website (**www.edieclaire.com**) or Facebook page (**www.Facebook.com /EdieClaire**). If you'd like to be notified when new books are released, feel free to sign up for her newsletter on the website. Edie always enjoys hearing from readers via email (**edieclaire@juno.com**). Thanks so much for reading!

Books & Plays by Edie Claire

Leigh Koslow Mysteries
Never Buried
Never Sorry
Never Preach Past Noon
Never Kissed Goodnight
Never Tease a Siamese
Never Con a Corgi
Never Haunt a Historian
Never Thwart a Thespian

Classic Romantic Suspense
Long Time Coming
Meant To Be
Borrowed Time

YA Romance
Hawaiian Shadows: Wraith
Hawaiian Shadows: Empath

Women's Fiction
The Mud Sisters

Comedic Stage Plays
Scary Drama I
See You in Bells